Also by Ian O'Neill:

'Jimmy First and Destiny's Watch'

'Jimmy First and the Time Conflict'

To Isabelle,

The Elf Boy Trilogy

Book One

The Heritage Bloodstone

Ian O'Neill

Ian O'Neill

New Generation Publishing

For my Golden Retrievers past and present,
Sonny-Boy, Rory, Murphy, Lucy and Henry.

Special thanks to Michele Anne for another wonderful front cover illustration and another special thanks to Caroline Byrne for her editor's eye and Gill Gravestock for her final proof read!

Chapter One - Green-Jack

'The Green Man represents an aspect of male energies to complement the female Mother Earth.'

Jack leant back against the green, furry bark of the old oak tree and looked out onto a sea of shimmering blue. The bluebells were in full bloom and it was a sight that never failed to gladden his heart and lift his spirits. Heywood Forest was just the most beautiful place to be in springtime as it burst into rich colour following the long, cold greyness of winter.

Jack Green didn't just live in the forest; he was of the forest. He was a part of it just like the trees, shrubbery and the wildlife that lived there. The old gamekeeper's cottage that he shared with his grandfather, Noah, was his home and had been for all of his life. He rarely went into the local towns and villages – he had no need. The animals in the forest were his only friends.

Noah nicknamed him Green-Jack because he always wore green and it was a play on his name. Jack could blend into the forest when the mood took him and even his animal friends wouldn't be aware of him. He'd never been to school in his life. Noah had taught him all that he needed to know to make his way through the world. He could read and write and he could most certainly look after himself.

Jack buttoned his jacket against the early evening chill and decided that it was time to go home. His grandfather would have his supper waiting on the table and would be sure to scold him if he was late. As he started to walk back along the path towards his cottage, he was distracted by the sound of a dog barking in the distance. There was nothing unusual about hearing a dog barking in the forest, but Jack heard something in the tone. Distress.

He sprinted off in the general direction of the barking,

keeping his eyes peeled for the dog. The panic in the animal's bark drove him on. The shrubbery and the undergrowth merged into a green blur as he sped along the pathway. It was as he approached the edge of the forest that he saw a golden retriever standing at the side of Miller's Pond barking hysterically. As he neared the pond he saw the reason why – a body lay face down in the green, slimy water.

Jack didn't hesitate and jumped straight into the pond, wading through the green slime and dragging the body out onto a patch of grass to the side of the path. It was only when he turned the body over he realised that it was a young girl. She wasn't breathing and her lips were already turning blue, so Jack sprang into action. He tilted her head back to open her airways, pinched her nose and clamped his mouth onto hers and forced air into her lungs, then quickly followed this with rapid chest compressions with both hands.

He alternated between mouth to mouth and chest compressions as he attempted to get her breathing. The dog stood to his side, barking and wagging its tail in anticipation. But Jack focused all of his effort and attention on the girl. He continued the resuscitation just the way Noah had taught him.

Keep trying, Jack. Keep trying …

He'd been working on her for several minutes but there was still no sign of her breathing. Jack's attempts became increasingly desperate as he searched for any slight trace of life in the girl. His own breathing became laboured and the sweat streamed down his forehead and dripped off the end of his nose. The dog sensed his desperation and its barking became more and more agitated.

'Come on – breathe,' he whispered to her.

But nothing. She lay there impassive and lifeless. She looked no older than Jack. She was fifteen or sixteen at the most. He couldn't let her die. Then he remembered something. He'd seen a fox hit by a car some years ago. The fox suffered a glancing blow and was sent spinning across the road. Its lifeless body lay wasted in the gutter.

Jack thought it was dead but went through the same process he'd just been using on the girl. As Jack willed it back to life, he felt an energy rising up deep within him. It was like electricity pulsating through his body and eventually it found its way to his fingertips. The fox suddenly jolted back into life. And Reggie the fox was still roaming the forest to that very day.

Jack refocused every ounce of his awareness and attention on the girl and continued the heart compressions. He searched for the same energy within himself that had saved Reggie. He felt a tingling sensation in his toes and a telling warmth building in his inner core. His hands kept working on the girl's heart and he kept willing her to wake up.

'Breathe,' he whispered, time and time again. 'Please …'

A wave of energy suddenly rose up from deep within him and surged through the entire length of his body, through his arms and into his fingertips and released into the girl. Her body jolted and she coughed and spluttered green, slimy water down the front of her T-shirt. Her whole body continued to convulse as she desperately tried to gulp in air.

Jack moved her into the recovery position and held her firmly. 'You're going to be OK,' he whispered, and her eyes flickered open. She started to cough violently and vomited more green, slimy water over his jacket. But he didn't care; he was just relieved that she was breathing again. He pulled her into a sitting position and patted her back as she coughed.

When she eventually calmed down, she looked up at Jack through watery eyes. The dog licked her face and furiously wagged its tale. It started to bark again but this time it was a happy bark. Its mistress was safe.

'What happened?' she croaked.

'I found you face down in the pond,' said Jack. 'When I pulled you out, you'd stopped breathing.'

3

The girl touched her forehead and winced. 'My head is killing me.'

Jack noticed a huge, dark lump on her forehead. He guessed what had happened as she was wearing a T-shirt, shorts and trainers. 'Were you running along the path?'

She nodded. 'I always go for a run with Sonny in the evening.'

'You must have hit your head on that branch that overhangs the path. You probably knocked yourself out and fell into the pond.'

'So how did you bring me round?' she asked.

'I, er, I used heart massage and mouth to mouth,' said Jack coyly.

The girl blushed slightly. 'You saved my life. I would have died if you hadn't come along.'

'You need to thank your dog,' said Jack. 'It was his barking that brought me here.'

The dog was now sitting by her side, and licked her face again. 'So I have you to thank, Sonny-boy. And you …?'

'Jack.'

'I'm Becky. I don't know how to thank you enough.'

Jack felt embarrassed. He hardly ever spoke to anyone other than Noah, and he most certainly had never spoken to a teenage girl before. She was drenched from head to foot and her long blond hair was matted in green slime but Jack thought she was beautiful.

'I'd better get home,' said Becky. 'My mum will worry if I'm late.'

She tried to stand up but staggered backwards. Jack caught her arm and steadied her. 'You're still very weak after your ordeal. I think you should rest for a while.'

'It's starting to get dark,' said Becky. 'I have to get home.'

'Well let me help you. Where do you live?'

'Grasslake village.'

'I'll come with you,' said Jack as he held out his arm. 'Hold on to me – just in case you feel dizzy again.'

Becky took hold of his arm and they set off very tentatively along the path towards the field on the edge of the forest. Sonny walked to heel by his mistress's side.

'I live on the far side of the field,' said Becky. 'Our cottage backs on to it.'

'I don't really know Grasslake that well,' said Jack. 'I rarely go there.'

'So where do you live?' asked Becky.

'In an old cottage on the other side of the forest. I live with my grandfather.'

'Which school do you go to?'

'I don't go to school,' said Jack. 'My grandfather teaches me all I need to know.'

'Lucky you,' said Becky. 'I go to Ridgeway Upper School in Staunton. I don't like it that much.'

'What don't you like about it?' asked Jack.

'Homework,' said Becky. 'The older I get, the more homework they pile onto me. I hate it, but my mum makes me do it.'

'My grandfather teaches me in the forest. We go on long walks and he tells me all about nature. But we never work in the afternoon. My grandfather rests and I do whatever I want.'

'But what about the authorities?' asked Becky. 'Don't they insist you go to school?'

Noah hated the authorities with a passion. '*Keep those people well away from your business, Green-Jack,*' he'd said to him on many occasions. '*They have no right meddling in things that have nothing to do with them.*'

'I leave that to my grandfather.'

They arrived at the back of Becky's cottage just as darkness descended. Becky opened the gate and let Sonny into the garden.

'I'll leave you here, if that's OK,' said Jack. 'I need to get home as my grandfather will have my supper ready.'

Becky's bright blue eyes sparkled as she looked up at him. 'What do you say to somebody that's just saved your life?'

Jack dropped his gaze to the floor. He felt embarrassed. Becky suddenly noticed the stain on his jacket. 'Did I do that? Please, let me clean it before you go?'

'It's nothing,' said Jack. 'I'll wash it when I get home.'

'Are you sure?' pressed Becky.

'I'm sure.'

Without warning she leant forward and kissed him on his cheek. Jack was glad it was dark as he felt his face burning with embarrassment. 'Thank you so much, Jack. If you ever need anything from me, you only have to ask.' Then she kissed him again.

Jack turned away and headed back across the field. His head was in a spin.

'Will I see you again?' called out Becky.

Jack smiled inside. He turned to face her. 'I'd like that.'

*

Jack didn't so much run across the ground as glide. He was running on air. He'd saved a girl's life. In fact, he'd saved a very pretty girl's life, and he felt wonderful. And she kissed him. He'd admired girls from afar but never dared to speak to them. He couldn't ever remember a feeling like it before in his life.

It was pitch black by the time Jack entered the forest, and even though he could hardly see more than a metre in front of him, he didn't slow at all. His instincts would guide him safely along the pathways and back home to his cottage. He'd lost count of how many times he'd run through the forest in the dark. It was all the same to Jack; daytime or night-time, the forest was his home and he knew it like the back of his hand.

As he neared the cottage, his mind turned to his grandfather. He knew that he would be angry when he saw him. Noah hated it when he came home after dark and had scolded him on many occasions. And as Jack approached the cottage, he saw his grandfather pacing up and down outside the front door. He knew by the look on his face that he was in for it.

'Where've you been, Jack? I've been worried sick.'

'I'm sorry, Grandfather, but I had to help a young girl.'

Noah looked aghast. 'What were you doing helping a young girl? What have I told you about keeping yerself to yerself? Do you ever listen to a word I say?' He saw the stain on his jacket. 'And what's that on yer jacket? Get yerself inside and get that jacket off and into the wash bucket.' He shook his head in despair. 'What am I going to do with you, Green-Jack?'

Jack walked in through the door and unbuttoned his jacket and put it into a large wooden tub under the sink. The enticing aroma of vegetable soup emanated from an old blackened cauldron hanging over a wood fire burning in a cast iron grate. The cottage was small but comfortable. A sink; two armchairs; two beds; a table and two chairs and some threadbare old mats on the floor.

Noah followed Jack into the cottage and closed the door. He walked over to the fire, stirred the soup that was simmering in the cauldron with a ladle before filling a large porcelain bowl. He placed the soup on the table alongside a spoon and plate that had several chunks of brown bread on it.

'Come on, Jack. Eat yer soup while it's hot.'

Jack sat down at the table and took a spoonful of soup and blew on it.

'I don't suppose I can tempt you into having some rabbit with it?' asked Noah.

Jack turned his nose up in disgust. 'They're my friends. How can you expect me to eat them?'

'Friends be blowed!' dismissed Noah. 'They're animals. We all have to eat and we all need the protein that meat gives us.'

'I get all the protein I need from nuts, fruit and vegetables,' said Jack. 'And do I look like I'm starving?'

Noah sat down in front of him shaking his head. He filled two mugs from a tarnished tin teapot and topped them up with milk. 'So how did you help this young girl?'

'I found her face down in Millar's pond,' said Jack. 'She'd knocked herself out. By the time I got to her, she'd stopped breathing. So I used the first aid just like you showed me. I gave her mouth to mouth and heart massage.'

'Is she OK now?'

'She's fine. I took her home which is why I was late. And don't worry, I didn't go inside her house.'

Noah smiled for the first time since Jack had returned home. 'Yer a good lad, Jack. But just be careful; there are some strange people out there.'

Chapter Two – Danger in the Night

Jack was aware of somebody shaking him; he heard a whispered voice. 'Jack, wake up lad.' He opened his eyes to see his grandfather kneeling down by his bed. He was about to speak but Noah put his finger up to his mouth. 'There are men outside and I'm not sure what they're up to,' he whispered. 'We need to get away from here.'

Jack wasn't fully awake and didn't comprehend what his grandfather was telling him. He felt a hand gently pull him into a sitting position. 'Get yer clothes on.' Jack climbed out of bed and pulled on his T-shirt, jeans and socks. He forced his feet into his trainers without undoing them. 'Where are we going?'

Noah rolled back one of the mats and pulled open a trapdoor underneath.

'But that's the cellar,' said Jack. 'They'll easily find us down there.'

'Just climb down the stairs, Jack, and don't ask questions.'

Jack grabbed his jacket and did as he asked. His grandfather followed him down the stairs and closed the trapdoor. He switched on a torch and shone it around the small cellar and settled on a small wooden panel in the corner. He knelt down and pulled the panel back before turning to Jack. 'This is a tunnel that leads into the forest. It's very narrow but big enough to crawl through.' He handed him the torch. 'Here take this and I'll follow you.'

Jack took the torch and dropped to his hands and knees and crawled into the tunnel. He stopped after a few metres and shone the torch back towards the entrance. His grandfather joined him in the tunnel and pulled the wooden panel back into place.

'Let's go,' he whispered and Jack began crawling on the dirt floor along the tunnel. He didn't particularly like being enclosed in such a confined space but swallowed his rising anxiety down and just kept moving forwards. He wasn't sure how far they'd gone or how long they'd be crawling when they came up against a dead end.

'Shine the torch upwards,' said Noah. Jack did as he asked and saw a ladder strapped to the wall. 'Climb up it, Jack, and when you get to the top push the trapdoor open.'

Jack climbed the dozen or so steps to the top of the ladder and pushed on the trapdoor. It took several attempts but it eventually creaked open. Jack climbed the last few steps and emerged into the middle of a cluster of tall shrubs and ferns. He shone the torch back down into the tunnel so his grandfather could see. As Noah climbed out into the forest, he whispered, 'turn the torch off, Jack. I don't want anyone seeing us.'

Jack turned off the torch as his grandfather closed the trapdoor and covered it with dead leaves and dirt. 'What do we do now?' asked Jack.

'We stay here,' said Noah. 'It's too dangerous to move in the forest in the dark.'

He and Jack huddled together under cover of the ferns. 'How did you know about the tunnel and what's it doing there?' asked Jack.

'Many years ago the forest used to be owned by a Lord of the Land. The gamekeeper would use the tunnel and surprise the poachers who were hunting deer.'

'Do you have any idea who those men were outside of the cottage?'

'I don't,' said Noah. 'But I'm sure they were up to no good. We'll stay here until the morning.'

*

Jack opened his eyes to a warm welcome from the early morning sun. He sat up and stretched and yawned. Sleeping outside never bothered him; he felt refreshed after a good night's rest. He looked for his grandfather but he was nowhere to be seen. He crawled out from under the ferns and checked all around for any sign of him. He was on his own – he could sense it.

Perhaps he's gone back to the cottage, he thought. So Jack set off through the thick green undergrowth towards his home. He avoided the main pathways just in case the men from the night before were still around so he expertly used the abundant green cover of the bushes and the tall ferns.

His light-hearted mood instantly disappeared when he entered the clearing where his cottage sat. All that was left of his home was a charred wooden frame and a pile of grey ash. A thin wisp of white smoke corkscrewed into the early morning sky. Noah sat on a log holding his head in his hands. Jack walked over and sat by him.

'Was it the men from last night?'

Noah looked at him, his dark, swarthy features wet with tears. 'Who else would it be? We've lost everything, Jack. Our home and a lifetime of possessions gone up in smoke.'

Jack put his arm around his grandfather's shoulders. 'We can rebuild it, you and I. We're not going to let anybody force us from our home.'

Noah shook his head. 'We've got to get away from here, Jack. It's too dangerous.'

'But you never run away,' said Jack. 'You've always taught me to stand up for myself.'

'This is different,' said Noah. 'These people, whoever they are, are totally ruthless. No, Jack lad, we've got to get away from here.'

'So where are we going to?'

'We'll go to my people. There are two camps not too far from here. I'm sure someone will put us both up.'

Jack knew his grandfather nearly as well as he knew himself and he could sense that there was something he wasn't telling him. And he really didn't like his family; they were the last people he wanted to be with.

'I don't want to stay with them.'

Noah looked surprised. 'Why ever not? They're family.'

'They may be but I've never felt they liked me.'

Hurt replaced the surprise on Noah's face. 'Why would

you say that?'

'Billy-boy and Danno were always teasing me and beating me up when I was a kid. They used to call me names.'

Noah laughed light-heartedly. 'That's just the traveller's way. They don't mean anything by it.'

'They said that I wasn't family and that I was a freak.'

Noah's mood changed instantly. 'Well they had no right saying that; yer as much a part of the family as those two little chancers.' He adjusted his trilby hat to the back of his head. 'Pay no attention to them, Jack.'

'What do you mean I'm as much a part of the family as they are?'

Noah readjusted his hat, and fiddled nervously with his neckerchief. 'It's just an expression. Don't pay any attention to me.'

'They said that you found me under a bush in the forest and that you weren't really my grandfather.'

'Don't listen to them, Jack,' pleaded Noah. 'They have mouths bigger than their brains. They'll be feeling the rough end of my boot when I see them.'

Jack was most at home when he was in the forest. He loved the company of the animals – they were his friends. He loved his grandfather dearly and would gladly give his own life for the old man's, but he didn't feel the same about the family. Even without the nasty comments from his cousins, he knew he was different. And he knew that his grandfather was keeping something from him. Noah couldn't make eye contact and that was a sure sign he felt uncomfortable.

'You've always taught me that the truth will never harm me, and that I should never be frightened of either telling it or hearing it. Whatever it is you're hiding from me can't be that bad.'

Noah dropped his gaze to the floor and sighed deeply. 'I can't tell you what happened last night unless I tell you why … and that will lead us both to a place neither of us wants to visit just yet.'

'How will I know unless you tell me?' said Jack. 'Surely it can't be that bad.' He lifted his grandfather's head and turned it towards him. 'If I'm adopted, just tell me.' Jack saw the tears welling in Noah's eyes. Whatever the secret was, it was going to cause him pain.

Noah reached into his pocket and pulled out his battered old tobacco tin. He flicked open the lid and pulled out a thin paper from a red packet and filled it with the brown tobacco strands. He rolled it into a cigarette shape before licking the edge of the paper and sticking it down. It was a process Jack had watched his grandfather do a thousand times over the years and it never failed to fascinate him. Noah struck a match and lit the 'roll-up' that was now hanging from his mouth. He inhaled slowly and blew the smoke out with a deep sigh. 'I'm not sure yer ready to hear this.'

'You've always taught me to face up to things,' said Jack. 'I'm ready.'

Noah placed the 'roll-up' in the corner of his mouth and began his tale. 'Yer not adopted, Jack, but yer not mine. Yer grandmother and I took you in over fifteen years ago. It wasn't done legally – the authorities were never involved.'

So that's why he hated them so much.

'Who gave me to you?'

'Yer mother. She was frightened. She said that she had to get away and asked if we would look after you. She said that she would come back for you when it was safe to do so.'

'So who is she, this woman?'

'We'd never seen her before and we've never seen her since.'

'Didn't she say where she was from?' pressed Jack.

Noah removed the roll-up from his mouth and flicked the ash that was building up on the end of it onto the ground. 'She said she was an Elf.'

Jack looked quizzically at his grandfather. 'An Elf?'

Noah's sad eyes filled with tears. 'That's what she said

and I believed her.'

Jack stood up and walked over to the smouldering remains of the cottage. He studied the grey ash as he mulled over what he'd just been told. He turned to his grandfather. 'You're telling me the truth, aren't you?'

Noah nodded. 'My own father often talked about the Elves. He said that you would only see them on moonless nights in the deepest and darkest parts of the forest. They avoid contact with humans and live their own lives in their own land - a land of mystery and magic.'

Jack took a deep breath and exhaled slowly. His mind was racing like a raging river. He'd always known he was different. Not just from his family but the people he saw in the forest. But an Elf? 'Why haven't you told me this before?'

'I hoped yer mother would come back for you. Then you would have seen for yerself. You're the image of her Jack - the same dark eyes; the same dark brown, wavy hair and the same sharp Elven features.'

Jack offered no arguments to his grandfather. He wore his hair long to cover his pointy ears. They were the main reason his cousins called him a freak. Billy-boy teased him by calling him Pixie ears. Then something suddenly occurred to him. 'What's this got to do with our cottage being burnt down?'

Noah puffed anxiously on his roll-up. 'I told you that yer mother was frightened. She said she was in danger and had to get away. As much as it broke her heart she left you with Rosie and me. She said that you would be safer with us.'

'I still don't understand,' said Jack.

'I'm certain that they were Elves in the forest last night. I couldn't see them clearly in the dark but they didn't move like humans. They crept silently in and out of the shadows like wraiths in the night. It was only because I couldn't sleep that I knew they were there. It was as they circled our cottage I heard one of them say, 'is the boy in there?''

Noah threw his 'roll-up' into the smouldering ashes of the cottage. His facial expression was a mix of disbelief and fear. 'They were trying to kill you, Jack.'

'Kill me? But why?'

Noah shook his head. 'I have no idea but I do know that we have to get away from here. I don't want us to be around if they come back tonight. We'll stay with the family for a while. You may not like them but at least you'll be safe.'

Jack's head was bursting with everything that he'd just learned. He was frightened but there was another more overriding emotion – curiosity. Where did he come from? Who was his mother? A mother, who until a few minutes ago, he never knew he had. He'd never asked his grandfather about his parents; he'd just accepted things as they were. He couldn't even remember his grandmother, Rosie.

No, he had to find out who he was. 'I'm not coming with you.'

Noah looked aghast. 'But you must. You need looking after.'

Jack shook his head. 'Whoever did this will think I'm dead. They didn't see anyone escape from the fire and would've had no idea about the tunnel. I'm going to find out where I come from, and I'm going to find my mother.'

'Jack, you'll never find the Elven world,' pleaded Noah. 'It's protected by magic. And as for yer mother, she could be anywhere.'

'I don't care,' said Jack. 'It's something I have to do.'

Noah changed his tack. 'Let me come with you? I can help.'

Jack shook his head. 'I have to do this on my own. I appreciate everything you've done for me but I need to find out who I am.'

Tears welled up in Noah's sad eyes. His face looked old and lined. 'Is there anything I can say that will change yer mind?'

Jack stared, first at the ground, and then at his

grandfather and said one word: 'No.'

Chapter Three – Cyril the Squirrel

Jack sat on a log under a beech tree looking across the clearing towards a brick built wishing-well. It was a place called Faery Crossing and the well sat at the intersection where two pathways crossed. Jack smiled as he remembered the numerous times as a young boy when he threw pennies down the well and made a wish. His grandfather would tell him that if he ever shared his wish with anyone, it would never come true.

Young boy? That was just it, he was never a boy. Tears welled up in his eyes again when he thought back to the morning. His grandfather had been distraught when Jack finally managed to tear himself away from him. He'd wandered aimlessly around the forest all day and eventually found himself at the crossing. Guilt assailed him all over again but he knew that he had to do this. He had to find out who he was.

He reached into his pocket and pulled out a small, blood-red, oval shaped jewel on a gold chain. His grandfather had given it to him as he said goodbye. It was his mother's; she'd given it to Noah when she'd left Jack with him all those years ago. It was his only connection with his past. He put the chain around his neck, fastened the clasp, and hid the jewel inside his shirt so that it couldn't be seen. He would always wear it close to his heart.

His thoughts turned to his mother. Noah said that she was frightened. But what was she frightened of? And why did she have to leave her people? And more disturbingly, why would the Elves want to kill him? Perhaps it was mistaken identity and they were after someone else. None of it made any sense to Jack but he was absolutely determined to find answers.

The shadows grew longer across the clearing as the light faded and darkness slowly descended. He felt the stirrings of hunger in his stomach for the first time that

17

day. How he would relish a plate of his grandfather's thick vegetable soup at that precise moment but he was going to have to settle for simpler fare that evening. As he was deciding where to begin his search for food, he felt something hit his head and bounce off. He peered up into the dense foliage of the beech tree, but couldn't see anything. Whatever it was that hit him, was lost in the grass.

He stood up and walked from under the tree and surveyed the clearing. Visibility was poor in the fading light, but he was sure he was on his own. People from the surrounding villages rarely ventured into the forest after dark. Just as he was about to walk across the clearing, something hit him on his forehead, right between his eyes. It hurt so much that it made his eyes water. He dried them on his jacket sleeve and looked around the clearing once again. A small spherical object on the dry dirt path caught his eye. He knelt down and picked it up - it was a hazelnut.

Realisation dawned. He looked up into the tree and called out, 'Cyril! I'm not in the mood for your games. At least have the decency to crack the nuts before you throw them at me so that I can eat them.'

The words were barely out of his mouth when a small furry creature leapt out of the lower branches of the beech tree and landed on Jack's head knocking him off balance. Jack ended up on his back on the grass and found himself face to face with a small grey squirrel. Jack made a grab for it but it was up and off across the clearing in a flash.

'Cyril! Wait till I get my hands on you!'

Jack scrambled to his feet and ran across the clearing after the squirrel. Jack was quick but Cyril was quicker and he managed to keep a safe distance between himself and his pursuer. He ran towards the wishing well and momentarily slowed down and looked at Jack as if he was taunting him. Just as Jack closed in on him, Cyril leapt up onto the side of the wishing well. Jack lunged for him but Cyril was too quick and jumped into the well.

Jack momentarily hesitated, expecting his friend to leap

out of the well and attack him again. He waited and waited but the expected assault never came. Jack tentatively crawled up to the wishing well and peeked over the top, anticipating the attack that he knew was coming. He peered into the gloom but there was no sign of Cyril. The silence unnerved him.

'Cyril! Stop messing around and show yourself. You've had your fun but I'm really not in the mood for your silly games.' Jack's plea was met with an echo followed by a stony silence. 'Cyril! I mean it. I haven't got time for this. Come on out of there now!'

Still nothing. Jack stepped back from the wishing well. 'That's it, I'm going. You're starting to bore me now.' He walked away expecting to see a little grey head peer over the top of the well, but it didn't happen. Now Jack started to lose his temper. He ran back to the well and shouted down into it. 'Cyril! I've had a really bad day and don't need this, so will you come out and stop being a pest!'

His voice reverberated loudly around the well and bounced back at him, but it didn't prompt an appearance by Cyril. Jack peered into the gloom and listened for any sign of movement. He heard absolutely nothing – it was as quiet as an empty church. An eerie feeling swept over him. He sensed something was wrong. Was Cyril lying injured at the bottom of the well, or worse? He saw a line of iron rungs cemented into the brickwork on the inside of the well, descending down into the darkness. He climbed over the wall and carefully lowered himself into the well.

It was difficult to see in the fading light and Jack painstakingly felt out the rungs with his feet. Fear gnawed at him but he wasn't about to abandon his friend so he began his hazardous descent into the dark abyss. He reckoned the well was around three hundred metres deep but had no feeling for his relative position because of the dark. He daren't look up for fear of losing his balance and there was no point in looking down into the sea of blackness below him.

His descent was slow and cautious. He knew that a

stream ran through the bottom of the well because of the numerous times he'd thrown pennies into it. But he didn't know how deep it was. He slowly lowered himself down, rung by rung, clinging onto the cold iron for all his worth. His foot suddenly felt the icy chill of water and he tentatively lowered himself down. The relief was instant when he felt firm ground underneath his feet. There was no more than thirty centimetres of water at the most. He leant back against the brick wall and breathed a huge sigh of relief.

His trainers and the bottom of his jeans were soaking wet but that was the least of his problems - it was so dark that he could hardly see his hand held out in front of his face. But Jack had been brought up in the ways of a traveller and he was prepared for most eventualities. He reached into his jacket pocket and retrieved a box of matches. Even though it was difficult to see in the dark, he fumbled open the box and managed to retrieve a match and strike it.

It took several seconds for his eyes to adjust and he was surprised to find himself staring into the mouth of a large cave. Jack was over 1.8 metres tall and he wouldn't have to bow his head to walk into it. The match burned out and he quickly struck another one and took a tentative step into the cave.

'Cyril,' he hissed. 'Are you there?' His question was greeted by silence. There was no sign of his friend. He noticed a metal flame torch in a holder on the cave wall. He took it down from its holder and lit the wick with the match. The torch immediately burst into flame casting its dancing light deep into the dark cave.

Why would there be a flame torch, he wondered? He reasoned that it must be for maintenance. He looked into the cave for Cyril but it was empty. The only sound was the gentle murmur of the stream and the drip, drip of water from the jagged cave roof. Cyril hated water but it wasn't that deep so he was unlikely to drown. But where was he?

Cyril had to be down here somewhere, as there was no

way he could have passed Jack on his descent into the well. He had no choice other than to go further into the cave and look for him. It wasn't an inviting prospect but he'd set his mind on finding his friend. His eyes and ears were on full alert as he slowly waded through the stream and further into the cave.

Jack called out as he walked along: 'I'm not angry with you, Cyril. So why don't you show yourself? Come on, you don't like confined spaces any more than I do. Show yourself and we can both go home.' But his friend wasn't responding. The flaming torchlight cast Jack's shadow on the wall of the cave, unnerving him as it looked like he was being followed. But he kept vigilant and he kept calm, despite the faint tingle of anxiety in the pit of his stomach.

He wasn't sure how long he'd been in the cave or how far he'd gone when something moved to his right catching his eye. He turned around quickly and saw Cyril sitting on a ledge on the cave wall.

'There you are. I've been going nearly frantic trying to find …'

But Cyril disappeared.

Jack felt the anger building up inside him and held the torch over to where Cyril had been sitting. He saw a hidden crevice in the cave wall, barely half a metre wide. He squeezed through the gap and into a small chamber, but there was no sign of Cyril. The chamber was around five metres square with a stone spiral staircase in its centre and no other entrances. Cyril must have climbed the stairs, reasoned Jack, so he followed him.

As he cantered up the steps he wondered what his friend was up to. Although Cyril was a great joker, for a fleeting moment Jack wondered if he was deliberately leading him somewhere. But this was Cyril and his sense of mischief knew no bounds. Just find him, thought Jack, and get back to the forest.

Jack eventually came out onto a small rectangular landing with an arch shaped wooden door facing him. And there was Cyril sat on a hand size square wooden panel on the door. Strange symbols were carved around the top of the door but Jack noticed something unusual - there were no handles or locks on it.

'So, my friend, you've had your fun and led me on a wild goose chase.' He held out his hand. 'Let's go back to the forest and you can share your stash of hazelnuts with me.'

But Cyril didn't move. He sat rock still, his furry nose twitching and his beady eyes locked onto Jack.

'Come on,' pleaded Jack. 'I've had a really tough day and I just want to eat and get some rest. Please, Cyril.'

But the squirrel wasn't moving. Jack reached up to where Cyril sat, but as he tried to grab him, Cyril jumped on his hand and forced it against the panel. Now Jack's not sure what happened next, but he suddenly found himself standing under a tall stone arch staring out across a tree covered meadow. A bright, fluorescent full moon cast its silver light across the meadow, illuminating candelabra shaped lanterns hanging from the branches of the trees. It looked beautiful.

He took a step back and looked up at the arch. He could just about make out some symbols and words written around its radius. He held the torch up in front of him. The words were in English and read: 'The Arch of Peace – In Freedom We Trust'. Jack turned a full circle trying to establish his bearings. One minute he was standing on a small landing, the next he was standing on the edge of a beautiful meadow. What happened?

He decided that it wasn't a good idea holding a flaming torch in his hand attracting attention to himself so he pressed it against the stone arch, starving it of oxygen so that it extinguished. As he placed it at the base of the arch, Cyril jumped up onto his shoulder. Jack tried to grab hold of him but Cyril jumped down and ran along the path that led from the arch and wound its way across the meadow. He stopped and turned to face Jack before looking back along the path. Jack walked up to him and knelt down beside him. 'What are you trying to tell me?'

Cyril did what he always did and twitched his nose and stared back at him. But he'd deliberately brought Jack to this place. Cyril jumped up onto his shoulder again and touched his nose on Jack's forehead. He looked along the path, before jumping down and scampering through the archway and disappearing.

Jack jumped up and ran over to the arch. He briefly thought about running after him, but he guessed that Cyril had brought him here for a reason. Although he was having trouble rationalising the day's events, his instincts were telling him to stay. How did Cyril know about this place? And why did he bring Jack here?

Was this his home? Was this where he came from? Was this the Elven land that his grandfather had told him about? But Noah had also told Jack that it was protected by magic and would be almost impossible to find. Cyril had brought him straight here without any problem.

He looked up at the moon and it was brighter than any moon he'd ever seen. The trees, although they looked like horse chestnuts, had luminous candelabras hanging from their branches. The grass was the richest green colour, as were the leaves on the trees. And then he realised that he felt different. The tiredness had gone; he felt alive and full of energy. His instincts were screaming at him; they were telling him that he was home.

He wanted to shout out at the top of his voice. The elation ran through him like a fast flowing river. He knew that something had been missing for the whole of his life, and this was it. His homeland. At the start of the day he was Green-Jack the teenage boy who lived in the forest. By the end of it he was someone totally different. Someone who he'd always known had been there, hidden somewhere deep down inside himself.

He was Green-Jack the Elf.

As he stared out across the meadow, the elation subsided. The events from the previous night crowded his thoughts. His people, the Elves, wanted him dead. They'd tried to kill him by burning his cottage down. When he embarked on this journey he knew that it was going to be dangerous. He was walking directly into that danger, but he had no choice. If he was going to find out who he was, then he had to follow this path.

Besides, he had one major advantage over his enemies. They thought he was dead so they had no further reason to look for him, at least he hoped that was the case.

His thoughts were distracted by voices coming from the other side of the arch. He crouched down low and dived behind bushes to the side of the path. He peered through the leaves and saw two people appear at the front of the arch. One was tall and slim; the other was short and stout. They were both dressed in dark blue jackets, black trousers and knee length black boots. Jack listened to their conversation.

'Vilner will kill us if he finds out.'

'And how's he going to find out. I'm not going to tell him, and as dense as you are, Laric, you're not going to tell him either.'

'But he has spies everywhere,' said Laric. 'He'll throw us both in the slammer for sure.'

'We had a short nap at the end of a long day - hardly the crime of the century. We both need our beauty sleep, Laric, and you need it more than most!'

A few seconds of silence followed. Laric broke it. 'Garwood, what's that torch doing leaning against the arch?'

'I've no idea,' replied Garwood. 'Is it a trick question?' he asked sarcastically.

'It wasn't there before our nap,' said Laric. 'Someone must have left it there.'

'Brilliantly deduced,' said Garwood. 'And that someone would have been an Elf returning from the human forest. Now put it back in its holder and stop bothering me.'

'But won't they tell Vilner that we'd left our post while on duty?'

'If they do, we'll just tell Vilner that we were

answering the call of nature.'

'But Vilner will be really angry with us if he finds out we weren't here.'

'Let's worry about that if and when it happens. Now do as I ask and put the torch back.'

Jack breathed slowly and deeply. Now he knew for sure. He really was in the land of the Elves.

Chapter Four – Waterswood

Jack crawled on his belly away from the arch and alongside a fast running stream towards a shallow waterfall. He found a secluded patch of grass surrounded by thick green bushes, halfway between the path and the stream. He needed to compose himself; he needed to gather his thoughts.

How did Cyril know that this was his home? Had he always known that Jack was an Elf? Did all the animals in the forest know of the existence of an Elven land? He remembered the fairy stories that his grandfather told him when he was a young boy. They took on a much greater significance for Jack now. His grandfather had always taught him to respect everybody, whether they were the same as you or different. Noah had known he was an Elf when he took him in, but he still treated him as one of his own.

And now he knew why his grandfather worried if he was late home. He must have always suspected that Jack was in danger because of what his mother had told him. Noah said that she was frightened, but of whom? Why would she be running away from her own people? And the question that bothered Jack the most, why would the Elves want him dead?

The same questions to which he had no answers kept coming back and the only way he was going to find those answers, was along that pathway across the meadow to wherever it led. Cyril had clearly conveyed that to him before he left, and that's where his destiny lay. But he had to be careful. Follow the direction of the path without actually walking along it. One thing that Jack could do well was to blend in with whatever cover was available.

He looked back towards the arch making sure that the two Elves couldn't see him, then crouched down low and moved stealthily from tree to tree to the side of the path. His eyes and ears scanned all around him for any threats.

The senses that had served him well on so many occasions in Heywood Forest were now on maximum alert. He felt alive and ready for anything that came his way.

The path across the meadow slowly wound its way upwards towards the brow of a hill. Jack looked up to the sky and saw that the moon was now joined by bright stars that glistened like jewels in the night. He assumed that it must be the same night-time sky that he'd grown up with but for some reason it looked different. The moon was whiter and the stars shone brighter. Perhaps it was the magic, he thought.

Nothing could have prepared him for the view he found when he reached the brow of the hill. The path continued its journey downwards across the meadow to the mouth of a valley. To the right, there were tall, snow-capped mountains that rose majestically into the night sky and on the other side, green rolling hills covered by thick, pine forests.

And in the midst of this beauty, tucked snugly between the mountains and the hills at the foot of the valley, was a picturesque village. The glow from the streetlamps merged with the candlelight flicker from the cottages to create a fairy-tale scene. All it needed was snow to make it look like a Christmas card. Was this his home? Was this where Cyril was guiding him to? He couldn't think why anyone would ever want to leave such a beautiful place.

But he needed to keep his wits about him. He had to be aware of potential dangers at all times. He continued his journey downwards through the meadow and eventually arrived at the mouth of the valley. It was going to be tricky to remain unseen as the path into the village was lined by a stream on one side and rocky shingle on the other. There was no natural cover.

So Jack used whatever shadow was available and managed to get to the edge of the village undetected. This was where the challenge became greater. Surely there would be guards just as there were at the arch. He'd been lucky that those guards were inept; he couldn't rely on luck again. At least now he had some idea of what he was up against.

A lone lamppost stood at the entrance to the village, spreading its flickering candlelight along the approaching path. If he chose this route he was going to be totally exposed, but a quick reconnaissance of the area showed him that there was no other way in. Did he want to risk climbing over a wall and finding himself in somebody's back garden, or worse, in a place full of guards?

The path to the village was clear – he listened intently. A solid silence greeted him. He'd take a chance and run into the village. Jack was quick and even if he came across more guards he was sure he could outrun them. Decision made and off he set. He ran the twenty metres to the lamppost and took a sharp left along a narrow lane. The dirt path had given way to cobblestones and he was glad that he was wearing rubber-soled trainers as he ran noiselessly along the lane.

Quaint thatched cottages lined the lane but Jack didn't have time to admire them. This was about working out the lie of the land and hopefully finding somebody who could help him. The lane split and he chose the left fork for no other reason than instinct. If he could find a place to hide on the outskirts of the village that would be ideal. He looked behind him to make sure that he wasn't being followed, just as he prepared to take a sharp right into an alleyway.

He slowed slightly as he turned, which was just as well as he ran head on into somebody walking the other way. Jack managed to keep on his feet but the other person was knocked flat on their back. He was about to make a run for it, but thought better of it. What if they were hurt? He couldn't just run away and leave them there. He leant down and helped them back on to their feet.

'What's the hurry? Is there a fire somewhere?'

He found himself face to face with a female Elf. She had short, swept back blond hair and striking, blue eyes that glittered in the flickering streetlight.

'I'm sorry; I was, er, I was just …'

'I know there's a curfew but the LEOs couldn't catch a cold,' she said dusting the dirt from her jacket.

'LEOs?' queried Jack.

'Lore Enforcement Officers - they supposedly police our community.' She looked Jack up and down. 'I don't think I've seen you around here before. Do you live in one of the villages further along the valley?'

How did he answer that? He could see that she was studying him intently as he thought about his answer. She was the first Elf that he'd ever spoken to and he didn't want to mislead her. Besides, he was a terrible liar. His grandfather could tell he was lying even before the words were out of his mouth. So, he had no choice, he had to trust her with the truth. 'I come from Heywood Forest, in the human world.'

She looked surprised. 'I didn't know there were any Elves in the forest. How long have you lived there?'

'All my life,' said Jack.

'So what brings you to Waterswood?'

'I, er, I'm looking for someone.'

'What's their name? I'll probably know them.'

This was getting more difficult by the second. 'I don't know … it's complicated.'

The Elf eyed him suspiciously. 'You're not one of Vilner's spies are you?'

'I don't even know who Vilner is.'

'He's not someone you want to meet, take it from me.' Her demeanour softened slightly. 'What's your name?'

'Jack – or sometimes Green-Jack.'

She held out her hand. 'I'm Lilac … Lilac Wildflower.'

He took her hand and shook it.

'It's not a good idea for you to be wandering around Waterswood after dark. The LEOs are everywhere. They're not the brightest bunch but if they catch you they'll throw you in the lock-up, especially when they find out you're from the human forest.' She peered out of the alleyway and checked up and down the lane. 'I'll take you to a friend of mine. He'll give you a bed for the night. Make sure you stick close to me.'

He followed her to the other end of the alleyway and she turned left into another narrow lane. Even though she wore boots, she moved noiselessly across the cobblestones. She had a grace and poise unlike anyone Jack had ever met before. And she had an air of confidence about her that made him feel safe. He'd been fortunate that he'd bumped into her and not one of the LEOs.

He followed her along several narrow lanes as they made their way stealthily through the village. They turned a corner and a line of cottages stood at the end of the lane facing them. They marked the edge of the village and backed on to the rolling hills. One cottage at the far end stood out from the rest. It was a bee-hived shape as opposed to the rectangular shape of the others. Lilac walked up to the cottage and opened the front gate and ushered Jack through. She pointed to a candle in the bay window. 'Lomund lights that every night. He says that it lets friends and strangers know that they are always welcome.'

She tapped gently on the front door and checked back along the lane. The door opened and a tall elderly Elf stood there. 'Lilac, I thought you were going home.' He stepped back and waved them in. Jack followed Lilac through the door and stood in the middle of a small circular room. A round table and chairs were tucked up against the wall to one side of the door; two armchairs sat either side of an open log fire and two beds were on the opposite side to the table. It was very basic but comfortable. Not unlike the cottage he shared with his grandfather.

'I found Jack wandering in the village. He comes from the human forest and doesn't know his way around here so I offered to help him. And I didn't want him falling into Vilner's clutches. I was hoping that you would give him a bed for the night.'

Lomund smiled warmly. 'Of course. Have you eaten?'

Jack was starving. He hadn't eaten all day. 'Er, no,' he said coyly.

Lomund pointed to the table and chairs. 'Take a seat at the table. I have some mushroom soup in the pot.'

Jack sat down at the table and Lilac sat next to him. 'Jack's looking for someone. I told him that we may be able to help him.'

Lomund peered at Lilac over the top of his half-moon glasses. 'Now let our guest eat first before you start firing questions at him!'

*

Jack devoured three bowlfuls of mushroom soup; four large chunks of oatmeal bread and drank several glasses of rhubarb juice. As he finished the last drop of juice, Lilac smiled at him.

'I was beginning to wonder if you were ever going to stop. Even Tyler can only manage two bowls of Lomund's mushroom soup.'

Lomund sat down beside her and placed a teapot and three mugs on the table. 'He's a growing young Elf and needs to keep his strength up. A healthy appetite is a sign of a healthy mind and body.' He filled the three mugs with a steaming gold liquid. 'Roseleaf tea,' said Lomund. 'It's just what you need after a meal. It aids the digestion.'

Jack picked up his mug and took a sip of his tea. It was sweet and very refreshing – nothing like the strong, dark brown tea his grandfather used to make.

'So, are you going to tell us who you're looking for? I'm intrigued,' said Lilac.

'You'll find that Lilac lacks a little patience and subtlety,' said Lomund. He looked at her over the top of his glasses again. 'Now let our guest enjoy his tea and stop interrogating him!'

Jack liked Lomund. He had the demeanour of someone who had not only lived his life but had learned lessons from it. An aura of serenity and wisdom surrounded him like a shining light. His kindly grey eyes, wispy, thinning, grey hair, and a patchy grey beard covering a tanned, lean face, gave him an appearance not too dissimilar to Jack's grandfather, Noah. Jack felt safe enough to tell them his story.

'I've lived in Heywood Forest all my life. I shared a cottage with my grandfather, Noah Green. I found out today that he's not my real grandfather. My mother left me with him when I was a baby around fifteen years ago. Noah said that she was frightened and asked him to look after me until it was safe to come back for me. We haven't seen her since.'

'Where is your grandfather now?' asked Lomund.

'He's gone to join his family – they're travellers.'

'I assume that Noah is a human?'

Jack nodded his head. 'Yes he is. I only found out today that I'm an Elf.'

Lilac sat open-mouthed. 'You're kidding me! I knew the moment I saw you that you were Elven.' She leant across and pulled his thick brown hair back revealing his pointy ears. 'Didn't they give you a clue?'

Jack shrugged his shoulders. 'I just thought I had funny ears. My cousins constantly teased me about them. I suppose I always thought I was different but …'

'You didn't have trouble accepting you were an Elf? Most humans seem to think that we only exist in story books,' said Lomund.

'My grandfather was very open minded and he taught me to be the same. Yes, it was a shock when he told me but I knew that he would never tell me a lie. I guess it came as a bit of a relief.'

'So, what's your mother's name?' asked Lilac.

'That's just it,' said Jack. 'I don't know, but my grandfather said that I'm the image of her.'

Jack sensed Lilac and Lomund studying him intently. He pulled out the red jewel that was hanging on a chain around his neck. 'This is hers. She left it with my grandfather.'

Lilac leant forward and studied it; her face suddenly turned ashen. She looked up at Lomund, wide-eyed and open-mouthed. 'It's Ciara's …'

Now it was Lomund's turn to look shocked. 'Are you sure?'

'I'd recognise it anywhere. It's definitely her Bloodstone.' She held it up against the candle light. 'Can you see there's a letter 'S' embedded within it. When we were young we used to speculate what it stood for.'

They both looked at Jack with a new awareness. 'I can't believe I didn't realise,' said Lilac. 'You're the image of her.'

Jack felt like his heart would burst with joy. They knew his mother. 'You know her? Can you take me to her?'

Lomund and Lilac's expressions changed instantly. They exchanged pained looks. 'We haven't seen her for over sixteen years,' said Lomund. 'She disappeared without trace.'

'But she does come from here?' pressed Jack.

'She lived here with a friend of ours called Crystal Oak,' said Lomund. 'She never knew her real parents – Crystal took her in and was like a mother to her. She was devastated when Ciara disappeared.'

'Can I see Crystal?' asked Jack. 'I want to know all about my mother.'

'Not tonight,' said Lomund. 'The LEOs will be prowling the lanes of Waterswood. Lilac will fetch her in the morning. I think we all need a good night's sleep. You've had a long day and Lilac and I need to gather our thoughts.'

'There's one other thing that you need to know,' said Jack. 'Elves in the forest tried to kill me and my grandfather last night. They burned our cottage to the ground.'

Lomund and Lilac looked aghast. 'Are you sure they were Elves?'

'My grandfather was sure and he overheard them

saying to make certain that I was in the cottage before they burned it.'

Lomund turned to Lilac - he didn't try to disguise the alarm in his voice. 'You'd better bring Tyler and Crystal here first thing in the morning.'

Chapter Five - New Friends

Jack opened his eyes, it took him several seconds to fathom out his surroundings. The delicious aroma wafting across the room made him think for a moment that he was back home in his grandfather's cottage. It was the Sunday morning ritual where Noah would cook them both a huge fry up. So much had happened to him the previous day that he wondered if he'd been in the middle of some bizarre dream. Lomund's cheery face told him he was not.

'Lilac brought around some clean clothes for you. I left them on the cabinet by the bed. I've filled a bath for you so that you can freshen up. I'll have breakfast on the table in ten minutes.'

Jack saw an old tin bath in the corner of the cottage behind an open curtain. It was almost identical to the one that his grandfather had. He jumped out of bed, threw his clothes off and stepped into the bath and gave himself a good scrub down and felt all the better for it. He put on the clothes that Lilac had left for him – a white shirt, green jacket and dark pants. There were also some black, knee length, leather boots, and when Jack put them on, he felt like a real Elf. The leather was so soft that it was like he was wearing a pair of well-worn slippers.

Lomund put two plates of steaming hot food on the table. 'Take a seat, Jack, and eat your breakfast while it's hot. There's plenty of toast and I'll pour the tea in a minute once it's brewed.'

Just as Jack was about to sit down there was a loud knock at the door followed by a shout: 'Open up! It's the Lore Enforcement Officers.'

'It's Vilner,' whispered Lomund. 'What does he want at this early hour? Quick, Jack, hide behind the door. I'll get rid of him.'

Jack hid behind the door as Lomund slid back the bolts and opened it. A short, slightly built Elf with greasy, jet black hair stood glaring at him. 'A stranger was seen in the village last night. I have reason to believe that he is staying here with you.'

Lomund was calm and composed. 'And what would lead you to such an assumption?'

'The stranger was seen entering your cottage last night.'

Lomund smiled dismissively. 'Now if that was the case, Vilner, you would have been knocking on my door at the time and not waiting until morning. There is no stranger here so if you don't mind I would like to get back to my breakfast.'

Vilner took a threatening step towards him. 'In that case you won't mind me searching your cottage.'

Lomund rose to his full height and looked down on the weedy Vilner. 'I have absolutely no intention of letting you in my cottage, so why don't you leave me in peace and let me get on with my breakfast.'

A tall muscular Elf suddenly appeared by Vilner's side. 'I think that Torec might not agree with you,' he sneered.

His high pitched, whiny voice grated on Jack. Although he couldn't see him, the voice told him all that he needed to know.

Lomund looked down at Vilner with contempt but knew he was no match for the young and strong Torec. He stepped back and Vilner strode into the cottage followed by Torec. Lomund waited for the inevitable cry of triumph when he saw Jack, but it didn't come. He pulled the door back but Jack wasn't there.

Vilner searched every centimetre of the cottage. He even looked under the beds. He walked over to the table and pointed to the two plates full of food. 'If there's no-one else staying here with you, why are there two plates of food?'

It didn't happen very often, but Lomund was lost for words. How did he explain that? Just at that moment a short, stout Elf with a bright red, blotchy face strolled into the cottage. 'Vilner! How unpleasant it is to see you so early in the day. I hope that I don't have to look at your sour face for too long, or it will put me off my breakfast.' He turned to Lomund. 'Sorry I'm late.' He pointed an accusing finger at Vilner. 'I got held up by his thugs questioning everyone in the centre of the village about some imaginary stranger.'

He pulled the front door of the cottage open. 'Now if you don't mind, my friend and I would like to enjoy our breakfast.'

Vilner looked as if he was about to explode. His shoulders tightened and his face turned a deep red. 'I know that you're up to something. And when I find out what it is, I'll have you both up before the Council of Elders.' He then stormed out of the cottage and the stout Elf slammed and bolted the door behind him.

'Your timing is impeccable as ever, Tyler,' said a relieved Lomund.

'Lilac told me to get over here as soon as I could. What did you do with Jack?'

Lomund shrugged his shoulders. 'I don't know, I …' He was interrupted by a voice from above him. 'I'm up here.'

They both looked up to see Jack hiding in the wooden roof beams of the cottage. He swung down and dropped beside them. 'I thought I'd better make myself scarce when Vilner barged his way in.'

Tyler stood open mouthed for several seconds. 'I can't believe it – you're her double.'

Lomund put his hand on Jack's shoulder. 'Jack, this is my good friend, Tyler. He was also one of your mother's closest friends.'

Jack wasn't sure what to do but was taken aback when Tyler embraced him in a bear hug. 'Ciara's son will always be a friend of mine. Just ask if you need anything - and I mean anything!'

'Come,' said Lomund. 'It would be a shame to let our breakfast go cold. Tyler, you take mine. I'll cook some more.'

'I'd make enough for at least another three,' said Tyler,

'as Crystal and Lilac are on their way.' And sure enough there was a knock at the door. Lomund walked over and opened it and Lilac breezed in followed by another elderly female Elf, who Jack assumed to be Crystal.

'Please take a seat at the table. Breakfast is on its way.'

But Crystal stood rooted to the spot, her whole attention focused on Jack. She looked as if she'd seen a ghost. Jack started to feel slightly uncomfortable. As much as he wanted to be back amongst his own people, he had no idea how to handle the effect he seemed to be having on them.

'I thought you were exaggerating, Lilac, like you always do, but he really is the image of Ciara,' said Crystal.

'Can I suggest that we all eat a hearty breakfast and we can talk afterwards over a cup of Roseleaf?' said Lomund.

Jack sat at the table and looked at his plate. It was full of mushrooms, fried tomatoes, scrambled egg and what looked like two white cakes. Tyler noticed him pushing them with his knife. 'Oat cakes – they're delicious. And if you don't like them give them to me.'

'Leave him alone, Tyler,' said Lilac. 'Pay no attention to him, Jack. He would eat you if you stayed still long enough!'

Jack tried the oat cakes and they were delicious. He could taste herbs and a slight spice. It suddenly occurred to him that they were all eating the same as him. He always thought his refusal to eat meat was because of his love for his animal friends, but perhaps it was more genetic. Maybe Elves are vegetarians, he thought.

It was a strangely subdued meal and Jack couldn't help but feel self-conscious as he felt three sets of eyes on him as he eat. But Lomund's awareness came to the rescue and he placed a pot of Roseleaf in the middle of the table. He cleared the plates away and asked Lilac to pour the tea.

Jack studied Crystal discreetly as she helped Lilac. Her blue-grey eyes were bright and clear and she had a look of steely determination about her. Her grey hair was tied up in a neat bun on the back of her head. Her features were sharp and distinguished. Jack could see why his mother would look to her as her own mother figure.

Lomund sat down at the table and playfully slapped Jack on his shoulder. 'So, young Jack, let me welcome you to Waterswood – your home. I just wish that circumstances were different but I'm afraid that we live in challenging times. In all of my many years living in this village, I have never known such an oppressive atmosphere. Our rulers, the Council of Elders, think, for some reason that we need to be told what to do, and I can assure you that we do not.'

'I'll second that,' said Tyler raising his mug of tea.

'I am very disturbed by what you told Lilac and me last night,' continued Lomund. 'Are you sure your grandfather was correct about what happened to your cottage.'

'He would never say anything without being sure of his facts. I could tell that he was genuinely concerned for my safety and begged me to go with him to his own people. But I knew I had to find out where I came from and I had to find my mother, which is why I came here.'

'How did you find your way to Waterswood?' asked Crystal.

'My friend Cyril brought me here.'

Tyler looked surprised. 'A human led you to Waterswood?'

'Er, no,' said Jack. 'He's a squirrel.'

Tyler's face broke out into a huge grin. 'Cyril the squirrel! What an amazing name. I'm sure there must be a poem there somewhere.'

'You'll get used to Tyler,' said Lilac. 'He has aspirations of being a poet.'

'Aspirations, young Lilac,' protested Tyler. 'I am surely the best poet in Waterswood.'

'You're the only poet in Waterswood!' laughed Lilac.

'You see, young Jack, she just doesn't appreciate my creative talents.'

'Animals have great instincts,' said Lomund trying to

get them back on to the subject. 'I have no doubt that he always knew you were an Elf, which is why he is your friend.'

Jack felt a warm and comfortable feeling slowly building up inside him. He loved his grandfather dearly, and even though Noah wasn't a blood relative, Jack's feelings for him would never change. But this was different – he was amongst his own. Already he felt a strong bond with them. But there was one subject he was bursting to discuss.

He looked across the table to Crystal. 'Please tell me about my mother.' He reached into his shirt and pulled out the Bloodstone. 'This is all I have of hers and I know so little about her.'

Crystal nursed her mug of tea and breathed slowly for several moments. Jack could see that discussing his mother was going to cause her pain.

'Ciara lived with me for over eighteen years. I took her in when she was only a young child and we became like mother and daughter. I've never been so close to anyone in my life. We seemed to know what each other was thinking. She even trained to become a Healer and we were going to work together in my clinic in the village.'

She hesitated and sipped her tea for a moment. 'And that's how it was until around a year before she left. She suddenly became distant and spent less and less time with me. To be honest, I never knew where she was most of the time. She lost interest in her healing work and we stopped communicating. I kept asking her if I'd done something to upset her but she would dismiss it and say that everything was fine. But I can't help wondering if I missed something. She was hurting and for some reason couldn't tell me.'

'It wasn't just you, Crystal,' said Lilac. 'She became distant with me too. I very rarely saw her during that time.'

'I would put it down to adolescence,' said Lomund. 'Every young Elf goes through a period like that. It's when they're striving for their independence. Ciara loved you dearly, Crystal, so please don't blame yourself for her disappearance.'

Crystal looked at Jack through tear filled eyes. 'She didn't even tell me that she was pregnant. When Lilac told me about you this morning I could hardly take in what she was saying. And to be honest, I didn't believe her. That was until I saw you. There's absolutely no doubt you are Ciara's son. Not only do you look like her but you have her mannerisms.' Tears streamed down her cheeks. 'I just can't understand why she never told me.'

It disturbed Jack to see her so upset. It was obvious that she loved his mother dearly. 'My grandfather told me that she was frightened, not just for herself, but for me too. He said that she was broken hearted at having to leave me with him but that it was for the best. And she always planned to come back for me one day.'

A sombre Tyler stared grim-faced into his mug. 'Whoever it was she feared lived in this village. And I would bet that they are the very same people who tried to kill Jack the other night.' A tense, uneasy silence spread around the table. 'And I think we all know who is behind most of the nasty things that happen in this community.'

'Surely you're not suggesting Grimley is responsible for this?' said Lomund.

'Who else would it be?' asked Tyler.

'Grimley is capable of many things, but murder?'

'Who's Grimley?' asked Jack.

'The supposed leader of the Council of Elders and head of our community,' said Tyler. 'Grim by name and grim by nature.'

'Well our main concern must be for Jack's safety,' said Crystal. 'We have to get him away from Waterswood. Vilner's LEOs already know that there's a stranger in the village. It's not safe for him to be here.'

'I agree,' said Lomund. 'But where can we take him that's safe from them.'

'Back to the human forest,' said Crystal. 'Vilner has no influence there. It will give us time to decide what to do.'

Jack couldn't believe what he was hearing. 'No!' he pleaded. 'I've only just found you. Please don't send me back to the forest. For the first time in my life I feel like I belong.'

'Surely there must be somewhere outside of Waterswood where we can take him that's safe?' said Lilac.

'Crystal's right,' said Lomund. 'I'm sorry, Jack. I know you don't want to leave but we must keep you safe. We don't know who tried to kill you but they almost certainly came from this village.' He tried to console Jack. 'It will only be until we find out who's responsible.' He placed his hand on Jack's shoulder. 'Having only just found you, the last thing we would wish to do is to send you away again.'

Jack understood the reasons why he had to go but his heart still ached. He'd only just found his home village, and now he was being sent away. But he trusted the people sat around this table and he knew that their only concern was for his safety. 'OK, I'll go back to the forest, but I want you to come for me as soon as it's safe to do so.'

'I give you my word,' said Lomund.

'We'll wait until nightfall and then I'll take you back to the arch,' said a serious looking Tyler.

*

Chapter Six – Custody

Jack had spent the whole day thinking of reasons why he should stay in Waterswood, but as hard as he tried, he couldn't come up with any viable arguments to put to his new friends. The only reason they were asking him to go back to the human forest was because of his own personal safety, or lack of, in Waterswood.

It had been decided that Tyler would take him around the village perimeter and along the path that followed the foot of the Waterdown Hills. Vilner's LEOs would be patrolling all of the entrances to the village and the Arch of Peace had a permanent guard, likely to be Laric and Garwood. The plan was that Tyler would distract the two guards while Jack sneaked through the arch unnoticed.

As nightfall came, the dread that had lurked in the pit of Jack's stomach all day came to the surface. He felt physically sick. How he wished he could stay, but … Lilac and Crystal had left Lomund's cottage straight after breakfast and gone about their usual daily work so as not to arouse Vilner's suspicions.

Jack stood at the door to Lomund's cottage proudly wearing his new Elven clothes and Tyler was furtively checking the lane for any sign of the LEOs. Lomund placed both hands on Jack's shoulders and looked him directly in the eyes.

'It pains me to have to send you away. I promise you if there was any alternative and you could stay, that's what would happen. We must find out who is behind the attempt on your life and until we do, we have to keep you safe.' He pulled Jack close and hugged him warmly.

Tyler suddenly appeared at the door. 'It's all clear – we must go.' Jack did his best to smile at Lomund before following Tyler out of the door and through the gate. Tyler led him around the back of the cottage and along the path that followed the foot of the Waterdown Hills around the village perimeter. 'The LEOs rarely venture along here.

They think it's haunted,' whispered Tyler.

'Why would they think that?' asked Jack.

'Because I told them,' winked Tyler. 'Come, let's get you safely across that meadow and out through the arch.'

The moon was bright and full and flooded the village in its silver light. Jack stopped and looked down onto the array of cottages that was Waterswood. As strange as it seemed, he felt homesick. A place that he'd known for only a day had already become his home. Tyler put his hand on Jack's shoulder and gave it a reassuring squeeze.

'Don't worry, Jack, you will soon be back. I give you my word.'

Jack forced another smile and nodded before following Tyler along the compacted dirt track towards the edge of the village. Jack pushed his unhappiness at leaving Waterswood to one side and focused all of his attention on getting safely back to his forest.

It was as they approached the outer perimeter of the village that Jack stopped and grabbed Tyler by the shoulder. 'I can hear voices,' he whispered.

'Are you sure?' asked Tyler.

'They're up ahead,' said Jack. 'Wait here - I'll go and check.'

'Let me,' said Tyler.

'No offence,' said Jack, 'but I'm lighter on my feet. And I'll make sure they don't see me.'

Tyler reluctantly nodded his agreement and Jack left the pathway and stealthily moved through the bushes. He crept through the undergrowth with the guile of one of his animal friends from Heywood Forest. He was impossible to either see or hear. He crawled on his belly in between two blackthorn bushes and looked along the path. Four LEOs were huddled in a group behind a perimeter fence that backed onto the cottages.

Jack smiled to himself. He could have spotted them with his eyes closed. He crept back to Tyler and told him what he'd seen.

'Are you sure there were four?' he asked.

'Absolutely,' said Jack.

'Mmmm,' said Tyler as he stroked his chin. 'We're going to have to find another way out.'

'What about going through the wood on the hill?' asked Jack.

Tyler shook his head. 'It's as black as a raven's backside in there at night. It's hard enough to find your way through it during the day as the trees are so densely packed. I think we'd be better taking our chances by going back into the village. I know some safe passages in between the cottages that will take us out onto Golden Meadow. Follow me.'

Jack followed Tyler back along the path and turned down a narrow alleyway in between Lomund's cottage and his neighbour's. He hesitated at the end of the alleyway and checked that the lane was clear. 'This way,' he whispered to Jack, and stepped out onto the lane.

They crept along the lane for several metres before turning off into another narrow alleyway. 'The LEOs rarely check these,' said Tyler. 'As long as we avoid the main lanes we should be OK.' Jack followed Tyler along a series of lanes and alleyways as they slowly wound their way towards the village perimeter.

Tyler stopped at the end of an alleyway on the edge of the village and pointed across the lane towards a narrow entrance. 'That leads to the meadow. It's never guarded. A few more minutes and we'll be out of the village.'

Jack was relieved. The tension was draining him and as much as he didn't want to go back to the forest, he most certainly didn't want to get captured by the LEOs. They ran across the lane and straight into the alleyway, although in Tyler's case, it was more of an amble. Jack ran into the alleyway and turned back to see where Tyler was.

A cry rang out from behind him. 'Stop! Don't move!'

Jack turned around and saw Vilner slowly walking along the alleyway towards him. He reacted instantly and ran back across the lane and shouted to Tyler: 'It's Vilner. Run!'

He grabbed Tyler by his arm and dragged him in the opposite direction. But Tyler was struggling. He didn't have the physique or the fitness to run for any distance. They turned a corner and he almost collapsed onto the ground. 'It's no good; I'll never be able to outrun them. You should leave me Jack, and take your chances,' he wheezed.

'I'm not leaving you. Surely there's somewhere we can lie low for a while.'

Tyler was struggling to breathe and couldn't get his words out. 'Lilac's cottage is just around the corner. We could hide there.'

'Let's go,' said Jack as he pulled Tyler back up. Jack near lifted him off his feet and half carried him along the lane. They turned a corner and Tyler pointed to a pink cottage in front of them. 'That's Lilac's.'

Jack pulled Tyler across the road and through the gate and up to the front door and knocked loudly. The door opened and Tyler almost fell through. Jack followed him in and the door was immediately shut behind them. He heard a voice that he didn't recognise from across the room.

'I was beginning to wonder what had happened to you. You're much later than I expected.'

A tall Elf, with his long, grey hair tied back in a ponytail, stood in the corner staring at them. His cold, grey eyes penetrated deep into Jack's soul. Jack looked across the other side of the room and saw Torec holding Lilac with his hand across her mouth.

'So, Tyler, are you going to tell me who your friend is?'

Tyler looked at him with contempt. 'I wouldn't tell you the time, Grimley.'

A vicious sneer crossed Grimley's lips. 'As disrespectful as ever, Tyler. Perhaps a few days on bread and water and a few nights on a hard stone floor might teach you some manners.'

'For you? I doubt that very much,' spat Tyler.

Grimley raised his eyebrows. 'We shall see.' He walked over to the front door and opened it. Vilner stood there with two LEOs. 'Take Tyler to the jailhouse and give him our most uncomfortable cell.'

'My pleasure,' sneered Vilner and walked over to Tyler and grabbed him by the arm. Tyler immediately snatched it back. 'Get your filthy hands off me you little worm.'

Vilner turned to his two officers. 'Arrest Tyler and take him to the jailhouse.' Two burly Elves strode into the room and grabbed Tyler and unceremoniously bundled him out of the door. Tyler protested vehemently and struggled, but he was no match for their combined strength.

Grimley turned to Vilner. 'You can stand down the extra patrols. Just keep the usual numbers on duty. Tell your officers that I'm very pleased with their night's work.'

'Why thank you, Grimley,' snivelled Vilner. 'I will pass your compliment on to them.'

Grimley shut the door behind Vilner and turned his attention to Jack. 'Please, take a seat,' and pointed towards one of the fireside chairs.

Jack had taken an instant dislike to Vilner. His whiny voice and sneaky manner were both traits that he hated in people. And Grimley was even worse. There was something sinister about him. The way he talked and the way he looked at you were unnerving. But Jack chose to show he wasn't scared.

'I'd like you to tell your officer to release Lilac. It makes me feel uneasy seeing her held like that.'

Grimley nodded towards Torec. 'Release her.' He took his hands from Lilac and stepped away from her.

Lilac glared at Grimley. 'How dare you invade my cottage and let that brute manhandle me?'

'What do you expect if you insist on breaking council lore?'

Lilac shook her head in disbelief. 'So welcoming a visitor into our village is all of a sudden a crime?'

Grimley walked over to the table and pulled a chair out and sat down. 'These are dangerous times, Lilac Wildflower. We cannot allow strangers to come into our community without first checking who they are and what business they have with us.' He pointed Jack towards one of the fireside chairs. 'Sit down.'

Jack did as he asked and sat in one of the fireside chairs. He tried his best to relax but it wasn't easy with Grimley's grey eyes boring deep into him.

'So, do you have a name?'

Jack could hear Noah's voice in his head. *Never let anyone put you down, Green-Jack. You're as good as any person on this planet.*

'I only share my name with people I like,' said Jack defiantly.

'Mmmm,' said Grimley. 'It seems that disrespect is catching.' He leant forward and locked his evil grey eyes onto Jack. 'Let me tell you what happens to young Elves who don't show me the respect that my position demands. They get taken to Darkenwold – and I can assure you that it's not a pleasant place. I would suggest that it is a place to be avoided.'

Lilac looked horrified. 'Grimley, why would you do such a terrible thing? Jack is only a ...' She stopped mid-sentence and put her hand over her mouth. 'Oh, Jack, I'm so sorry, I just ...'

'Don't worry, Lilac. It makes no difference whether he knows my name or not.'

A self-satisfied smile contorted Grimley's lips. 'So, Jack. Where do you come from?'

Jack didn't hesitate. 'Waterswood.'

Grimley sat back in his chair. The smile was replaced with a grimace. 'I haven't time for your tiresome games. You will be taken to the jailhouse for the night and will appear before the Council of Elders in the morning. I will recommend that you be sent to Darkenwold for a week. Then you will be brought back to Waterswood for further questioning. If you still refuse to co-operate, you will be sent back to Darkenwold indefinitely. Torec, take him to the jailhouse.'

The big Elf strode over to Jack and grabbed him by his arm and roughly pulled him to his feet. Although Jack wasn't as strong as him, he was more nimble. He yanked his arm away and darted for the door. He pulled it open only to find the two burly guards that had arrested Tyler blocking his way.

'There is no escape from me, Jack. The sooner you start co-operating, the sooner we can be more civilised towards you.'

Lilac confronted Grimley. 'You can see that Jack is only young, Grimley. Why don't you make allowances for the fact that he may be frightened? Please don't send him to Darkenwold. He won't survive in there.'

'I'm afraid that I don't agree with you, Lilac. I don't see fear in this young Elf, I see defiance. A week in Darkenwold will cure this character flaw.' He addressed the guards. 'Take him to the jailhouse.'

The two guards grabbed Jack by his arms and lifted him off his feet before whisking him out of the door and into the dark, cold Waterswood night.

Chapter Seven - The Hearing

Jack sat on a hard, cold, stone floor, alongside a tray of uneaten food; although food was probably too generous a description. It was a bowl of watery soup and a chunk of stale bread that was as hard as a house brick. He sipped water from an earthenware mug and dwelt on the situation he found himself in. It was hardly the homecoming he'd hoped for, but at least he was sure that he'd found the Elf who wanted him dead.

Grimley. But what he didn't know was why?

Grimley knew who Jack was the moment he set eyes on him. Jack saw the recognition in his evil, grey eyes. He knew that he was Ciara's son. Lilac, Crystal, Tyler and Lomund had all said that he was her double; it stood to reason that Grimley would see the same likeness.

He focused his mind on his immediate problem. He was going to be taken to this place, Darkenwold. He saw the horrified look on Lilac's face when Grimley said it, so it wasn't going to be pleasant. Jack smiled to himself. That was the understatement of the decade. It was going to be a living nightmare. So how was he going to get away from Waterswood?

Tyler was in custody. Hopefully, Lilac was still free. She would tell both Lomund and Crystal. All was not lost, he was sure that they would come up with something.

He thought about his grandfather. If he knew the predicament Jack was in he would be beside himself with worry. But Noah had taught Jack many lessons in life. In fact, he taught him everything he knew. *Never give up hope, Jack lad. Not until the last breath in your body says its final farewell ...*

*

The door burst open and Torec and another LEO strode into the cell. 'The Elders are ready for you.' Jack was about to stand up but found himself roughly pulled to his feet by the two guards. They half dragged, half walked Jack out of the cell and marched him along a door-lined corridor. They stopped in front of a heavy iron door at the end of the corridor and Torec knocked twice. Jack heard the sound of bolts being drawn back and the click of a lock. The door creaked open and a prison guard looked Jack up and down before nodding to Torec. Jack was pushed out of the door and into a cobblestone courtyard surrounded by high walls.

Jack briefly thought about making a run for it but saw that there was nowhere to run to. He was marched over to the large, double iron gates at the far end of the courtyard and Torec once again knocked twice. A small panel was drawn back. A pair of eyes appeared in the opening and scanned the three of them. The panel was slammed shut and Jack heard the sound of bolts sliding back again. The hinges squealed in protest as the gates were slowly pulled open. Jack looked out onto a cobblestone square with a wishing-well at its centre that was identical to the one on the Faery Crossing in Heywood Forest.

The square was surrounded by several tall, ornate, wooden thatched buildings. Jack guessed that it was the village centre. The guards dragged him through the open gates, across the cobblestones and up the steps of a large domed building on the far side of the square. They pushed open two tall wooden doors and pulled him into a spacious oak panelled foyer. An elderly, female Elf with short, grey hair sat behind a desk writing on some notepaper.

'We have the prisoner for the hearing,' said Torec in dull, flat tones.

'Take him into the courtroom, Torec,' said the Elf. 'The Elders will be ready shortly.' Jack was bundled through a door and into a chamber full of lines of empty chairs. Torec marched him to the front of the chamber and threw him into a chair that faced a long bench raised on a platform.

'Move and I'll break your legs,' he growled.

Jack looked up into his stony face and knew that he meant it. A part of him wanted to defy him but at the same time he didn't want to provoke him. He prayed that Lomund would be at the hearing to tell him what he should do.

A door opened behind the bench and a line of elderly Elves walked in. Torec yanked Jack to his feet and hissed, 'show respect for the Elders.'

They were all dressed in long white robes. Jack thought they looked like aged clones. Grimley sat in the middle of the bench, with five Elders sat either side of him. A self-satisfied smirk spread across his lips as he looked down at Jack. He didn't speak at first and studied him intently for several minutes. Jack could tell that he was enjoying himself.

'So, Jack, I trust that the accommodation and food were to your liking?'

Jack smiled defiantly. 'I've known worse.'

'Have you indeed,' said Grimley. 'Well I think that we may be able to introduce you to worse still.' He looked along the line of his colleagues. 'As I told you, defiant and aggressive. Not the sort of Elf we want stirring up unrest here in Waterswood. I don't see any point in any further questioning. We will take a vote on whether we send him to Darkenwold. I think that my original assessment of a week may be too short - a month may be more appropriate. Raise your right hands if you agree.'

Ten hands rose into the air as one. Grimley didn't attempt to hide his satisfaction and glared at Jack in triumph. 'You will be taken from here and confined in Darkenwold for one month. We will then reconvene this hearing and see if you've managed to learn any respect for this court. Take him away, Torec.'

Just at that moment the door at the rear of the chamber burst open and Crystal Oak came striding into the courtroom. 'Grimley! What the hell do you think you're doing?' She pushed Torec away from Jack and put her arms around him. 'Jack, are you OK?'

'I'm fine – just a little tired, that's all.'

She glared at Grimley and the other Elders. 'You are meant to be the upholders of our lore, and here you are treating it with contempt.'

Grimley waved his hand dismissively at her. 'Crystal Oak, why must you always be so tiresome? Concentrate on your duties as a Healer and allow us to get on with the work of protecting our community.'

Crystal stood directly in front of him. 'Your role is to uphold our lore and make sure that it is administered fairly and justly. You know that you cannot hold a hearing without people in the public gallery.'

'We have Torec and Ranion as witnesses.'

'They're guarding Jack!' cried Crystal. 'They're hardly independent witnesses.'

'Well, I'm sorry, Crystal Oak – our decision has been made. Jack will be sent to Darkenwold for one month.'

Disbelief etched Crystal's face. 'A month in Darkenwold! Whatever has Jack done to deserve that?'

'He has been disrespectful to me and the Elders. We cannot tolerate such behaviour. He must be taught the error of his ways.'

Crystal stepped up onto the platform and placed her hands on the bench and pushed her face right into Grimley's. Jack saw his unease as he leant back from her. 'If you don't suspend the hearing this minute, I will go from here and call a public meeting in the square. I will tell them about this farce and call for a challenge to the Elders.' She looked at him with a steely determination. 'I think you know the consequences of that better than I.'

Grimley looked as if he was about to wave her away, but one of the Elders rose to his feet. He had long, white hair and a long, white beard. Jack thought he looked like Old Father Time.

'Crystal Oak has a point, Grimley. A challenge to the Elders at this time could prove to be very destabilising. Perhaps we could call a recess and reconvene later when the public are in attendance.'

Grimley's face flushed an angry red colour. Jack thought that he was about to explode. He looked along the line of Elders and they all seemed to retreat into their seats. 'One hour,' said Grimley. 'I will delay the proceedings for one hour.' He stood up, threw his chair out of the way and stormed out of the chamber.

Crystal walked over to Jack. 'I will gather the village. I will do my best to make sure that you get a fair hearing.'

*

Jack sat in a small room to the side of the courtroom. Torec and Ranion stood either side of the door staring impassively into space. They hadn't uttered a single word to him the whole time he'd been in the room. He had no idea what to expect at the hearing but was reassured that Crystal was going to ensure that it was fair.

There was a knock at the door and the Elf who'd been in the foyer came into the room. 'The Elders are ready for you, Jack. If you'd like to follow me.'

He stood up and followed her into the chamber. The rows of empty chairs were now filled with chattering Elves. The background chatter ceased as soon as they saw Jack. Every eye in the chamber watched him as he took his seat in front of the bench. He wanted to look around for Crystal and Lomund but he felt conspicuous in front of so many strangers.

The female Elf stood at the front of the chamber facing the gallery. 'Would you please all be upstanding for the Elders?' Chairs scraped on the wooden floor as the Elves stood up. The Elders filed through the door at the front of the chamber and once again took their places behind the front bench. Jack studied Grimley and thought that he still looked very tense. He hoped that was a good sign.

Grimley waved his hand for them to sit back down and looked across to the female Elf standing to the side of the front bench. 'Rosebud, would you please read out the accusation.'

She looked across to Jack. 'Would you please stand?' Jack stood and made a point of looking straight at Grimley. Rosebud read from the piece of paper she was holding.

'You are accused of entering Waterswood illegally and without permission. That you deliberately avoided capture by the Community Lore Enforcement Officers and that when you were finally apprehended, you were rude and disrespectful to the Head of the Council of Elders.'

Grimley nodded towards her. 'Thank you Rosebud.' He locked his evil grey eyes onto Jack. 'Perhaps we can resume from where we left off before we were so rudely interrupted earlier this morning.'

Jack suddenly heard a voice from the back of the chamber. 'May I approach the bench?' He looked around to see Lomund ambling through the middle of the gallery towards him. The old Elf gave Jack's shoulder a reassuring squeeze as he stood beside him.

'May I offer the Elders my sincere apologies for being late,' he said as he bowed his head. 'It takes longer and longer to get these aching bones up and out of bed in the morning.'

Grimley looked contemptuously at him. 'I have no interest in your aching bones, Lomund. Will you please take your seat in the gallery and allow the hearing to proceed.'

'Ah,' said Lomund. 'This hearing cannot proceed without the Defence Council. And I haven't had a chance to brief my client of his rights yet.'

Grimley bristled at the suggestion. 'The accused is not entitled to a Defence Council as he isn't a resident of Waterswood.'

'You surprise me, Grimley,' said Lomund. 'As the leader of the Council of Elders, I would have thought that you would have a better grasp of our lore. It quite clearly states that any Elf, regardless of their origin, is entitled to representation if an accusation is made against them.'

The Elf that looked like Old Father Time rose to his

feet again. 'He's correct in his assertion, Grimley; legal representation is a right for all Elves.'

Grimley shot him a look that could kill. 'When I want your council, Bailey, I will ask for it.' Bailey shrank back into his chair and lowered his eyes. Grimley looked first at Jack, and then at Lomund. 'Very well, I will give you thirty minutes with your so-called client, then the hearing begins.'

Lomund bowed low. 'I thank the Elders for their patience and understanding.'

*

Jack sat at a table as Crystal massaged his shoulders. 'You're very tense, Jack. You're going to need all of your energy to deal with this hearing.'

A serious looking Lomund sat across from him. 'I have a very bad feeling about this. I doubt that you will get a fair hearing. Grimley intimidates the Elders and they are never going to undermine him, especially in public. But what bothers me most is why he's so intent on sending you to Darkenwold.'

'Why does that bother you?' asked Jack.

'Because I don't think he intends you to come out of there.'

The knots in Jack's shoulders weren't responding to Crystal's soothing massage which was hardly surprising after what Lomund had just said. 'Is Darkenwold really that bad?'

Lomund exchanged uncomfortable looks with Crystal before continuing. 'Waterswood and all the other Elven communities are sustained by ancient magic. It's what separates us from the human world. Elves were once accomplished artisans in the use of magic but sadly, that is no longer the case. It takes years of hard work and practice to be able to work with such power. It's a skill that can never be truly mastered.

There were instances where individual Elves were

overwhelmed by the magic. They were unable to keep control of the wild powers that underpin it. Sadly, it sent them insane. They were a danger to themselves and to the community so they had to be contained. The Elders built an institution in a remote valley some miles away from here. The victims of the magic were incarcerated there, and sadly, will never see the cold light of day again.

At Grimley's insistence, the Elders banned the Elves of Waterswood from working with magic. It is now an illegal practice in our community. Not for the first time in his life, I believe that Grimley is wrong. Magic is an important part of our heritage. It is what makes us who we are – part of the world of Faery.'

There was little familiar in this new world that Jack found himself in. He knew it was going to be difficult when he set out on his quest but he was in a situation that he neither relished nor understood. But his grandfather had taught him well. He could deal with most things.

'I'm sure I could survive a week, or even a month in such a place. I was taught from a young age how to look after myself.'

'Once you were in there, it would be easy for Grimley to arrange for a nasty 'accident' to happen to you.' Lomund shook his head. 'We cannot risk you going into that place.'

'So you also think that Grimley wants me dead?'

'I didn't agree with Tyler when he first suggested it but the fact that Grimley wants to send you to Darkenwold has changed my mind. It is now even more important that we get you away from Waterswood.'

'That's not going to be easy,' said Crystal. 'There are LEOs all around the courtroom. We'll never get Jack out of there.'

Lomund addressed Jack directly. 'When we return to the hearing, I will join you at the front of the courtroom. I will tell the Elders that you have recognised that you were disrespectful to Grimley and that you will accept whatever punishment they deem appropriate.'

Jack looked horrified. 'But …'

'Don't worry, Jack,' continued Lomund. 'It's just a ruse to put them at ease.' He turned to Crystal. 'I want you to take a seat next to Rosebud to the right of the front bench and discreetly open the window behind you while I address the Elders. When I give you the signal, Jack, I want you to dive through the open window into the hedges outside, and run like the wind through the village and towards the hills at the rear of my cottage. When you reach the edge of the village, continue up the hill towards the forest at the top. As you approach the forest you will see a tree standing out on its own. This is the Tickle Tree, so named because of her light, feathery leaves. The tree is one of my oldest friends. Tell her that I have sent you and that you seek refuge. She will open her branches and hide you until we come for you.'

Jack's head was spinning with everything that was happening to him. His homecoming hadn't turned out anything like he'd hoped. But he had friends that he could trust in Lomund and Crystal. They would see to it that he came to no harm.

He nodded. 'I'll do whatever you ask.'

'We'll keep you safe,' said Lomund. 'No matter what it takes.'

Chapter Eight – Escape

Lomund stood alongside Jack at the front of a hushed courtroom as he addressed the Elders. Grimley eyed him suspiciously as he started to speak.

'I thank the Elders for their indulgence and for allowing me the time to consult with my client. Jack now has a better understanding of the workings of our lore and realises the importance of the procedures that we have to follow. He recognises that the lore is there to protect him and that the Elders have a duty to protect the community as a whole. He also …'

Grimley raised his right hand and gestured for Lomund to stop. 'I'm very pleased that your client recognises the importance of our lore but can we return our attention to why we are here today. Would you please get to the point and tell me how he is going to plead?'

Lomund bowed his head. 'I apologise, Grimley, but I just wanted you to know that Jack fully understands the process we are about to go through.'

'And how is he going to plead?' persisted Grimley.

'I was just getting to that,' said Lomund. 'But I needed to acquaint myself with the facts of the accusation before I could advise my client. Jack explained that he was both confused and frightened when he was first confronted by the Lore Enforcement Officers, which is why he may have come across as disrespectful to you, Grimley.'

Jack looked out of the corner of his eye and saw Crystal discreetly opening the window. The moment of his escape was near.

Grimley looked at Jack. 'Are you now ready to answer my questions?'

Jack's heart thumped like a bass drum in his chest. He was preparing himself to run. 'Yes I am,' he said as calmly as he could.

Grimley looked almost disappointed, but he repeated his question of the night before. 'So, Jack, where is it exactly that you come from?'

Jack saw that Crystal was back in her seat. He felt Lomund squeeze his arm – the signal to run. 'There is something that I'd like to say first,' said Jack.

'And what is that?' asked Grimley.

'Goodbye!' Jack sprinted the short distance to the window and dived through. He hit a thick privet hedge just outside the window and bounced onto the cobblestone path beyond. He jumped to his feet and quickly found his bearings and headed towards the hills at the rear of the village. As he sped down the road, a cry of 'Stop!' rang out behind him.

He didn't bother turning around to see who it was and ran as fast as he could, turning left and right along a series of lanes as he kept running in the general direction of the hills. He relied on his instincts to guide him and kept to the lanes as he didn't want to risk any narrow alleyways where it would be easier to apprehend him.

As he approached the village perimeter, he saw Lomund's 'bee-hive' cottage in front of him. He spotted the alleyway that he and Tyler had used the previous evening and decided that was the quickest route to the foot of the hills. He ran along the alleyway and into the hedges beyond. He expertly used the cover of the bushes to make it more difficult for his pursuers to follow him.

As he climbed the hill, his pace didn't slow. He kept to the bushes where he could, as it gave him much needed cover. And one thing that Jack could do well was blend in with his surroundings. As he approached the top of the hill, he looked for the tree that Lomund had mentioned.

And sure enough, it was just as Lomund had told him. A tall tree that had a dense covering of leaves that stretched almost all of the way to the ground stood out alone in front of the forest. He ran up to her and hesitated for a few seconds as he caught his breath. A quick look behind told him that he'd left his pursuers a long way back, but he knew they would be arriving soon.

He looked up to the tree and in his clearest voice said,

'Hello Tickle Tree. My name is Green-Jack and Lomund has sent me. He told me that you would give me the sanctuary that I so desperately need.'

The tree seemed to study him for a moment before she opened her lower branches to reveal what looked like a staircase. Jack didn't hesitate and climbed onto the branches and quickly made his way to the top of the tree. He found a comfortable spot and lay back into the feathery leaves. The tree enclosed itself quickly around him making it impossible to see him from the ground.

Which was just as well, as a matter of minutes later, he heard loud voices down below him. 'He must have run into the forest. We'll have to spread out and start our search. Kliner, you wait here and tell the back-up officers where we've gone.'

Jack lay back into his feathery nest and was surprised at just how comfortable it was. He wondered why he'd never made friends with any of the trees in Heywood Forest. *Maybe that's something I can put right in the future*, he thought.

*

It was dark when Jack woke. He rubbed his eyes and stretched, before listening for any sign of the LEOs. An owl hooted in the distance, and the wind rustled the leaves; other than that it was quiet. He looked down onto the flickering lights of Waterswood and wished that he was staying in the warm comfort of Lomund's cottage.

But the Tickle Tree had also welcomed him with open arms, or more accurately, open branches. He was comfortable and he was safe. What more could he ask for? His stomach rumbled. Food – he was starving as he hadn't eaten since the previous night in Lomund's. The Tickle Tree seemed to read his mind as a bag mysteriously appeared within the feathery leaves next to him.

He opened it and found a chunk of bread, some cheese and a small flask. He removed the stopper from the flask and took a drink. It was rhubarb juice. He bit into the bread and broke off a lump of cheese. Hunger always made food taste so much better, he thought. As basic as it was, it hit the spot nicely.

Jack drained the last drop of rhubarb juice and put the stopper back into the flask. He placed the flask in the bag and left it on the branch next to him, only for it to disappear into the feathery mass. Jack shook his head. *What an amazing tree,* he thought.

*

The long, lonely days and endless nights merged into each other. Jack lost track of how long he'd been hiding in the Tickle Tree. He slept most of the time, mainly because there was nothing else to do. The LEOs kept up their relentless search for him in the forest so he had little choice other than to keep hidden high up within the dense, feathery leaves of the Tickle Tree.

Sometimes in the dead of night, the tree would sense that there were no LEOs in the area and would make a staircase so that Jack could climb back down to the ground and stretch his legs. But the tree never let him stray far and would pull him back with her long reach when she sensed danger.

And the food parcels kept appearing at regular intervals. They would mysteriously appear within the feathery leaves when he was hungry and disappear when he'd finished. It wasn't the life he'd imagined when he set out to find his homeland but he was grateful for small mercies. He was safe.

Jack lay back in the feathery bed that the tree made for him every night and prepared himself for sleep. He thought about his grandfather as he did every night just before sleep beckoned. But just as he was about to drop off, he heard a voice from down below him.

'Jack! Are you there?'

Jack opened his eyes and sat up. He was about to answer

then changed his mind. What if it was a trap? Perhaps it was the LEOs trying to lure him out of his hiding place. As he contemplated his options, the Tickle Tree made his decision for him. A staircase of branches appeared again, leading down to the ground. Jack had grown to trust the tree so tentatively stepped down the feathery staircase. As he approached the bottom, Crystal suddenly appeared.

Jack surprised himself and grasped her in a hug. She wrapped her arms around him and kissed him affectionately on the cheek. 'Are you OK, Jack?'

He stepped back from her. 'I'm fine, just a little lonely. The Tickle Tree has looked after me like a King, but she isn't that great a conversationalist!'

Crystal smiled. 'You have that same sense of mischief as your mother. She would be so very proud of the way you handled yourself in custody.'

'So what's happening in Waterswood?' asked Jack.

'Grimley was furious after you escaped and immediately sent all of the LEOs out to search for you. He was convinced that you were hiding out in the hills, but seems to have changed his mind. The village is swarming with LEOs tonight and they're carrying out cottage to cottage searches. I was with Lomund and we decided that this was our opportunity to get you away from Waterswood and back to the human forest. I crept out the back of his cottage and came straight here.'

Jack was both relieved and disappointed to hear that he was leaving. Crystal tenderly touched his face. 'It won't be for long, Jack, I promise.'

'I know it's the right thing to do, especially after finding out what Grimley had in store for me, but I just …'

'We will get to the bottom of this,' reassured Crystal, 'but it's going to take time. Now we must go. We're going back to the arch via the Waterdown Forest.'

'Tyler said that it's too dark to find your way through the forest at night.'

A wry smile crossed Crystal's lips. 'Although he would never admit it, Tyler is afraid of the dark. We'll follow

Ledger's Stream through the forest and around the edge of Golden Meadow to the Arch of Peace.'

'Won't it be guarded?' he asked.

'Laric and Garwood are there. I don't think the word 'guard' describes either of them. Now it's time to go.'

Jack turned to the Tickle Tree and was sure that her branches were sagging. It struck him that she looked sad. He reached out and took hold of one of her branches. 'I can't thank you enough for what you've done for me. I promise that I will come back one day and we can spend some time together in less difficult circumstances.'

The tree reached out and embraced Jack in her branches. He felt the tears moisten his cheeks. She was his first ever tree friend. She let go of Jack and Crystal took his hand. 'Stay close to me, Jack.'

She led him into the forest and along a narrow pathway in between the dense, dark undergrowth. The moonlight barely penetrated the tightly packed forest canopy making it almost impossible to see where they were going. Jack was used to Heywood Forest at night but this was something else and he fully understood why Tyler didn't relish the prospect of a night-time stroll through it.

But Crystal seemed assured and easily found her way along the covered pathways, eventually bringing them out into the bright, silver moonlight on the edge of Golden Meadow. A gentle breeze wafted the sweet fragrance of the golden flowers over them providing a stark contrast to the damp, musty smell of the forest. The reflection of the moon rippled across the surface of Ledger's Stream illuminating the way towards the Arch of Peace.

Jack had so many unanswered questions swirling around his head. He'd only spent a day with his new friends and the rest of the time either on the run, in captivity or in hiding on his own. But he had a strong feeling that the bond between him and his new found friends was strong. They were always going to be part of his life. He was at least sure of that.

He watched Crystal as they walked alongside the

stream. She had strong features and carried herself with an assurance of someone who was confident in her own abilities. It was obvious to Jack why Ciara had adopted Crystal as her mother. He decided to make the most of the short time he had with her.

'Can you tell me about the Arch of Peace?'

'It's supposed to be a symbol of our freedom,' said Crystal. 'It's a magical barrier between our world and the human world. You must have placed your hand on the small wooden panel on the door to enter here?'

'My friend Cyril the squirrel did it for me,' said Jack.

'The arch only allows Elves into our land. Our ancestor's intention was that it would be an open gateway through which we could leave at any time. But I'm afraid that Grimley put a stop to that once he became head of the Council of Elders.'

'Why?' asked Jack.

'Because he doesn't believe in freedom – he believes in rules and discipline. He forbids any changes to our lore. He uses it as a means to suppress us rather than as an instrument to allow us freedom of expression.' She shook her head. 'I'm afraid that Waterswood isn't the carefree community that I remember as a young Elf.'

'Do you think Grimley was the reason behind my mother deciding to leave Waterswood?'

'I'm as certain as I can be, as is Lomund. Sadly, we don't have any proof as yet, but we will.'

As they skirted Golden Meadow, Jack saw the arch in the distance. The silver light of the moon illuminated the grey stone structure, giving it a look of pure majesty. You didn't have to be told that it was special; it was inherent in the craftwork of the ancient Elves who built it. It was magnificent.

Crystal stopped in the middle of a group of bushes alongside the stream as they approached the arch. She whispered in Jack's ear: 'wait here while I deal with Laric and Garwood. It will take five minutes at the most.'

'Be careful,' said Jack.

Crystal smiled at him before stepping out of the bushes and walking towards the arch. Laric and Garwood sat on a bench seemingly in a world of their own. Garwood eventually noticed her and called out, 'Halt! Who goes there?'

'It's me, Crystal Oak.'

They both stood up and walked over to her. 'You shouldn't be here, Crystal. You know the Elders have imposed a curfew at night,' said Garwood.

'Yes I do,' said Crystal, 'but I couldn't sleep and decided to go for a stroll. I walked through Golden Meadow and suddenly found myself here.'

'I should really arrest you and take you back to the guard room, but Vilner is tied up looking for that renegade Elf, so he's got other things on his mind. Go back home, Crystal Oak, and we'll say nothing about it.'

'That's very kind of you,' said Crystal. She reached into her pocket and took out a small silver flask. 'There's a sharp chill in the air tonight. Here, try this. It will warm you from the inside.' She removed the stopper and held up the flask to him.

'I'm not sure we should be drinking on duty,' said Laric. 'Vilner will …'

'Vilner's not here,' said Garwood as he snatched the flask from Crystal and took a large mouthful of its contents. 'My, Crystal Oak, that's good. In fact,' he said, just as he was about to take another swig, 'that's very good.'

Laric's reticence suddenly disappeared as he snatched the flask from his colleague's hand and also took a large mouthful. Garwood snatched it back and took another drink. The flask went back and forth between the two of them until it was empty. Crystal took the empty flask back and replaced the stopper.

'It's time for me to go. Enjoy your night. And thanks for not telling Vilner.' She walked back towards where Jack was hiding, and called out to him. 'Jack, it's OK to come out now.'

He left the cover of the bushes and looked for the two LEOs. 'What about Laric and Garwood?' he whispered. Crystal pointed towards the arch. Both of them were fast asleep at its base. 'There was a sleeping draft in the flask. They'll sleep for an hour or two at the most.'

'But what about when they wake up?' asked Jack.

'It's a special draft. They won't remember a thing. They'll think that they've just had a nap like they do most nights.' She took a torch down from the holder on the side of the arch, and lit it with sparks from a flint wheel. 'Now take this and go back to the forest. Don't talk to anyone and find somewhere to hide. We will come for you as soon as it's safe to do so.'

'How will you know where to find me?' he asked.

'We'll find you,' smiled Crystal. She hugged him and kissed his cheek. 'I have a strong feeling, Green-Jack, that one day, you will lead our people to freedom. Now go and take care of yourself.'

Jack returned the hug and saw the tears running down her cheeks as he stepped back from her. 'Don't leave me too long,' he said doing his best to force a smile before stepping through the arch and disappearing.

Chapter Nine – Exile

Jack ran down the stone steps as fast as he could. He didn't like confined spaces at the best of times, but this was even worse as he knew it gave him less room for manoeuvre if he was confronted by LEOs. When he reached the bottom he listened for any sign of pursuit. Once he was sure he was on his own he eased his way through the crevice in the wall and out into the tunnel. He listened intently again – the only sound was the gentle murmur of the stream. He waded slowly through the water holding his flame torch out in front of him. The tunnel was clear for as far as he could see. As tempting as it was to run, it was too risky because of the numerous potholes that peppered the stream floor, so he walked as fast as he dare towards the well shaft.

Anxiety sharpened his senses as he continuously looked forward and behind for any sign of the LEOs. He just wanted to get out of that tunnel as quickly as he could. As he approached the well shaft he extinguished the torch and put it back into a holder on the tunnel wall. His heart was in his mouth as he peered up towards the top of the wishing-well. A solitary, single ray of silver moonlight lit up the shaft and Jack breathed a huge sigh of relief when it was empty.

Go for it, Jack. There's no point in waiting.

He slowly climbed the metal rungs, taking care with his foot placement as his boots were wet. If there were LEOs placed at the top he would have nowhere to run, but what choice did he have? He hesitated as he approached the top of the well; his ears and eyes on full alert. Just as he was about to climb the last few rungs and step out of the well, Jack heard voices. He instantly froze.

'How long are we going to have to keep coming here?'

'Until he's captured. I heard that Grimley was white with rage when he escaped from the courtroom.'

'I was there. I think Vilner copped it and still is for not

catching him.'

'Where do you think he is?'

'My guess is he's hiding in the Waterdown Hills.'

'So why are we having to come here every night?'

'Vilner says he may try to get back to his old home.'

'Well I don't know, Kardan, he looked like any normal Elf to me.'

'What do you mean by that?'

'According to Grimley, this Jack is a danger to us all. He says that he could destroy Waterswood.'

Jack couldn't believe his ears. *Destroy Waterswood?* He lost concentration and his feet suddenly slipped from the iron rung and he let out an involuntary cry. He was momentarily dangling by one hand in the well shaft, but managed to hold on and place both his feet back on the rung. His relief was short lived, as when he looked up, there were two faces staring back down at him.

'I think you'd better come up here,' said one of them.

Jack briefly thought about going back down the well shaft, but where would he run to? He reluctantly climbed the last few metres to the top of the well and jumped over the wall. Two LEOs stood in front of him.

'Now don't try anything. We're both fully trained officers.'

Jack thought about making a run for it but they both looked fit and strong. He doubted that he would be able to either overpower, or outrun them. 'I'm not going to try anything. All I want to do is to live peacefully in Waterswood but for some reason, Grimley won't allow it.'

The two LEOs exchanged uneasy looks. 'We're just following orders.'

'I overheard you talking just now,' said Jack. 'I heard you say that Grimley thinks I could destroy Waterswood. Why would he think that?'

The two LEOs stared blankly back at him. 'We just do what we're told. We're going to have to take you back to Waterswood.'

'You do know that Grimley's going to put me in

Darkenwold.'

They both looked horrified. 'Why would he do that?'

'He obviously wants me dead as he also had my cottage burned down in this forest.'

The two LEOs shook their heads in bemusement. The tall guard with long, blond hair tied back in a ponytail turned to his colleague. 'Did you know about this, Mildun?'

He shrugged his shoulders. 'Vilner doesn't tell me anything. He just gives me orders.'

Jack sensed their unease. 'If you take me back I'm as good as dead.'

The two guards looked at each other again. 'We have no choice other than to take you back to Waterswood.'

'Do I really look like I'm a threat to anyone or anything? All I want to do is come home and live in peace.'

'You were born in Waterswood?' asked Kardan.

'No, but my mother was.'

'Who's your mother?' asked Mildun.

'Her name's Ciara.'

'Ciara! I grew up with her,' said Kardan. 'She disappeared some years ago.'

'I seem to remember that you had a bit of a thing for her,' smiled Mildun.

'She's a fine Elf,' said Kardan. 'I never understood why she left.'

'It was down to Grimley,' said Jack. 'She was frightened of him for some reason. All I want is the opportunity to find her.'

Kardan looked to his colleague. 'I can't take him back to Waterswood to be put into Darkenwold. I couldn't live with myself.'

'But if we let him go and Grimley finds out, it will be us going there.'

'How's he going to find out?'

'I suppose if we turned our backs and he was to run off.'

Kardan turned to Jack. 'Good luck – and give my regards to your mother when you find her.'

'I can't thank the two of you enough. I hope that one day I have the opportunity to return the favour.'

The two LEOs turned away and sat on the edge of the well. Jack took his opportunity and ran at full speed towards the edge of the clearing and into the forest. His arms pumped like pistons as his legs ate up the ground beneath him. He followed familiar concealed paths through the undergrowth that only he knew, and didn't stop until he reached the outer perimeter of the forest.

He hid under the branches of a beech tree as he caught his breath. He leant back against the rough tree trunk and thought through his options. Where was he going to stay? He didn't mind sleeping out in the open but that would make it easier for the LEOs to find him. No, he needed somewhere safe and secure to hide until his friends came for him. He continued around the forest perimeter and weighed up his options as he ran.

Jack had learnt many skills from Noah. He knew how to look after himself and he knew how to blend into the forest, to become a part of it. He moved with the guile and instincts of many of the wild animals that lived there. And it was these instincts that had saved him on many occasions. He remembered when some village boys chased him through the forest many years ago, but Jack soon lost them. He hid amongst the ferns and bushes and watched as they ran by.

But when they chased him again the next day, he realised that other actions were necessary. He called upon the assistance of his friend, Reggie the Fox. Reggie turned into a 'man-eating' fox and ran at the gang snarling and growling like a wolf. They never bothered Jack again.

He smiled at the memory, but he needed to call on those same resources if he was going to keep out of the clutches of the LEOs. He continued to run around the forest edge but came to a sudden halt when he reached a clearing. He thought his heart was going to break. The charred skeleton of his cottage stood in the moonlight like a ghost of its past. He remembered all the happy times he spent there. Grimley had a lot to answer for. It was one thing having a problem with Jack but burning down his grandfather's home? Jack shivered when he thought about what could have happened if his grandfather hadn't been awake that night.

*

Jack sat under the cover of the weeping willow to the side of Millar's Pond. It was daylight and he hadn't slept a wink all night. The conversation between the two Elven guards kept going around and around his head. He already knew that Grimley wanted him dead, but why would he think that he was a danger to Waterswood? It didn't make any sense. How he wished that he could talk it over with Lomund or Crystal. Or even better still, his mother. He was sure that she was the key to everything.

But he had a more pressing problem. It was only a matter of time before Grimley sent the LEOs into the forest. As adept as Jack was at surviving in the forest, if he stayed there, sooner or later they were going to find him. As he deliberated his options, his attention was distracted by a rustle in the branches of the willow tree above him. He was onto his feet in an instant and about to run when a small, grey creature landed on the ground in front of him.

It was Cyril.

Jack thought that he would explode with happiness. He picked up his furry friend and hugged him. 'Cyril! How glad am I to see you?'

Cyril twitched his nose as his dark beady eyes scanned all around for signs of any threats.

'My homecoming didn't quite work out as I hoped. I've had to come back here for a while. But it's so good to see you my friend.'

Cyril jumped back down on the ground and hopped around under cover of the tree.

'It's all right, my friend, there's nothing for you to be wary of. Most of the threats to you are asleep.' Jack's stomach rumbled reminding him that he hadn't eaten since the previous evening. 'I don't suppose you'd like to share your stash of hazelnuts with me?'

Cyril didn't hesitate and immediately ran into the forest. He returned five minutes later and placed three hazelnuts into Jack's hands. 'Cyril, you're a lifesaver,' said Jack as he gratefully ate the nuts. He repeated the journey several times until Jack took the edge off his hunger. 'That will do for now, Cyril. There's only so many nuts I can eat in one go!'

He sat back down under cover of the willow tree and returned his attention to his troubles, as Cyril cleaned his paws beside him. A return to Waterswood was out of the question. Grimley was almost certainly going to send his LEOs into the forest after him. The challenge he faced was how to keep out of their clutches until his friends came for him.

He had to get away from the forest. Perhaps he could find his grandfather and stay with his people? It was an option that didn't exactly fill him with enthusiasm. And it would be difficult for his friends to find him. No, his heart wasn't in it. His gut-feel told him it was the wrong thing to do.

It was as he stared into the murky green water of Millar's Pond, that the idea came to him. He remembered what Becky had said after he'd saved her. *'If you ever need anything from me, you only have to ask.'* Perhaps he could stay with her in the village? The LEOs would never risk going into a human community and he wasn't that far from the forest, so he could keep a look-out for his friends. He could only ask – if she said no, he'd lost nothing.

He knelt down by Cyril and ruffled his head. 'I have to go away again, my friend. But don't worry, I'll be back. And thanks for the nuts – you're a lifesaver!'

Jack stepped out from under the willow tree as Cyril scampered back into the forest. He quickly surveyed the area to make sure that he was on his own and set off towards Grasslake Village.

*

Jack hesitated outside the gate at the rear of Becky's cottage. Doubts crept into his mind. Would she really want to help him? And even if she did, what could she do? Her parents were unlikely to allow a strange boy to stay in their house. Perhaps it wasn't such a good idea after all.

He thought back to the last time he stood at the gate. His life was so uncomplicated then. He was just a young traveller boy without a care in the world. Then he remembered how he felt after Becky kissed him. He blushed at the memory. He shook his head and decided that he would find somewhere else to go. The last thing Becky needed was to be burdened with his troubles. As he turned to walk back towards the forest, he heard the gate open. A golden retriever came bounding up to him. It was Sonny-Boy.

Jack knelt down and made a fuss of him and in return got his face severely licked as Sonny jumped all over him, his tail wagging frantically. Jack looked up to see Becky standing at the gate. She was wearing faded blue jeans and a lilac top. Her silky, long, blond hair cascaded over her shoulders and her bright, blue eyes sparkled like azure jewels. She was as beautiful as the morning sun.

Her face lit up and broke into a warm smile. 'Jack! I was beginning to think that I would never see you again.'

'I've been away for a few days. I've only just got back.'

'Did you go somewhere nice?' she asked.

How did he answer that? 'It was OK, but I needed to get back home.'

'Would you like to join Sonny and me on our walk? We're going to the forest.'

He really didn't want to risk going back there, even though the LEOs had almost certainly returned to

74

Waterswood. 'I'd rather not go to the forest. Would you mind if we went somewhere else?'

'You look tense – is there anything wrong?'

He couldn't tell her the real reason for being there. Besides, would she believe him if he did? 'There are some people I want to avoid.'

Concern etched her face. 'Are you in some sort of trouble?'

Jack shook his head. 'My grandfather has returned to his people and I didn't want to stay with them. So I ran away and they're looking for me.'

'Who are these people?' asked Becky.

'They're travellers. I really don't like them. My cousins did nothing but bully and tease me as a kid and I don't want anything to do with them.'

'Where are you going to stay?'

Jack shrugged his shoulders. 'I'm not sure. I was hoping that you'd know somewhere.'

She thought for a moment. 'If you can do without your home comforts for a while, I know just the place. Follow me.'

She led him along the back of the cottages towards a rusty old corrugated iron fence. She stopped by the corner and pulled the fence back. 'In here.' They stepped into the field beyond and Sonny-Boy followed. 'A local farmer owns this field but he hasn't used it for years.' She pointed towards a rickety old wooden barn in the far corner. 'It's not much, but we can make it comfortable. It will do for a few nights until we decide on something more permanent.'

They walked up to the barn and Becky pulled open the door. It was only held on by the upper hinge as the wood had rotted around the lower one. Jack propped the door up against the barn and followed Becky inside. Wooden benches lined the far wall and various rusty gardening implements were scattered around the floor. 'Some of the villagers used to have allotments here. They used the shed to store their tools and the vegetables they grew. I'll go home and get some things for you and I'll bring a broom back to sweep the floor.' She smiled at Jack. 'Don't worry; we'll turn this into a little palace for you.'

*

Four hours later, following a lot of hard work from both Becky and Jack, what once had been an old barn, had been transformed into a comfortable abode for one. The floor had been swept clean; the old tools and sacks that littered the floor had been thrown out; a cosy sleeping bag lay on one of the low benches in the corner, and a beanbag and small table had been added. Becky had even put up some curtains at the window.

'There,' said Becky, 'I told you, it's a palace.'

Jack leant against one of the benches and surveyed his new home. 'I don't know how to thank you enough, Becky. It's just perfect.'

'You saved my life, Jack. It's the least I can do. Now, what about food? Have you eaten today?'

'Just a few hazelnuts,' said Jack.

'I can go home and make you a sandwich. Is there anything you don't like?'

'I don't eat meat,' said Jack.

Becky brought him a cheese sandwich and a bag of crisps, along with a can of fizzy orange and some chocolate cake that her mum had made. Jack was starving and made short work of the food as Sonny-Boy sat at his feet studying every mouthful. Jack gave him the occasional crisp much to Sonny's gratitude.

He sat back on the beanbag and sipped his drink. 'That was great, Becky, thanks. Why does food always make you sleepy?'

'Why don't you take a nap this afternoon? I still need to get you one or two things, and I can bring you back some more food later.'

'Thanks Beck …'

'And don't thank me. I wouldn't be here if it wasn't for you.'

Chapter Ten - Elves in the Night

Becky and Sonny came back in the evening and she brought Jack a flask of vegetable soup for his supper. It reminded him of the soup his grandfather used to make. All that was missing was his grandfather's protestations to try and persuade him to have meat with it. The memory made him smile. How he wished his grandfather was there to advise him.

He followed his soup with a slice of apple pie that Becky's mum had made. It was absolutely delicious. He sat on the bench sipping his orange drink while Becky sat on the beanbag. Sonny lay on the floor at Becky's feet with his chin on the ground, emitting the occasional contented sigh as his eyebrows danced up and down.

Jack had slept the whole afternoon and into the early evening. Avoiding capture by the LEOs had been an exhausting experience. He felt safe in the shed, at least for the time being. Becky had done him proud and had remained true to her word. They'd known each other for only a few weeks but she was already a close and trusted friend. He'd made more friends in the past weeks than in the whole of his life. Up until that point, his grandfather had been his only true friend.

'Won't your mum and dad wonder where you are?' asked Jack.

'My mum is cool as long as I have Sonny with me. My dad decided that he preferred being with his secretary rather than my mum and me some years ago, so it's just the two of us'

'I'm sorry,' said Jack. 'I didn't realise ...'

'That's OK,' said Becky. 'It happened over five years ago. I'm over it now. He made his choice; he's the one who has to live with the consequences.'

'How is your head?' asked Jack changing the subject.

She pulled her hair away from her forehead. The lump and bruising had gone. 'My mum kept me off school for a few days afterwards and I rested the whole time. And thanks to you, I made a full recovery.'

Jack raised his can of drink. 'And thanks to Sonny-Boy.'

'And to Sonny-Boy,' laughed Becky.

Jack drained the last drop of orange from the can and placed it on the bench next to him.

'Can I ask you a question?' asked Becky.

'Of course,' said Jack.

'Your clothes are … well they're a bit unusual.'

Jack had forgotten about his change of clothes. They felt so natural and comfortable that he hadn't considered how they would look to anyone in the human world. 'It's to do with my nickname. My grandfather has called me Green-Jack since I was a young-un. I love green and these boots are just so comfortable. Do I look strange?'

Becky giggled mischievously. 'You look like an Elf in a picture book I used to read as a child.'

Jack felt himself blushing.

'And he was a very handsome Elf,' she added.

Jack turned an even deeper shade of red. He needed to change the subject, and quickly. 'How long can I stay here?'

'No-one ever uses this field anymore. I can't see why you can't stay for as long as you need. Do you have any plans?'

'I'm waiting for some friends. I'm not sure when they'll get here. It could be days; it could be weeks.'

Becky looked disappointed. 'Where will you go?'

How did he answer that? 'It's a small village a long way from here. It's the other side of Glenchester.'

'So will I see you again?'

'Of course,' said Jack. 'I have two friends I need to keep in touch with.'

She smiled. 'I'm glad.' Sonny sat up and barked. 'So is Sonny!'

*

78

Jack lay back on top of his sleeping-bag staring at the image of the moon through the curtained window. Two weeks had passed since his escape from Waterswood, although it felt much longer. Becky had looked after him like a Lord during this time. She brought him breakfast every morning before school and returned with his supper after school. And at weekends she and Sonny spent most of the day with him. His only exercise was a stroll around the field each evening as he didn't want to risk going anywhere near the forest.

Waterswood was never far from his thoughts. Grimley was sure to be leaving no stone unturned in his relentless pursuit of him. How was he ever going to be able to return to Waterswood with Grimley as Head of the Council of Elders? Why was he so convinced that Jack would destroy Waterswood? It was a question that wouldn't leave him.

He pulled out the Bloodstone that hung around his neck and held it between his fingers. He was so relieved that the LEOs didn't search him when he was arrested in Waterswood. They would have surely confiscated it and it would have felt like they had taken a part of his mother from him. She had worn this very same jewel around her own neck and that made it all the more special to Jack. He held on to every link he had to her no matter how tenuous.

He put the jewel back into his shirt and relaxed onto his makeshift bed. It wasn't the most comfortable bed he'd ever slept on but it was good enough. He closed his eyes and readied himself for sleep. Even with all of the danger that he faced, sleep always came easy. He remembered how his grandfather used to constantly complain about not sleeping, which was a mystery to Jack especially as Noah managed to snore most of the night! It was a nice memory to go to sleep on.

Just as he was about to drop off, he heard a twig snap outside in the field. Jack was out of his bed in an instant and discreetly pulled back the curtain and peered out of the window. Two shadowy figures moved through the field. He was sure they were Elves. His worst nightmare was upon him.

The LEOs had found him.

He thought through his options. Perhaps he should make a run for it? He quickly dismissed the idea. There were almost certainly more LEOs out there – he'd run straight into them. *Come on, Jack, think!* They were planning to surprise him, but perhaps he could turn the tables and surprise them. He crept across the wooden floor and hid behind the door. Whoever it was circled the shed and stopped outside. He held his breath and waited.

The door slowly opened and Jack readied himself. The wooden floor creaked as they stepped into the shed. Two tentative footsteps later and he made his move. He grabbed an arm and pulled it behind the intruder's back and put his hand over his mouth. He turned to face the door and hissed, 'back off or I'll break his arm!'

The companion stepped cautiously through the door and whispered, 'Jack, it's me, Lilac.'

'Lilac?'

He heard a match strike and she held it up to her face. Sure enough, it was his friend from Waterswood. So who was he holding? He took his hand from his mouth. 'I'd appreciate it if you would let go of my arm, young Jack, as I think you're about to break it!'

It was Tyler. Jack let go of his arm and embraced him. A bemused Tyler retorted, 'first you try to break my arm and now you're crushing my ribs!'

Jack let go of Tyler only to fall into Lilac's embrace. 'Don't mind him, Jack. He's just grumpy because he hasn't eaten this evening.'

'I've got some cakes,' said Jack as he picked up a tin and handed it to Tyler, who instantly pulled the lid off and set about the cakes inside. Jack sat down on the bench next to Lilac. 'It's such a relief to see you both. How did you find me?'

'Crystal put some Elf dust on your jacket. She gave me some of the same dust and it sort of guided us here. It's difficult to explain but you just follow your instincts.'

'Well I'm just glad you're here. Is it safe to go back to Waterswood?'

'That's not why we're here, Jack,' said Lilac. 'I'm afraid that it's got worse since you escaped. Grimley's fury is out of control. The LEOs are on continuous patrol around the village.'

'I only got out of the slammer today,' mumbled Tyler through a mouthful of cake.

'We met at Lomund's along with Crystal. It was obvious that the security situation was only going to get worse, so we decided that Tyler and I would leave Waterswood immediately. We arranged for some friends to create a diversion and we escaped through the forest with Crystal.'

'I thought you were scared of the forest, Tyler,' said Jack.

'That is a complete lie,' said Tyler as he scowled at Lilac, 'put around by my so-called friends!'

'So why did you hang on to mine and Crystal's hands the whole time we were in there?' she laughed.

'I just wanted to make sure that you were both safe,' said an unconvincing Tyler.

'Anyway,' continued Lilac, 'Crystal drugged Garwood and Laric, as she did when she helped you, and we escaped through the Arch of Peace and came straight here.'

'Did you see the LEOs by the wishing-well?' asked Jack.

Tyler momentarily stopped eating. 'There were no LEOs by the well when we came through.'

'I ran into them when I escaped.'

'Why didn't they capture you?' asked a confused Lilac.

'They did but I managed to persuade them to let me go. I got the impression that neither of them had much time for either Vilner or Grimley.'

'Did they tell you their names?' asked Tyler.

'Kardan and Mildun,' said Jack.

'They're both decent sorts,' said Tyler.

'I seem to remember Kardan had a bit of a thing for

Ciara,' said Lilac.

'And that's what finally persuaded them to let me go.'

'Well I'm just glad they did,' said Tyler, 'as I really don't think you want to return to Waterswood at this uncertain time.'

'And there's something else,' said Jack. 'I overheard them talking. Apparently Grimley thinks I'm going to destroy Waterswood and that's the reason he wants me dead.'

Tyler put the cakes down on the bench next to him and looked across at Lilac. Even in the dark Jack could see the concern on their faces.

'There's something we need to tell you,' said Lilac. 'We won't be taking you back to Waterswood.'

'So why are you here?'

'We're going to find your mother,' said Tyler. 'We're going to find Ciara.'

A warm feeling swept over Jack. It felt as if he was in the middle of an amazing dream. *I'm going to find my mother.*

'Only she knows why Grimley wants you dead. Her own life was in danger which is why she fled Waterswood. Both Lomund and Crystal are convinced that she holds the key to this,' said Lilac.

The anticipation built up in Jack like a breaking wave approaching the seashore. 'Where do we start? She's been gone for nearly fifteen years.'

'Syd Gumboot,' said Tyler. 'He left Waterswood some twenty years ago. He couldn't put up with Grimley and his rules. He was great friends with Ciara. We think she may have gone to him.'

'Do you know where he is?'

'Er, not exactly,' said Tyler coyly. 'We'll be relying on the dust.'

'Will it still work after all of this time?'

'I think we're about to find out,' said Tyler.

Jack felt as excited as a little boy on Christmas Eve. 'When do we leave?'

'Immediately,' said Lilac.

Jack's excitement momentarily cooled. 'I can't leave now. I have to say goodbye to Becky.'

'Who's Becky?' asked Lilac.

'She's the girl who found this place for me.'

'We must use this time to put as much distance between us and Waterswood as we can,' urged Tyler. 'We need to leave now.'

But Jack was adamant. 'I owe Becky so much - I could have fallen into the hands of the LEOs without her. Can't we leave first thing in the morning?'

'Very well,' said a reluctant Lilac. 'We leave in the morning. But let's make the most of this time and get some sleep.'

Chapter Eleven - Journey West

Jack stood outside Becky's back gate anxiously looking towards the forest. Would the LEOs really risk searching for him in broad daylight? He didn't have to ask the question. Grimley would stop at nothing to recapture him and would take whatever risks that were necessary to see that happened.

As much as he wasn't looking forward to saying goodbye to Becky, he was relieved that she couldn't unwittingly become involved in something that had absolutely nothing to do with her.

The gate opened and Sonny came bounding through. As soon as he saw Jack he ran up to him, his tail wagging furiously. Jack knelt down and made a fuss of him and Sonny rolled over on his back inviting him to rub his tummy.

'He'll let you do that all day,' said Becky as she came through the gate. 'I didn't expect to see you waiting for me. Not that I'm complaining as it was a nice surprise. Are you going to risk coming for a walk with me?'

'Er, I don't think so,' said Jack nervously. 'I, er, I have something to tell you. My two friends turned up last night. They're going to take me to a safe place away from here.'

Becky couldn't hide her disappointment. 'I thought you were going to be staying for a while. I was … I was looking forward to you being around.'

'I will come back,' said Jack. 'I promise. It's just not safe for me to stay here at the moment.'

Sonny sat at Jack's feet, swapping stares between him and Becky. He could sense the sadness in the air. Becky wiped a tear from her eye.

'I will never forget what you've done for me over the last few weeks. I don't think I could have got by without you,' said Jack.

Becky forced a smile. 'We always seem to be thanking each other.'

Jack stepped forward and embraced her. Her hair was soft and smelt as fresh as a new day. He could feel her heart beating rapidly in her chest. The heart that had stopped beating the first time he met her. He stepped back and looked into her crystal blue eyes. She handed him a plastic carrier bag. 'I brought some food for you.'

He was about to thank her but she put her index finger up to his lips. 'Just promise me that you'll come back.'

He didn't hesitate. 'I promise.'

*

Jack followed Lilac along the edge of a field of golden corn. Tyler lagged several steps behind them.

'My legs are much shorter than yours. I have to take twice as many steps as you two,' complained Tyler.

Lilac turned to Jack. 'You'll soon get used to him. He's not happy unless he's moaning.'

'I'll have you know, Lilac Wildflower, that I have the sensitivity of a poet and the heart of a lion. I can rise to any challenge that presents itself to me.'

Lilac raised her eyes to the sky and smiled at Jack. But Jack wasn't hearing them. His mind was on Becky.

'You're quiet, Jack. Are you OK?' enquired Lilac.

'Do you think that the LEOs will go after Becky?'

Lilac shook her head. 'Vilner isn't known for either his judgement or his subtlety, but he would never risk a confrontation with the humans. Elves avoid contact with them at all costs. They don't acknowledge our existence which is the way we like it.' She patted him reassuringly on his back. 'Don't worry about her. She will be fine.'

'Do you think the LEOs will come after us?'

'Almost certainly. Especially once they know that Tyler and I have left Waterswood,' said Lilac.

'And will they be able to track us?'

'They have some specialist trackers so the answer is yes. But we don't need to worry about that. Syd will know how to avoid them.'

'The sooner we find him the better,' chimed in Tyler. 'I need a rest. My feet are hurting.'

Lilac shook her head in exasperation and smiled grimly at Jack, and whispered, 'and we've only just started.'

They travelled the whole day, only briefly stopping to eat the food that Becky had given Jack. They kept to the field perimeters, forests and woods, and avoided the open countryside where possible. Jack was surprised to find that there were Elf trails everywhere. These were trails that humans wouldn't be aware of. He thought he knew Heywood Forest like the back of his hand but Lilac told him that there were trails known only to the Elves.

'They're Faery trails,' said Lilac, 'protected by magic.'

As the sun settled in the west, and the grey, orange-lined clouds filled the sky, they set up camp on the edge of a forest. Lilac lit a fire while Tyler filled a metal pot with water from a nearby stream. He added dried vegetables to the pot and made a thick vegetable stew.

He served up three bowls of steaming stew, along with some chunks of oat bread. 'Enjoy my friends.'

And it was good. Although Jack was so hungry he would have eaten the grass off the ground. Lilac made a pot of Roseleaf and the three friends sat chatting around the glowing embers of the fire as darkness descended.

'This is my favourite time of the day,' said Tyler.

'Only because if you were at home you would be sitting with a glass of Peardrop,' said Lilac.

'Lilac Wildflower, you are so cynical at times. My life doesn't just revolve around Peardrop. I appreciate the softening light and the space to think. It's when I write some of my best poetry.'

'When you're drunk,' said Lilac. 'The only trouble is that the rest of us can never understand it!'

'You see, young Jack. What I have to endure at the hands of one of my closest friends.'

Lilac leant across and kissed him on his rosy cheek. 'You wouldn't have it any other way.'

'For once, Lilac Wildflower, I agree with you.' He raised his mug of Roseleaf to her and took a healthy mouthful.

Jack liked the banter between Lilac and Tyler. It took his mind off his troubles. 'Do you know if we're any nearer to finding Syd?' he asked.

'It's difficult to say,' said Lilac. 'I've sensed Elven presence along some of the trails, but no more than that.'

'I think you'll find that Syd will find us,' said Tyler. 'We just have to put ourselves in the general vicinity.' And this prompted him into verse … 'I wander lonely as an Elf, In search of my old friend, Through forest and dell, It's hard to tell, When this trek will ever end …'

'Goodnight, Tyler,' said Lilac cutting him short and wrapping herself in her blanket.

*

Days and nights merged into one another as they journeyed ever further westwards. Thankfully the weather held and they didn't have to cope with rain. Tyler moaned the whole journey as Lilac warned he would, but she maintained her optimism at finding Syd even though two weeks had passed.

'Are you sure Syd still lives in the human world?' grumbled Tyler.

'Lomund said he does, and that's good enough for me,' said Lilac curtly.

'Well I'm not sure how long I can carry on like this. We've stretched our food to its limit. You should know better than most that an Elf marches on its stomach.'

'In your case grumbles on its stomach,' whispered Lilac under her breath.

'I heard that,' said Tyler. 'I can't help the fact that I'm a sensitive soul. We creative people are like that.'

Jack was tired. He'd been on the run continuously for over a month and it was taking its toll on him. Tyler was right about the food. He could tell that they hadn't expected to be searching for Syd for over two weeks. They were reduced to eating cheese and dried biscuits for the last five days. It wasn't enough to sustain them, especially as they were walking the whole day.

It was early evening and the three of them sat around a fire in the midst of a forest, sipping the last of the Roseleaf. Jack trusted Lilac, and even though Tyler moaned constantly, he felt sure that when the chips were down, he would come through. He sensed the tension between his two colleagues and attempted to ease the atmosphere.

'I guess you were both close to Syd when he lived at Waterswood?' he asked.

'Lilac was sweet on him,' teased Tyler.

'Don't listen to him,' said Lilac. 'We grew up together. Syd lived with Lomund, while I lived with Rosebud. We were like brother and sister. Syd was very independently minded and he challenged the Elders at every opportunity. Of course, that didn't go down well with Grimley, so he constantly harassed Syd to the point where he had enough. It must have been around twenty years ago that he left Waterswood and vowed never to come back. Grimley was furious and sent the LEOs after him, but Syd was too smart for them. He managed to avoid capture and has never been back since.'

'So how do you know he's in the human world?' asked Jack.

'There are travelling Elves who sometimes pass through Waterswood. Although Grimley's oppressive regime has put a stop to that. They would often stay with Lomund and told him that Syd had settled in a forest in the human world.'

'That was years ago,' interrupted Tyler. 'He could be anywhere now.'

'Well I don't remember you coming up with any alternatives when Lomund suggested it.'

Tyler sat in front of the fire wrapped in a thick blanket. Jack thought he looked thoroughly miserable.

'I'm sorry, Lilac. I know that I must sound very negative but I didn't think we would be travelling quite so far. I think you would agree that my physique isn't cut out for long journeys.'

'I'm sorry too,' said Lilac. 'If I'm honest, I thought we'd have found Syd by now.'

Jack suddenly felt guilty. 'It's my fault that you're both here. Perhaps I shouldn't have come back.'

'Nonsense,' said Lilac and Tyler in unison. 'You're the breath of fresh air that Waterswood needed,' continued Tyler. 'We'd all fallen into a pit of indifference and sat back and let Grimley bully us. I think I talk for us both when I say that you're the best thing to happen to our community for a long, long time.'

Lilac raised her mug in the air. 'I'll drink to that.'

'I'm sure the world will look a much better place after a good night's sleep,' said Tyler.

*

Jack felt something sharp on his neck. He opened his eyes and saw an unshaven face with a threatening scowl looking down at him.

'Now don't make any sudden movements, like, or I won't hesitate to slash yer throat,' he hissed.

Jack had absolutely no intention of doing anything that would put his life at risk.

'Sit up nice and gently, like,' said the stranger.

Jack did as he asked.

'And now stand up … slowly, like.'

Jack rose slowly to his feet. The stranger moved around to his back whilst keeping the knife pressed tightly to his neck.

'Wake yer friends.'

Jack's heart beat like a drum in his chest. There was no way he could do anything with a knife at his throat. 'Lilac, Tyler, wake up,' he whispered.

Lilac's eyes flickered, but Tyler continued to snore

loudly. Lilac peered at Jack through half open eyes and didn't appear to register the situation.

'Get up, my little beauty,' growled the stranger. 'And no sudden movements, like, or yer friend's dead.'

Lilac's eyes suddenly snapped open and she sat up. 'Who are you?'

'That's no concern of yours,' said the stranger. 'Just do as I say, like, and yer friend will be fine. Now on yer feet.'

Lilac looked nervously at Jack and slowly stood up.

'Now turn around, like, and put yer hands behind yer back.'

She did as he asked. The stranger dangled some cord in front of Jack with his free hand. 'Now tie her hands. And don't try and fool me by tying them loose.' Jack stepped forward and the stranger kept the knife pressed to his throat. As he wrapped the cord around Lilac's wrists he heard a hollow thud from behind him. The knife fell away from his throat and the stranger dropped to the ground like a felled tree.

Jack turned around and found himself standing face to face with an Elf holding a heavy lump of wood in his hand. The stranger lay rock still on the floor with blood pouring from a wound on the back of his head. The Elf threw the wood on the ground and stepped in between Jack and Lilac.

'We need to get away from here, and quick. He's got two accomplices that he works with and they won't be far away.'

Lilac threw the cord from her wrists and turned to the Elf. 'Syd?'

The Elf stopped and studied her in the dark. 'Lilac?'

'Oh my god, it's Syd Gumboot,' she screeched, and wrapped her arms around him. Syd responded in kind and they both hugged each other.

He stepped back and looked her up and down. 'You haven't changed a bit. You're still as pretty as a spring flower.'

'And you haven't changed, Syd Gumboot. You're still

as charming as ever.' Syd turned his attention to Jack. 'And who do we have here?'

'This is my friend, Jack,' said Lilac.

Syd held out his hand and Jack grabbed it in a firm handshake just like his grandfather had taught him. 'You look strangely familiar, my friend. Are you from Waterswood?'

'He's Ciara's son,' said Lilac.

'You have the look of her,' said Syd, 'although it's a good few years since I last saw her.'

Syd looked like he could have been Jack's brother. He had the same mop of brown hair and the same sharp features. The only difference was his milky white skin that glowed in the pale moonlight.

'We must go,' urged Syd. 'I'll take you to my friend's cottage. You'd better wake your friend, Lilac.'

'He's your friend as well,' retorted Lilac. 'You wake him.'

Syd walked over and knelt down by the sleeping Tyler. 'On my life, it's the worst poet in Waterswood.' Syd gave him a firm shake. 'Wake up Tyler you old rascal.'

Tyler sat bolt upright, his eyes mad and wide. 'Whoaaaaa! What's happening? Where are you Lilac? Jack?'

'Just me, I'm afraid,' said a smiling Syd.

Tyler peered at him in the gloom and his face suddenly burst into a broad grin. 'Syd Gumboot. What a sight for sore feet and aching limbs you are. How good is it to see you?' He looked up at Lilac. 'I told you that Syd would find us.'

Lilac grimaced. 'Tyler Goldsmith, I'll swing for you!'

'I'm sorry, my friends,' said Syd. 'We're going to have to get away from here now. Lilac, you can have your argument with Tyler later!'

Chapter Twelve - Narky Norris

Syd took them to the edge of the forest and followed a path across the middle of a meadow. The moon was full and bright, which was both a curse and a blessing. The path ahead was illuminated, but at the same time they would be easier to follow. Syd kept glancing anxiously behind him as they crossed the open meadow, as did Jack. He most certainly didn't want to meet that nasty character's accomplices. There was a joint sigh of relief when they reached the other side of the meadow and were under the cover of the tall beech trees that lined it.

Tyler struggled to keep up and moaned constantly that his feet hurt and that he was too old to run for sustained periods. Lilac restrained herself to constant eye rolling whilst Jack and Syd did their best to help him along. They must have been travelling for just over an hour when Tyler's stamina finally gave out.

'Please,' he wheezed. 'Let me rest. I'm going to have a heart attack if we carry on without a break.' Syd checked again to make sure that they weren't being followed. 'Very well - we'll take five minutes to catch our breaths. But we must keep going. I don't feel safe out here at night. My friend's cottage is still another hour away. I want to get there by daybreak if possible.'

'Who is your friend?' asked Lilac.

'His name is Norman Norris, but everyone calls him Narky. You'll soon find out why.'

'It's not a name I remember in Waterswood,' said Lilac.

'He doesn't come from there,' said Syd. 'He's from a long line of Elven travellers. He's lived his whole life in the human world.'

'How did you meet him?' asked Jack.

'It was when I first came to the human world after I left Waterswood. I spent many weeks just wandering through the woods and forests, not sure where I was going. Narky came across me when I was camping near to his home one night. Lomund had told me about the travelling Elves and how they would take care of me. Narky took me in as he said it wasn't safe for me to camp out in the open so I stayed with him until I built my own place deep in Warewood Forest. He's been my one of my best friends ever since.'

'And when …?'

'No more questions until we reach Narky's,' said Syd climbing back to his feet. 'We'll be safe there.'

Jack helped Tyler back to his feet. Syd stood the other side of him and between them they managed to keep him going. They followed a path along the perimeter of a pine forest and skirted several corn fields. Syd eventually led them across a field of rapeseed towards a copse in its centre.

The copse was surrounded by jagged hawthorn and bramble bushes which were virtually impossible to penetrate. But Syd knew where he was going and found a non-existent gap and crawled through, followed by his three friends.

'I do hope we're nearly there,' complained Tyler, 'I'm dead on my feet.'

'Five minutes, my old friend,' said Syd, 'and you'll be sat in a comfortable armchair with a mug of Roseleaf in your hand.'

'Narky has Roseleaf tea?' asked Tyler.

'Of course,' said Syd. 'He may reside in the human world but he lives the life of an Elf, just as if he was in Waterswood.'

They headed towards the centre of the copse and down into a sheltered hollow. A gnarled old oak tree stood in its middle surrounded on either side by compact evergreen bushes. Jack sensed a change in the atmosphere. He couldn't put his finger on it but he knew that it was different.

Syd pointed towards the thicket. 'Narky's home.'

'He lives in a bush?' asked Jack.

'You're not looking carefully enough,' said Syd mysteriously. 'Look deep into the oak tree and the bushes around it.'

Jack wasn't sure what it was he was supposed to be looking at but he did as Syd asked. He peered into the thicket in a vain attempt to see what it was Syd was getting at. Just as he was about to give up, Lilac suddenly exclaimed out loud, 'there's a cottage!' She pointed to the trunk of the old oak tree. 'That's the front door.'

The words were no sooner out of Lilac's mouth when Jack saw it. The door in the oak tree was as plain as the nose on his face. The cottage appeared around it as if a mystery veil was magically removed. It was a cottage that wouldn't have looked out of place in Waterswood.

'How?' asked a stunned Jack. 'It's like … magic!'

Syd smiled enigmatically. 'And that's exactly what it is, Jack. We don't want nosy humans prying into our lives.' He looked across the copse towards the east and saw the tip of the sun peering over the faraway hills. 'Let's hope that Narky is up as I surely don't want to be the one who wakes him.'

Syd knocked twice on the door and stepped back. A few seconds later they could hear a voice from inside. 'Who can that be at this unearthly hour? I'm too old to be getting up at the crack of dawn. I'll tell whoever it is to come back later.'

The door opened and a wizened old Elf wearing a stripy nightshirt stood staring at them. Age had stooped his back and his brown skin was leathery from long years of exposure to the sun.

'Syd Gumboot! What time do you call this? You know I don't get up so early these days.' He looked at Jack, Lilac and Tyler in turn. 'And you have the audacity to bring friends as well. How many times have I told you that this isn't a hotel?'

'I'm sorry, Narky, but my friends are in need of a safe place to stay. I saved them from Finn Tarr only a few hours ago.'

Narky's demeanour changed instantly. 'Why didn't you say?' He stepped back from the door. 'You'd better come in – and don't bring that mud on your boots with you. Clean them on the stone outside. I haven't got time to clean up after you.'

Syd winked at his friends and cleaned his boots on the stone, as did the others. By the time they walked into the cottage, Narky was fully dressed in his day clothes.

'I suppose you'll be expecting me to make you breakfast. Syd, you can set the table.' He turned to Jack, Lilac and Tyler. 'Make yourself comfortable – the food will be on the table in half an hour.'

'Would you like me to make tea?' asked Lilac.

'The kettle's on the range. You can fill it from the hand-pump outside. And don't use too much tea. It's getting harder and harder to get hold of. And don't forget to warm the pot before you add the hot water. And ...'

'Mmmm, I think our Lilac may have just met her match,' whispered Tyler in Jack's ear, trying his best not to gloat and failing.

*

For all of Narky's complaining, he knew how to serve up a grand Elven breakfast. It was a real Waterswood spread. Fried mushrooms, fried tomatoes, scrambled egg, potato cakes and toasted oat bread, all washed down by Roseleaf. Jack hadn't eaten so much since his breakfast with Lomund.

Narky got up from the table and sat down in an armchair by the fireplace. He took an old clay pipe from the hearth and lit it with a wooden spill. He sat back and quietly puffed on the pipe, surrounding himself in plumes of grey smoke. Lilac stood up and started to clear the plates from the table.

'Sit down,' said Narky. 'They can wait until you've digested your food. You young Elves have forgotten how to relax.'

'Not all of us,' said Lilac. 'Tyler seems to have mastered the art. He's permanently relaxed!'

'So are you going to tell me who you are?' said Narky through a cloud of pipe smoke.

'I'm Lilac and ...'

'Syd's already told me your names,' said Narky dismissively. 'I want to know who you are, and more importantly, why you're here?'

'Can I ask a question first?' said Jack. 'Who is Finn Tarr?'

'He's a bounty hunter,' said Narky. 'And he's a human.'

'I gathered that from his traveller's accent,' said Jack. 'But why would he be after Elves.'

'Because they're worth gold to him,' said Narky.

Jack, Lilac and Tyler exchanged confused looks.

'It's our friend Grimley,' said Syd. 'He thinks any Elves living in the human world pose a risk to Waterswood.'

'Why would he think that?' asked Tyler.

'He says that humans are beneath contempt. They are uncultured beings who destroy our world with their greed and lust for power. According to Grimley, any Elf living in the human world could give away the secret of Waterswood,' said Syd.

'So he employs human thugs to keep the secret,' said an exasperated Tyler.

'The travelling community are outcasts in the human world,' said Jack. 'They live outside of mainstream society and are a very insular people. Grimley would know that which is why he's chosen them to do his dirty work.'

'Well I don't think they've been very effective at catching runaway Elves,' said Tyler. 'I haven't seen any returned to Waterswood.'

'Finn and his men have captured at least a dozen Elves to my knowledge in the last six months,' said Syd.

'Well they haven't been coming back to Waterswood. We'd know if they were,' said Tyler.

'So where would they be taken to?' asked Lilac. She looked at Tyler and saw a pained expression suddenly cross his face. She answered her own question. 'Darkenwold!'

'Surely he wouldn't be that ruthless,' said Jack.

'He was prepared to incarcerate you there,' said Tyler.

'But he wants me dead,' said Jack.

Both Syd and Narky's faces were cloaked with disbelief. 'Why would Grimley want a young, innocent Elf dead?' asked Syd.

'He seems to think I'm a danger to Waterswood. I'm not sure why.'

'So where do you come from?' asked Narky. 'You have a familiar look about you.'

'I was brought up in Heywood Forest by a traveller called Noah Green. I only found out recently that I am an Elf. My mother comes from Waterswood. Her name is Ciara.'

'Ciara,' repeated Narky. 'Of course – that's why I think I know you. She was here many years ago. She never mentioned a son.'

Jack felt the anticipation building within him. Narky must have seen Ciara after she left him with Noah. 'Do you know what happened to her?'

'She met up with a young Leprechaun called Seamus O'Shoehorn who was staying with me at the time. She went to Emerald Island with him.'

'Why would she do that?' asked Jack.

Narky knocked the ash from his pipe on the hearth and refilled it with tobacco, before lighting it with another wooden spill. He sat back and thoughtfully drew on the pipe and filled the room with clouds of grey smoke again. 'I could tell that she was frightened. She wouldn't say why but it was obvious to me that she wanted to get as far away from Waterswood as she could. Seamus is a charmer, as are all the Leprechauns I've ever met. He would fill her head with tales about the deep blue lakes and the tall grey mountains that reached to the sky. He would tell her about the velvet grass that was as green as the purest emerald. So one day she took off with him and I've never seen her since.'

'Do you have any news of her?' asked Jack.

Narky shook his head. 'Nothing I'm afraid.'

His mother was starting to feel more like folklore than reality to Jack. He was beginning to doubt if she ever really existed. Just as he thought he was getting nearer to finding her, she seemed to get further away. And where was this place 'Emerald Island'? How would he get there? Did he want to? Perhaps it was better that he forgot about her and returned to his life with Noah.

'Ciara's a fine Elf,' said Narky as if he was reading Jack's mind. 'It takes a mother of great courage to leave her child with somebody she barely knew. She sensed that Noah would look after you, and by the look of it, he did a fine job. She knew the danger that you were both in and decided that you would be safer with him. My advice, for what it's worth, Jack, is to go to Emerald Island and find her. She is the key to what has happened to you both.'

'But how am I going to get to this place?' asked Jack.

'Don't you worry about that,' said Narky. 'I will arrange it.'

Jack looked to Lilac and Tyler. 'Will you be coming with me?'

They both smiled. 'Try and stop us,' said Tyler.

Narky lay his pipe down on the hearth. 'Now I suggest that you use the day to rest. I think it will be safer to travel during the night. Syd and I will take you to where you need to be.'

Chapter Thirteen – Troy

Jack sat on the edge of his bed quietly sipping a mug of Roseleaf. He'd stopped trying to make any sense of all that had happened to him over the previous weeks. If he dwelt on his situation too long it only made him angry. Grimley had robbed him of his mother – he would never forgive him for that.

But now he was about to embark on a journey which really was a step into the unknown, not that any of his recent experiences had been a walk in the park. He had no idea where Emerald Island was, until Syd had explained to him that it was the island of Ireland. Noah had told Jack that he had Irish relatives in the travelling world, not that he'd ever met them.

His mother had gone off with this Leprechaun called Seamus O'Shoehorn. Only a matter of weeks earlier he would have laughed at the suggestion that Leprechauns even existed. Now he was going on a journey to their homeland.

Lilac sat down next to Jack on the bed. She put a reassuring arm around his shoulder. 'You've hardly said a word all day. Are you OK?'

'I'm just a little tired,' he said unconvincingly.

'You know that you don't have to do this?' she said sympathetically.

'I want to. When I started on this journey I promised myself I would find out who I am. I have to see it through, Lilac.'

A warm smile lit up her face. 'I'm glad, but I just wanted to make sure that you were sure.'

'Come on you two,' said Narky. 'You haven't got time to chat.' He held up two rucksacks. 'I've packed these for you. We leave in five minutes.'

*

As they walked through the copse, Jack looked back towards the cottage just as it melted back into the darkness. He marvelled at the wonderful new world that he now lived in. It seemed that there was magic everywhere. He just wished that he could have been introduced to it so much earlier in his short life.

Narky stopped on the edge of the copse, just in front of the wall of bramble and hawthorn. 'Now, I will be taking you across the field and onto a secret trail that I know. We are going to a very special place – a sacred place. I will tell you all when we get there. I want to be there by daybreak so we need to keep up a brisk pace. Keep close together, and if anyone lags behind, we won't be stopping for them.'

He led them through an invisible gap in the brambles and hawthorns and across the field of yellow. Then he kept to the field edge before turning on to a hedge- lined pathway. 'This is a Faery Trail,' he said. 'Humans don't know of its existence so we can't be followed.'

'Why don't humans know about magic?' asked Jack.

'Because they don't have our awareness,' said Narky curtly. 'Now no more questions. Save your energy for the journey ahead.'

The night was dark and moonless due to the low, thick cloud overhead. The only sounds being the occasional rustle in the hedgerows caused by the stirrings of the nocturnal creatures hiding there. Jack kept all of his senses on full alert. He was going to make sure that they weren't surprised again as they were in the forest the previous night.

They walked in silence for an hour. It was Tyler that spoke first. 'I'm sorry but I'm going to have to rest. I'm not made for journeys over such difficult terrain.'

But Narky gave him short shrift. 'Get used to it,' he said gruffly. 'We've got at least another six hours until we reach our destination. If you can't keep up, we'll have to leave you behind.' And surprisingly, Tyler shut up.

The journey through the night was uneventful much to everyone's relief. Narky kept to Faery Trails where possible, and when they strayed into forests and woods, both Jack and Syd made sure that any company they had was of the animal world and not the human kind.

They arrived at an open, rolling meadow just as the sun rose. They set up camp amongst the horse chestnut trees on the edge of the meadow. Syd and Narky built a small fire and soon had a cup of refreshing Roseleaf for everyone. Lilac prepared a breakfast of bread, fruit and cheese and they sat in the middle of the trees quietly eating.

Once they finished, Narky went through the ritual of lighting his pipe and made himself comfortable by leaning against the trunk of one of the tall trees. He sat mindfully staring at the plumes of grey smoke emanating from his pipe for several minutes, before addressing his friends.

'This is a place of great mystique and magical power. I don't know of a more sacred place for Faery people in the human world. We are sat at the junction of two of the most powerful Ley lines that straddle the planet Earth. Their Elven names are, Armantos and Garamaton. Armantos is the arc of magic, and Garamaton channels the magic around the planet.'

He hesitated as he drew on his pipe. 'Garamaton leads directly to Emerald Island, the spiritual home of the Faery world.' He looked at Jack, Lilac and Tyler with a burning intensity. 'And that is the route you will be taking.'

Jack was filled with anxiety and anticipation in equal measures. He was getting nearer to his mother or at least he hoped he was. He could sense the apprehension in Lilac and Tyler. They wanted to find Ciara as much as he did. But how were they going to travel to this Emerald Island? They were about to find out.

'Faery folk have their own means of transport in this world. Humans use mechanical contraptions that pollute our environment. They do not respect and love this planet as we do. Our methods of transport are more in tune with the natural rhythm of our planet. I will summon the flying horse, Troy. He will be your means of transport to

Emerald Island.'

'Did you say flying?' asked Tyler.

'It's perfectly safe,' said Narky. 'The magic that surrounds Troy will make sure that you cannot fall.'

Tyler shook his head indignantly. 'My feet stay well and truly stuck to the ground. I will leave flying to the birds.'

'But we have to find Ciara,' said Lilac. 'You promised Jack that you would go with him.'

'That was before I knew that I would have to fly on the back of a horse. I'm sorry, I will stay here.'

Jack couldn't hide his disappointment. It was important to him that both Lilac and Tyler joined him on his journey. 'I know that I have no right to ask you, and I know that we have only been friends for a short while, but I really want you to come with me. I felt an instant bond with both you and Lilac when I met you. For the first time in my life I thought that I'd met people that I identified with and who identified with me. If the answer is no I will understand and it will never affect our friendship, but this journey just won't be the same without you.'

Tyler hung his head and looked both uncomfortable and embarrassed. He looked across at Lilac; her crystal blue eyes urged him to change his mind. He held his head in his hands and audibly groaned. 'Very well – I will come to this island with you.'

Lilac let out a shriek of joy and threw her arms around Tyler and kissed him. Tyler reacted in his customary fashion and extricated himself from her. 'The one condition being that Lilac refrains from showing me affection. I feel much more comfortable when she's teasing me.'

'You know you love it,' said a beaming Lilac.

'Very well,' said Narky. 'It is time for me to summon Troy.' He rose slowly to his feet and walked from the clearing and out into the meadow. He closed his eyes and stood still for several seconds before raising his arms into the air and parting them as if he was welcoming some invisible guest.

> *'Oh great horse that flies the sky*
> *Spread your wings and hear my cry*
> *T'is to Emerald Island my friends must go*
> *Ride the wind and follow the crow'*

Narky slowly lowered his arms to his side, and stood rock still and eyes closed for several moments before walking back to where his friends sat in the clearing. He resumed his position leant against the tree and cleaned his pipe. He refilled and relit it and sat quietly puffing and contemplating the huge clouds of grey smoke that surrounded him.

'So what happens next?' asked Tyler.

'We wait,' said Narky.

*

And they did – for most of the day. Jack hated waiting for anything. His grandfather often berated him for his lack of patience. *'You'll be giving yourself ulcers the way you're pacing around. Sit down and relax – it won't come any slower if you do.'*

He wondered when he would next see his grandfather. He would be flying to another land soon, further away from the man who had brought him up. The man who taught him everything he knew about life. Lessons that were sure to hold him in good stead for the journey into the unknown that awaited him.

Lilac looked after them all during the day. She constantly made cups of Roseleaf and served up a delicious vegetable stew for lunch. But Jack just wanted to get on his way. Tyler had openly shown his fear about flying on the horse. Jack hadn't been quite so open about his own fears. If he was honest, he was as frightened as a dormouse at a cat show.

Narky stood on the edge of the clearing looking west

across the meadow. In two hours' time it would be dark. Jack stood beside Narky and followed his gaze.

'So when will Troy make his appearance?'

'When he's good and ready,' snapped Narky. 'You young Elves could do with learning the art of patience. We're not the only people who are in need of his services. He spends his whole life flying the skies of our world.' Narky's gruff countenance softened a little. 'He will come, Jack, I promise you.'

Just as they both turned to walk back to the others, Jack heard a voice that he recognised, but wished he didn't.

'What have we here? A nice group of Elves for the taking, like. Rich pickings this night, my lovely lads.'

A tall man with long, straggly, black hair appeared out of the cover of the trees. He walked slowly towards them, a vicious grin revealing unsightly brown teeth. An ugly raised purple scar stretched across his unshaven face. He stopped in front of Jack.

It was Finn Tarr.

'So we meet again my young Elven friend.'

Jack scowled at him. 'I'm no friend of yours. You're not welcome around here, so why don't you go and find somebody else to intimidate.'

'Brave words for a young'un,' sneered Finn. 'But I don't think you have what it takes to back them up.'

Jack swung his right fist at his head, but Finn was too quick and neatly side stepped it.

'I don't think you want to be doing things like that without first checking what yer up against.'

Jack followed Finn's eyes and saw two other men standing in the trees holding shotguns; one pointed at him and the other pointed at his friends in the clearing. Finn took a step towards Jack and dealt him a stinging slap around his face that sent him sprawling across the grass.

Finn looked in turn at Tyler, Syd and Lilac, who watched on in horror at the callous violence inflicted on Jack. 'So which one of you gave me the lump on the back of my head?' He looked them up and down like a vulture studying its prey.

'It wasn't the old one, and it wasn't you, my beauty,' he said looking at Lilac. He focused his evil grey eyes onto Syd and Tyler. 'I think the fat one was asleep, so by a process of elimination, it must have been you with the brown hair.'

He beckoned Syd with his index finger. Syd looked anxiously at the man holding the shotgun, and gingerly walked over to Finn and stopped just in front of him. A gratuitous smirk spread across Finn's face, and without warning he threw a punch at Syd's head. But Syd was too quick; he neatly sidestepped the blow and grabbed Finn's arm and threw him judo style facedown onto the grass. Syd held onto Finn's arm for all of his worth and pulled it so far back that he nearly wrenched it from its socket.

Finn screamed out in agony and shouted to his friends: 'Don't just stand there, shoot the Elf trash!'

But Syd made sure he kept Finn directly in the firing line.

'We can't get a clear shot at him,' said one of Finn's friends. 'You'll be sure to get hit!'

'Then shoot one of the others. They're worth the same dead or alive.'

Narky stepped forward directly into the firing line. 'Syd, in the name of common sense, what are you doing? Why are you stooping to their level?'

'But ...' said Syd.

Narky waved away his protests. 'It's not our way. Let him go.'

Syd reluctantly let go of Finn's arm and stepped back. Narky helped Finn back to his feet. The bounty hunter looked at Syd; pure hatred contorted his face. 'Yer going to regret that. I'll be handing you over in pieces.'

'Tell your men to lower their guns!' barked Narky.

'I don't think you're in any position to give orders. I think you'll find that it's me who holds all of the cards, like.'

'Your weapons are of no use here,' said Narky. 'Now for god's sake go and leave us in peace.'

Finn massaged his sore shoulder as he stared intently at

Narky. 'Shoot him in the legs.' The words were cold and unfeeling. One of his friends raised his shotgun and pointed it at Narky and slowly squeezed the trigger. Jack grimaced and waited for the deafening bang but nothing happened. The man tried to unleash the other barrel but again nothing happened.

'What are you playing at, Billy? Just shoot him,' urged Finn.

A bewildered Billy stared back at him. 'It's not working, Finn. I don't understand it. I cleaned it this morning …'

'Ahh, yer useless,' cried Finn, as he turned to his other friend. 'Hookey, do the deed and let's get these to the meeting place.'

Hookey raised his shotgun to his shoulder and tried to fire both barrels, but again nothing happened.

'Now do you believe me?' said Narky. 'You do not understand about this place. Take your friends and go before it's too late.'

'I don't think so,' said Finn as he withdrew his knife from his belt.

Lilac suddenly shouted, 'Look!' and pointed towards the meadow. Jack turned in the direction she was pointing. His mouth dropped open – he could hardly believe his eyes. A huge black horse with wings spread high and wide was gliding gracefully across the meadow towards them. It was Troy.

Finn and his men stood mesmerised as the horse drew nearer. Jack hadn't seen anything so magnificent in all of his life. Troy gently touched down on the ground and trotted forward several steps before coming to a standstill barely ten metres from them. He lowered his long elegant wings onto the ground and proceeded to graze on the grass.

'What the hell is that?' asked Finn.

'I already told you,' said Narky. 'There are things here that you will never comprehend, now for the sake of us all, just go!'

Finn approached Narky with his knife raised. 'And I told you that you don't call the shots around here, I do!'

But before he'd taken two steps, Troy reared up onto his hind legs and opened his wings to their full span. He screamed as only a horse can do. Jack was sure that he was going to attack Finn. The two huge wings fanned the air around the bounty hunter causing him to drop his knife and fall backwards onto the ground.

Billy and Hookey threw their guns down to the floor and ran off across the meadow. 'Come back you cowards!' roared Finn. 'I'll cut yer yeller livers out and fry them over a camp fire!' But it was too late, his friends weren't coming back.

Narky walked over and helped Finn back to his feet. 'Take this as a warning and leave us Elven folk alone. We are a peace loving people and have no interest in your human ways.'

Finn picked his knife up from the grass and placed it back in his waistband. He looked at the circle of Elves in turn, before settling on Narky. 'This isn't over, not by a long way,' he said and strode purposefully across the meadow after his retreating friends.

Troy had resumed his grazing and took little interest in the proceedings. Lilac ran up to Narky and embraced him. 'I thought he was going to kill you.'

Narky extricated himself from her embrace and Jack thought he saw a faint trace of a smile on his lips. 'There was no need to worry, Lilac. I knew what I was doing. Now let me introduce you to Troy.'

He reached into his rucksack and retrieved a handful of carrots and walked over to Troy. He stroked his head and fed him the carrots. 'It's good to see you again my old friend. Time doesn't seem to change you.' Troy nodded his head and neighed, although Jack thought it sounded more like a laugh.

Narky addressed his friends. 'So, this is your travelling companion who will be taking you to Emerald Island. His name is Troy and he is the truest friend you could ever have.' Troy nodded his head and whickered in agreement. 'Now pack your rucksacks and load them onto his back. You'll be leaving as soon as Troy's finished grazing.'

'Why so soon?' asked Jack.

'Because as I told you before, Troy has many more Faery folk in need of his services. You're not his only concern. Now do as I ask and don't keep him waiting.'

Jack packed his rucksack, as Tyler and Lilac packed theirs. Troy knelt down so that they could strap their packs to his back.

'Now, Jack,' said Narky, 'you climb aboard Troy's back, Tyler next and Lilac last.'

Jack did as he asked and sat astride Troy's huge back. Tyler followed him and immediately wrapped his arms around Jack's waist. Lilac was last and she also grabbed a firm hold of Tyler. Troy slowly rose to his feet. Tyler panicked.

'Whoaaaaa!'

'Tyler,' said Lilac in her best parental tone, 'we haven't even left the ground yet. Can you please calm down? You're holding onto Jack so you'll be OK.'

I'm not sure I will, thought Jack. *He's crushing my ribs and I can hardly breathe.*

'There's absolutely nothing to worry about,' said Narky. 'Troy does this every day of his life and he's never lost a passenger yet.'

'There's always a first time,' said Tyler, turning whiter by the second.

Narky ignored his remark and addressed the three of them together. 'Troy will take you to Seamus O'Shoehorn's village. It's called Cill-Arney.' He looked directly at Jack. 'I really hope that you find your mother there.' He and Syd shook them all warmly by the hand before stepping back.

'Make sure you come to see us when you get back,' said Syd.

'We'll do our best,' said Lilac. 'And thank you both for all that you've done for us.'

'And thanks from me,' said Jack. 'I hope the next time you see me I'll have my mother with me.'

Tyler sat in grim faced silence with his eyes firmly closed and holding onto Jack as if his life depended on it. Troy bowed his head towards Narky and Syd before turning to face the west. He walked slowly over towards the centre of the meadow and stopped. He stood quietly looking westwards for several seconds as if he was composing himself for the journey ahead.

Troy then raised his giant wings either side of himself and broke into a trot. Jack grabbed the coarse hair of his mane and held on for dear life. The fear that was lurking deep within him threatened to surface. He knew there was no point in fighting it so let it take its course.

The trot turned into a gallop and before he knew it he felt himself rising gracefully into the air. Jack's fear suddenly subsided and was replaced by exhilaration. He looked down and saw the green meadow below slowly fading behind him. The dark, grey-blue sky above was marbled with flashes of red and yellow. The setting sun glowed like a huge orange balloon ahead of him.

His life that had been so mundane and predictable until a few short weeks ago had changed beyond recognition; fear and uncertainty replacing routine daily life. But given the choice he wouldn't change any of it.

Troy's huge wings slowly and rhythmically beat against the cool evening air, taking Jack nearer and nearer to the Elf that gave him life. His mind focused on what he was going to, not what he was coming from. He was soon to be reunited with the only blood family he had in the world, his mother. He reached inside his tunic and held the Bloodstone in between his fingers and made a wish …

Chapter Fourteen - Cill-Arney

Jack sat on an upturned log sipping his first mug of Roseleaf of the day as he contemplated the beautiful blue lake and the grey-green mountains. A clear, blue, cloudless sky provided an idyllic backdrop to the breath-taking scenery. The grass was as green as green could be, as were the leaves on the trees. This was Emerald Island, the green island, the spiritual home of Faery.

Tyler sat next to Jack sipping a small glass of Peardrop. Narky had given him a bottle to help sustain him on his journey. And the truth of it was that Tyler needed it. As Jack and Lilac relaxed into their journey and enjoyed the spectacular sights, Tyler's anxiety increased, and he spent the whole journey with his eyes clamped firmly shut.

Lilac fed Troy the last of the carrots that Narky had given them before they left. It was the least they could do for their friend who'd flown almost continuously for four days and nights. Nothing seemed to bother him. High winds, torrential rain, and the rough seas below, didn't faze him. Their journey continued ever onwards until they arrived on Emerald Island early that morning.

Troy finished the carrots and carried on grazing on the lush green grass. Once he'd had his fill he drank from the clear, blue lake. He looked at them and nodded his head as he turned to the east. It was time for him to go. Lilac kissed him on his nose and embraced him. 'Until we meet again, my friend.'

Tyler patted him on his neck. 'Although I didn't enjoy the experience, I can't thank you enough for bringing us here safely.'

Jack wrapped his arms around Troy's neck and whispered to him: 'Thank you so much my friend. You brought me to my mother and I will never forget you for that. Take care and fly safely.'

Troy neighed, or was it laughed, and stood on his hind legs and spread his magnificent black wings to their full span. As his front hooves hit the soft ground he immediately broke into a trot before rising gracefully into the air. The three friends waved their farewells and watched as he slowly disappeared over the tall range of mountains to the east.

They sat back down on the log and Jack refilled their mugs with Roseleaf. 'I feel a poem is called for,' said Tyler. 'An Ode to Troy'. He closed his eyes and composed himself for a moment. 'Oh jet black rider on the wind, Our destinies now inextricably twinned, You fly so proud across our skies, The air of hope shines in your eyes, The servant of the Faery folk, As timeless as the ancient oak, Always listening for the heartfelt cry, A duty of love that will never die ...'

Jack and Lilac looked first at each other and then at Tyler. Lilac had tears in her eyes. 'That's beautiful, Tyler.'

They sat in silence as they drank their tea, each lost in their own thoughts. Jack was just a matter of hours away from meeting the mother that he never knew. It was difficult to put into words the feelings coursing through him at that moment. Any doubts that had surfaced during the previous weeks had gone. He was ready to be reunited with her.

Tyler finished his tea and washed his cup in the lake. 'Well if you two are ready, I think we should go for a stroll.'

'Where to?' asked Lilac.

He slung his rucksack over his back. 'We should walk around the lake and take in the scenery. Narky seemed to think that it was more a case of the Leprechauns finding us, rather than of us finding them. Shall we go?'

They wandered around the lake doing as Tyler suggested and enjoying the scenery. Jack was full of a mix of different emotions. The anticipation of meeting his mother was burning a hole through him. He thought he was managing to hide it but Lilac touched his hand.

'It's difficult not to be overwhelmed with feelings at this moment. I'm all churned up inside too, so I can't imagine what it must be like for you.'

'Well, when you're a poet,' chimed in Tyler, 'you use those emotions to write poignant verse.'

'Credit where credit's due,' said Lilac, 'your last offering was poignant. I'm not sure that describes most of your poems.'

'You have a cruel tongue, Lilac Wildflower. Your words wound me like the assassin's knife.'

'Well I won't tell you what your words do to my ears sometimes!' laughed Lilac.

'You see, Jack,' said Tyler. 'She just doesn't appreciate the prodigious talent that stands before her.'

Jack loved the teasing between Lilac and Tyler. It had sustained him over the last few weeks. And at that moment it poured soothing balm onto his frayed emotions. He was about to meet the mother he'd never known and couldn't think of two other people that he would rather have with him.

*

They continued around the lake's shore for the remainder of the morning and didn't see another soul. Nothing was said between them but they were all feeling distinctly uncomfortable with the situation. Lilac suggested they stop for a cup of Roseleaf not because she particularly wanted one, but more in the hope that it might help relax them.

They sat around the fire and sipped their tea in silence. Jack stared into the deep blue of the lake and tried to lose himself. He didn't want words in his head; he just wanted to be. He'd been fighting with the conflicting emotions flowing through him all of the morning and it was exhausting him. His grandfather had taught him to clear his mind when he was troubled. It was a technique that had proved to be very helpful over the years.

He'd been sitting quietly for several minutes when he saw something moving out of the corner of his eye. He focused on a cluster of gorse bushes just across from them.

Something wasn't quite right.

'Tyler,' whispered Jack. 'I think there's someone hiding in the gorse bushes behind us.'

'Probably a rabbit,' dismissed Tyler. 'Just relax and drink your tea.'

'But Tyler,' persisted Jack. 'How many gorse bushes have you seen with a bright ginger top?'

'Everybody knows that gorse bushes are yellow. Now let me rest and enjoy my tea.'

Lilac heard the exchange and looked over to the bushes. 'He's right, Tyler, there's definitely something odd about one of those gorse bushes.'

Tyler threw the dregs of his tea into the lake and put his mug down. 'I don't suppose I'm going to get any peace until I check it out.'

Tyler walked over to the gorse bush that Jack pointed to and stood in front of it. He reached down and touched the ginger top of the bush. All of a sudden a face appeared and a little man jumped up.

'Whoaaaaa!' cried Tyler as he took a hasty step backwards and fell on his backside.

The little man said, 'and a good day to you all,' as he held his hand out to Tyler. 'Rory McNory at your service. Pleased to make your acquaintance.'

It didn't take much of a guess to know that Rory was a Leprechaun. He was just over a metre tall and was wearing an emerald green suit with black boots. An unruly mop of bright ginger hair sat on top of a freckly face, although to be honest, there was more freckle than face!

Tyler sat up and grabbed Rory's outstretched hand. 'Tyler Goldsmith – pleased to meet you. And my two friends, Lilac Wildflower and Jack, sometimes known as Green-Jack.'

Rory walked over and shook their hands warmly. 'You're Elves if I'm not mistaken. Welcome to Emerald Island – the spiritual home of all Faery folk.' He noticed the mugs that Lilac and Jack were holding. 'I don't suppose there's a sup of tea going?'

Jack was fascinated by Rory's accent. He didn't so much speak as sing to them. There was a rhythm and soft cadence to his voice. And it amused Jack that he pronounced 'I' as 'oy'!

Tyler climbed back to his feet and washed his mug in the lake. He filled it from the metal pot that was on the fire and handed it to Rory. The Leprechaun took a healthy mouthful and swilled it around his mouth before swallowing. 'I have to say that's a grand sup of tea. Nearly as good as the Shamrock tea that we drink in Cill-Arney.'

Jack couldn't wait to ask him about his mother. 'Rory, can I ask you a question?'

'Ask away,' said Rory.

'My mother, Ciara. Is she staying in Cill-Arney?'

Rory choked on the mouthful of tea he was in the middle of swallowing and spat it onto the grass. The smile instantly disappeared from his face. 'I think I'd better take you to the Muldoon.'

*

Rory led them away from the lake, through a shadowy pine wood and down a steep slope into a tree-lined glen, with a rapid stream running across its floor. In the distance, they could hear the tranquil sound of a teeming waterfall. As beautiful as all this was, Jack's mind was elsewhere. Rory hadn't uttered a word since Jack mentioned his mother. It didn't take a psychic to realise that something was wrong. But what was it?

He tried to stop himself from thinking the worst but he was finding it difficult. Each time the anticipation built and he thought he was getting nearer to finding her, something got in the way. Neither Lilac nor Tyler ventured any opinion, their silence speaking volumes.

They followed a narrow pathway alongside the stream at the foot of the glen and eventually came out in front of a towering waterfall. The midday sun reflected in the cascading waters casting a stunning rainbow across the glen.

'That is absolutely beautiful,' said Lilac. 'Badger's Fall seems so sedate in comparison.'

'It's all relative, Lilac,' said Tyler. 'Badger's Fall is also beautiful, but on a smaller scale.'

'If you say so,' whispered Lilac under her breath.

'You see,' continued Tyler, 'I see the world through the poet's eye – I see beauty in all its guises.'

Lilac looked at Jack and rolled her eyes. Jack forced a smile but wasn't really in the right frame of mind for light-hearted chatter.

Rory turned from the stream and led them onto a narrow path that wound its way slowly up the side of the glen. Rugged gorse bushes and fragrant purple heather lined their way. When they reached the top they came out onto an open clearing, surrounded by tall, ragged pine trees that cast their shade across a ring of quaint thatched cottages with green and brown walls. A tall wooden tower with a large brass bell perched at its top stood proudly in the centre of the village.

Rory turned to them and said, 'welcome to Cill-Arney where there will always be a sup of tea and a warm welcome waiting for you.' He pointed to a lone cottage on the far side of the village. 'That's where the Muldoon lives. He's the head of our community. I'll introduce you.'

They walked over to the cottage and Rory knocked twice on the green door. Jack's head was almost level with the roof – there was no way he would get into such a small space without crawling on his hands and knees. The door opened and an elderly Leprechaun appeared. He was the same size as Rory, although twice his weight, with thinning, grey hair and a bushy grey beard. A pair of half-moon glasses were perched on the end of his nose. 'Good day to you Rory.' He looked at Jack, Lilac and Tyler. 'And who is it we have here?'

Rory pointed to them in turn. 'Green-Jack, Lilac and Tyler. Elves from Brittany Island I believe.'

A cheery smile lit the Muldoon's face and he shook

them all warmly by the hand. 'Rory, ring the bell. Let's give our guests a traditional Cill-Arney welcome.'

Rory ran over to the bell and tugged the rope that hung from it. Several deep clangs resonated around the whole village and beyond. The effect was instantaneous. The doors to the cottages were flung open and scores of Leprechauns ran into the middle of the village.

And when they saw Jack, Lilac and Tyler, an almighty cheer rang out, and they all burst into spontaneous song. The whole village centre was filled with singing and dancing Leprechauns. Jack's melancholy mood was instantly dispelled by the pure energy of their welcome. Young, old, male and female clamoured to welcome their Elven visitors.

Eventually a stout, elderly female with rosy red cheeks made her way to the front of the singing throng and gestured with her arms for them to calm down. It took several attempts but silence eventually reigned. 'On my life,' she said. 'You'd think that we never have guests in Cill-Arney.'

'We don't, Auntie Bridie,' said a young bright-eyed Leprechaun standing in front of her.

She gave him a playful slap on his shoulder. 'And I'll have less of your cheek, Sean McSpawn.' She turned to her three bemused looking guests and bowed her head. 'A thousand welcomes to you from us all in Cill-Arney. It is a pleasure to see you here. My name is Auntie Bridie and I try my best to keep everybody in check.' She gave Sean a disapproving look. 'Although I don't always manage it.'

Tyler stepped forward and bowed low. 'The pleasure, my dear, is all ours. Please may I introduce my friends, Lilac Wildflower and Green-Jack.' He took Bridie's hand and kissed it. 'And I am Tyler Goldsmith, resident poet in the Elven village of Waterswood on Brittany Island.'

Bridie's rosy cheeks turned rosier as she retracted her hand. 'Now, my lovely Leprechauns, let's lay on a spread to remember for our esteemed guests.' And they all disappeared off into different directions, leaving the three

Elves on their own with Rory and the Muldoon.

The Muldoon pointed to a semi-circular bench outside his cottage. 'We can sit and talk while the meal is being prepared. The bench may be a little small for you but it will be comfortable enough.'

They sat down around the bench and a young colleen, (female Leprechaun), appeared holding a tray with five mugs perched on it. 'Shamrock tea,' said Rory. 'It will refresh you and give you a healthy appetite.'

'I don't think Tyler has ever had any trouble with his appetite,' joked Lilac.

Tyler did his best to look indignant, but ended up smiling. He sipped his tea and said, 'I must say, this is very refreshing indeed. There's a hint of mint which livens the pallet.'

'Muldoon,' said Rory in a serious voice. 'Young Jack here is looking for his mother.'

'And who may that be?' asked the Muldoon.

'Ciara,' replied Jack. 'We're told that she came here with a Leprechaun friend called Seamus O'Shoehorn.'

The Muldoon carefully placed his mug on the bench beside him. He studied Jack for a moment. 'You have the look of your mother. I should have realised. Your information is correct. Your mother did indeed come here with Seamus, and most welcome she was too.' He thoughtfully stroked his beard as he spoke. 'She was very frightened when she arrived here. It was obvious to us all that she was running from something, or someone. She had her heart set on finding the Elven homeland on Emerald Island.'

Tyler exchanged confused looks with Lilac. 'I wasn't aware there was an Elven homeland on Emerald Island.'

'Legend says that there is,' said the Muldoon. 'Seamus had told Ciara about it which is why she came here, although no Leprechaun has ever found it.'

'Our friend, Narky, said that Emerald Island is the spiritual home of the Faery world,' said Lilac.

'And he would be right in that,' said the Muldoon. 'It is

a strong source for Faery magic, sure enough'

Jack sat quietly taking all of this in. As disappointed as he was that his mother wasn't there, he also understood the reasons why she would want to look for the Elven homeland. Perhaps she was looking for help to challenge Grimley? 'When did she leave here?' he asked.

'Only a matter of weeks after she arrived,' said the Muldoon. 'Seamus went with her, as did O'Reilly, our most experienced guide in these mountains.'

'O'Reilly knows the mountains like the back of his hand,' chipped in Rory, 'which is why he went with them. But we've heard nothing of them since the day they left, well other than through Brendan.'

'Who's Brendan?' asked Jack.

'He's known as the lonely Leprechaun,' said the Muldoon. 'He lives on his own in the mountains. He saw them just after they left here – they stayed the night with him.' The Muldoon turned to Rory. 'Go and fetch Sean. He can tell them about his many searches in the mountains.'

Rory jumped up and ran across the clearing to one of the cottages and knocked on the door. The Leprechaun that had been cheeky to Auntie Bridie appeared. 'Sean, the Muldoon wants you to join us.'

Sean followed Rory over to where they sat. He had a bounce in his step and a glint in his eye, and according to Auntie Bridie, had a smile that could charm the birds from the trees. He shook hands with Jack and Tyler. 'Sean McSpawn at your service.' Then he set his eyes on Lilac. 'And who is this vision of beauty?'

Lilac blushed and avoided Tyler's mocking look.

'Sit down, Sean,' said the Muldoon, 'and try to concentrate on the task in hand.' Sean dutifully obeyed and sat down next to Rory. 'Young Jack here is Ciara's son. He arrived in Cill-Arney expecting to find her here. Could you tell him about your attempts to find her?'

Sean's cheeky smile instantly disappeared to be replaced by a more serious expression. 'I really liked your mother, Jack. She had an engaging way about her – in fact we all loved her. So when she said that she wanted to find the Elven homeland, several of us volunteered to help guide her. O'Reilly was chosen to join her and Seamus, and take it from me, nobody knows the mountains better than O'Reilly.

Well they'd been gone for several months without any word back when the Muldoon asked me to go and look for them. I trekked west and followed their tracks to Brendan's and beyond. I found the remains of several camp fires which I guessed were theirs, but the trail went cold.'

'What do you mean 'it went cold'?' asked Jack.

'It suddenly stopped on the edge of a forest. I tried several times to pick it up again but failed miserably. We've been back several times since in the hope of finding them, but I'm afraid they all came to nothing.'

'Could you find this forest again?' asked Jack.

'O'Reilly may be the best tracker in Cill-Arney, but I'm the second best. I'll find it.'

Jack turned to Lilac and Tyler. 'I want to go there – will you come with me?'

'Do you need to ask?' said Tyler.

'I really think you need to rest here a while before you take on such an arduous journey,' suggested the Muldoon. 'The mountain terrain is physically and mentally demanding.'

'I'm sorry,' said Jack, 'but my mother could be in real danger so I can't afford to delay any longer than I have to. We will rest tonight and leave tomorrow. I came here to find my mother and that's what I'm going to do.'

Chapter Fifteen - The Lonely Leprechaun

The Leprechauns laid on a lunch quite unlike anything that Jack had ever seen in his life before. The food just kept on coming. Tyler had the appetite of a hungry horse but even he had to give in after the third helping of Auntie Bridie's apple pie.

And then their farewell supper – more food, but this time accompanied by copious amounts of alcohol. Jack hated alcohol – the smell of it made him sick. The Leprechauns tried to ply him with a disgusting clear liquid called Poteen. Jack thought it smelt and tasted like white spirit. When that failed, they tried another spirit called Ishka Baa (water of life). But Jack found that equally as repulsive.

Finally, they tried the black stout - a glass of jet black liquid with a foamy white head. Now Jack thought that it looked inviting, so he tried a healthy mouthful, but it didn't taste as good as it looked. So he settled for a glass of lemonade with a difference – it was red!

A young colleen called Cara took a shine to Jack. She had long dark hair as black as a raven's wing and green eyes that sparkled like precious emeralds. She sidled up to him as he chatted to Sean and Rory, fluttered her jet black eyelashes framing dazzling green eyes and said, 'Green-Jack, you have the look of the rebel about you.' She giggled mischievously. 'And doesn't this colleen just love a rebel.' She grabbed his hands and pulled him into the middle of a dancing throng of Leprechauns. 'Let me show you how we dance in Cill-Arney.'

She hitched up her long green dress and started to jig in front of him. Before he knew it, they were both circled by laughing and clapping Leprechauns. The rhythm of the fiddle, tin whistle and the bodhran (small drum) were electrifying. It lifted him up and carried him along and when she grabbed his hands, he started to dance with her, which was amazing for someone who had never danced in his entire life until that moment. Lilac and Tyler joined in the dancing and by the end of the night, Tyler was singing along with the Leprechauns, which was made even more amazing by the fact that he knew neither the words nor the melodies!

It was the morning after the night before and Jack was staring out across the blue lakes and the tall, grey, mystical mountains that surrounded Cill-Arney. He stood alone with his thoughts on the edge of the village. The Leprechauns were amazing people and you couldn't fail to be affected by the warmth of their welcome. As tempting as it was to stay for a while, he was on a quest to find his mother and that had to be his focus.

The Muldoon had tried his best to dissuade him from leaving Cill-Arney so soon but Jack was adamant he wanted to keep the momentum going. It was agreed that Sean and Rory would be their guides and Jack was reassured by that. He'd known them for less than a day but he already had a deep regard and trust for them both. He took in the beautiful scenery as he dwelt on the challenges that lay ahead.

'It's beautiful, isn't it?' Lilac appeared by Jack's side and followed his gaze across the lakes and mountains.

'It certainly is,' he agreed. 'It seems a shame to be leaving so soon, but …'

Lilac held his hand. 'I know, Jack. Both Tyler and I are aware of how hard this is for you, but we're going to stay with you no matter where it takes us.'

Jack put his arm around her shoulder and held her close. 'I wouldn't be here without you both.'

Before she could answer, they were interrupted by a jovial Rory. 'Come on you two - the Muldoon wants a word before we leave.'

Jack and Lilac followed him back to the centre of the village, where the whole community were gathered to wish them well on their journey. Auntie Bridie stood at one end of a long table crammed with food: sandwiches, pies, vegetables, fruit. It was like the banquet from the previous day. Sean stood by her cramming it into two small rucksacks.

'I think you'll find it's not all going to fit,' commented Tyler.

Sean winked at him. 'It'll fit.'

A very serious looking Muldoon called for their attention. The silence was instant and they all looked to their leader as he prepared to speak.

'I think you all know that I would prefer that Jack and his friends rested here at Cill-Arney with us before embarking on their journey into the mountains. As much as I may wish that, at the same time I understand Jack's desire to leave immediately. The disappearance of his mother, Ciara, and our own Seamus and O'Reilly has long been a source of worry and concern for us all.' He turned his attention to Rory and Sean. 'I will be looking to you both to use your experience in the mountains to make sure that you all remain safe. Next to O'Reilly, you are the most experienced trackers we have here in Cill-Arney. Please, for all of our sakes, don't take any unnecessary risks.' He beckoned the two of them over and embraced them both. 'Now all that remains to be said is, keep safe, keep fed and keep well.'

Sean and Rory strapped their rucksacks to their backs and they both hugged Auntie Bridie. 'Now don't you be doing anything daft, the two of you, otherwise you'll have me to answer to,' she scolded.

'I think I'd rather face a wild, hungry bear than the wrath of Auntie Bridie,' whispered Rory under his breath.

Cara walked up to Jack and handed him a gold coin. 'Here, Green-Jack, keep this close to your heart. It will bring you good luck.' She reached up and stood on her tiptoes and kissed him full on the lips. Jack turned a deep shade of crimson and mumbled a 'thank-you'. He looked at the coin – it had a Leprechaun's head engraved on one side and a Shamrock on the other.

Rory whispered in his ear, 'that's a very precious gift, Jack me lad. We're all given one at birth.'

Jack kissed the coin and placed it in the breast pocket on the inside of his jacket. He strapped his rucksack on his back and joined Tyler and Lilac. Tyler rose to the occasion and addressed them all. 'Good Leprechauns of Cill-Arney, we thank you all from the bottom of our hearts for the warmth and gracious hospitality that you have shown us over the last day. I expect to be coming back here in the not too distant future with our mutual friends. And always remember that there will be a warm welcome waiting for you at Waterswood if you ever stray across the water to Brittany Island.'

'Well we haven't time to chat all day,' said Sean. 'I want to be at Brendan's cottage before sundown, and it's a good day's walk in the mountains.' He turned to the assembled Leprechauns. 'Until we see you all again,' and led the group across the clearing and down the path towards the glen.

The goodbyes from the Leprechauns resonated in their ears until they were halfway down the path and the sound of the cascading waterfall finally drowned them out.

Jack's recent life had been a series of goodbyes. First from his grandfather - then Waterswood, Becky, Syd, Narky and finally the Leprechauns. He'd left a part of himself with them all, but at the same time had a strong feeling that he would be reunited with every one of them again one day. His grandfather had taught him that sadness was a part of life that you should learn to embrace.

And he did. A solitary tear ran down his face and dropped onto his jacket. He wiped the trail from his cheek and felt the sadness in his heart at leaving such wonderful people behind.

Sean led them from the glen and back through the pine wood to the lake shore, towards the tall, grey mountains that lay to the west, just as the sun disappeared behind the dark, grey clouds that followed them from the east. Rory looked up at the sky and frowned at Sean. 'There'll be rain before the morning's out,' he said. 'We need to make as much progress as we can while the going's good.'

'A bit of rain never harmed anyone,' said Tyler.

Sean and Rory winked at each other and smiled to themselves. 'Let's see if he still says that when he's soaked to the skin after three constant weeks of it,' whispered Rory.

They journeyed along the blue lake and then into a desolate grey valley, that Rory called Lone Valley. As colourless as it was, Jack thought that it had a solemn beauty about it. He could imagine that a sunny day would change the whole atmosphere of the place. But then something occurred to him.

'Is there any chance we'll come across humans on this trail?'

Rory shook his head. 'Unlikely, but even if we do they probably won't even acknowledge us.'

'Have you had many dealings with them?' asked Jack.

'Only the once. Some years ago, I had a late night stroll around the lake. I was having trouble sleeping so I thought a breath of fresh air would help. I came across a human sitting on a rock by the water's edge who was obviously a little worse for wear with drink. So I thought that I would make sure that he was OK and walked over to him and said, 'How are you my friend?' Well nothing could have prepared me for what happened next. He jumped to his feet and dropped his bottle on the floor and screamed: 'Oh my god, I'm hallucinating! I'm seeing and hearing the little people!' And ran off like a frightened rabbit.'

'So what did you do?' asked Tyler.

'I picked up his bottle and had a drink from it. It was Ishka Baa, although not as good as the Leprechaun stuff.'

'Did you finish it off?' asked Tyler.

'It would have been rude not to,' smiled Rory.

They stopped around midday to eat by the edge of a small lake nestled in between the valley and the mountains. They had soda bread sandwiches washed down with rhubarb juice.

'I have to say that this bread is rather nice,' said Tyler.

'Auntie Bridie's soda bread,' said Rory. 'It's made

from buttermilk – it's what gives it a unique taste and texture.'

'Well I could get used to it,' said Tyler.

It was as they cleared up after their meal that the rain came. A slight drizzle at first but it quickly turned into the dreary mist that you only see in the mountains on the west of Emerald Island. Sean produced full length capes for them all, complete with hoods.

'Auntie Bridie and the colleens made these for you. Take it from me, you'll be glad of them by the end of the day.'

And they were. The rain was relentless. Not heavy but a constant drizzle that soaked deep into their beings. Tyler walked by the side of Sean and Rory, and said, 'the next time I say that a bit of rain never harmed anyone would you both politely tell me to shut up. I don't think I've ever felt as cold, wet and miserable as I do at this moment.'

'Don't worry, Tyler,' said Sean. 'We can all make eejits of ourselves at times.'

Lilac joined them. 'What's an eejit?'

'A Leprechaun word for idiot,' said Rory.

'That sums up Tyler nicely,' she smiled.

Brendan's cottage was at the far end of Lone Valley on the edge of a lake called the Gleaming, and by the time they got there in the early evening, they were all mightily relieved to be getting out of the rain. Brendan's cottage was tucked neatly by a clump of willow trees near to the water's edge. A large barn stood to one side of the cottage.

Sean walked up to the front door and knocked twice. The door opened and an elderly Leprechaun with long, grey hair and a white beard stood there. Age had stooped his posture but a warm smile lit his face when he saw Sean.

'Sean McSpawn ye young rascal - it's grand to see ye.' He grasped Sean firmly by the hand. Then he noticed Rory. 'Ah Rory McNory – a sight for sore eyes if there ever was.' He stepped back from the door. 'Come in the pair of ye and get yourselves into the warm.'

'We've got friends with us,' said Rory. He pointed to them in turn. 'This is Jack, Tyler and Lilac. They're Elves visiting from Brittany Island.'

'And welcome as they are, as ye can see, my cottage may be just a little cramped for ye all. But I can put ye all up in the barn – I'll soon have it ready for ye.'

And he did. He lit a fire in the forge and hung a huge soup pot over it. Sean produced sleeping bags from his bottomless rucksack for everyone, and placed them on mattresses that Brendan had laid out. They hung out their wet capes to dry and crowded around the fire. The warmth was like food for their souls. Brendan gave them a mug of Shamrock tea each and sat down beside Jack.

'I'll soon have the soup ready and I have some soda bread just baked. And I made an extra-large apple tart this morning so we'll have that with some clotted cream.'

The meal when it came was just what they needed. Thick, steaming hot mushroom soup and soda bread followed by apple tart and clotted cream, all washed down with Shamrock tea and rhubarb juice. They sat in a semi-circle around the fire, digesting their food and enjoying the warmth.

'I can't remember the last time I ate so much,' said Tyler.

'Try last night,' said Lilac.

'I can always rely on Lilac to jog my memory,' he laughed, 'but that truly was a meal fit for Kings.'

'And Queens,' chimed in Lilac.

'Indeed,' he said as he raised his mug of Shamrock tea. 'To Brendan and all of the wonderful Leprechauns we've met since we've been on Emerald Island.'

'I think we can manage something a little more suitable for a toast,' said Brendan pulling a bottle from behind him. 'I'm sure the Muldoon introduced ye all to Ishka Baa when ye were in Cill-Arney.'

'He did indeed,' said Tyler leaning forward and holding out his mug.

Rory, Sean and Brendan joined him. Rory proposed a

toast. 'To the Elves and Leprechauns – long may they be friends.'

'Long may they be friends,' they all repeated as they sipped their respective drinks.

'So what brings ye all to Emerald Island?' asked Brendan as he relaxed back into his makeshift chair.

'We're looking for my mother,' said Jack.

'And that would be Ciara,' said Brendan.

'Yes it would,' said a surprised Jack.

'Only you have the look of her. The same hair and the same colour eyes. She's a fine Elf. It's so sad that she's missing along with O'Reilly and Seamus. I warned them about the foolishness of their search, but I'm afraid they wouldn't listen. Fear does strange things to us.'

'Why do you think the search for the Elven homeland was foolish?' asked Jack.

'Because the Elves on this island left centuries ago. They became disillusioned with our world and used magic to create their own. It will be impossible to find, a fact which I shared with Ciara. But I could see that fear drove her. She seemed desperate to find her homeland and would not listen to my warnings. When the three of them left my cottage all of those years ago, that was the last that anyone ever saw of them.'

'Do you have any idea of what may have happened to them?' asked Lilac.

Brendan sat quietly and thought for several moments. 'There are strange and mysterious places in the mountains that I have come across in my travels and I have always walked away from them. One such place is the forest that Sean came across in his search. There is something unnerving about that place and I didn't risk entering it and I suggest that ye do the same.'

'But Sean said that he tracked my mother, Seamus and O'Reilly there. Surely that's where we need to go?'

'I can understand why ye would want to go there, Jack. The desire to find your mother is a strong one. But I believe that if ye do, ye will meet the same fate and will be lost to us forever.'

It was the last thing that Jack wanted to hear. He'd already faced so many dangers in the quest to find his mother. But he'd come this far and wasn't about to give up on her. He turned to his friends. 'I don't expect any of you to enter this forest with me. I would fully understand if you take me to the forest edge, Sean, and let me find my own way from there. And that goes for you all.'

'I'm hurt that you would think I wouldn't come with you,' said Tyler.

'And me,' said Lilac.

Sean leant forward and looked Jack deep in his eyes. 'You have to remember, Jack, that Seamus and O'Reilly are like brothers to Rory and me. We care about them as much as you care about your mother. When we left Cill-Arney we knew it was never going to be easy, but we will continue this journey to wherever the road takes us.'

'I'll drink to that,' said Tyler as he raised his mug, and Sean, Rory and Lilac joined him.

Chapter Sixteen – Breannacht

When Jack woke it was still dark. A dull red glow from the embers of the fire was the only light in the barn. He had no idea what time it was but had an urgent thirst that needed quenching. He extricated himself from his sleeping bag and carefully tip-toed through the sleeping bodies to a table and filled a glass with water from a stone jug.

He downed the water in one and refilled the glass and sipped it slowly. The barn was filled with the unmelodic snores of Tyler, Sean and Rory. Lilac slept quietly in the sleeping bag next to Jack. He should have been tired after the long trek through Lone Valley the previous day, but for some reason he felt wide awake.

He needed fresh air; he needed space. He placed the glass back on the table and pulled his boots on and opened the creaky barn door as quietly as he could. The fresh air hit him instantly as he stepped outside and a cleansing breeze washed over him. The rain had thankfully stopped but the ground was damp and soggy. A full moon rested over the mountains on the far side of the lake and its milky white reflection stretched across the full length of the resting waters.

Jack found himself drawn to the water's edge and walked around the lake away from Brendan's cottage. The only sound was the occasional rustle of the leaves in the trees as the wind gently caressed them. A feeling of deep serenity took a hold of him; no worries; no concerns; no fears. Just peace.

The moon disappeared behind a dark, black cloud and Jack was suddenly plunged into darkness. He found himself in a world of shadow but still felt strangely at peace. As he continued his walk around the lake he noticed a subtle change in the wind. Shallow ripples traversed the lake's surface towards him causing the water to lap up over his boots.

The wind intensity continued to build and whistled

across the vast open space of the lake. Jack shivered and pulled his jacket tighter. The whistle soon turned into a low wail and he felt the subtle stirrings of anxiety deep down in the pit of his stomach. He had a pressing urge to go back to the barn but his feet felt as if they were glued to the soggy ground. His heart beat faster as the low wail turned into a blood curdling, anguished cry. It was the cry of someone in deep distress. Surely his friends in the barn must have heard it.

The hairs on the back of his neck stood to attention. 'Keep calm, Jack,' he breathed to himself. 'You're only a matter of a hundred metres or so from the others.' But the spine tingling anxiety channelled through the entire length of his body, setting his nerves on edge.

A swirling white mist suddenly appeared on the far side of the lake and moved slowly in his direction. It looked like a giant ball of cotton wool rolling precariously across the lake's surface. The wind continued to cry out in pained distress adding to his already anxious state. Centimetre by centimetre the mist edged its way towards him. The desire to run built up to fever pitch but his feet steadfastly refused to move.

The wind dropped just as suddenly as it started and the mist ground to a halt barely twenty metres from the lake's edge in front of him. All was still again and a strange calm descended upon him. He peered into the misty gloom and was sure that something stirred deep within it. He fleetingly thought the mist was playing tricks on his eyes, but then he saw it - a tall figure moving slowly towards him. His calm was replaced by a trembling excitement.

A face appeared out of the mist; it was the face of a beautiful woman. Her skin was as white as snow and her lips were the colour of blood. Her long, black hair hung loosely over a glistening white, full-length gown. She seemed to glide across the lake's surface and stopped just a few metres from where Jack stood and looked at him with a burning intensity.

His heart beat faster and his throat felt as dry as a

desert. He looked up into her face and saw pain buried deep in her dark eyes. He couldn't speak – he was mesmerised by the overwhelming presence of the beautiful woman standing in front of him.

'Welcome, Green-Jack.' Her voice was low and resonant – it melted over him. 'Welcome to my home.'

'B-but how do … how do you know my name?' he stuttered.

She smiled enigmatically. 'I've been waiting for you …'

Confusion numbed Jack's brain. Why would she be waiting for him? 'Who are you? What's your name?'

'My name is Breannacht. I am a Banshee.'

A Banshee?

She sensed his confusion. 'I am not of this world. I am a messenger.'

'A messenger of what?' asked Jack.

'I foretell death …' She tilted her head back and opened her mouth and the same anguished cry that he'd heard from across the lake, surrounded him like a shroud.

A terrible feeling of dread gripped Jack. 'Am I … am I going to die?'

'You are not,' she said firmly.

'I don't understand, I …'

'I am here as your guide. I am here to help you, Jack.'

Dread gripped him again. 'Is it my mother? Is she OK?'

Her dark eyes bore deep down into him. 'Your mother is alive but she is in grave danger.'

His mother was alive. A surge of adrenaline electrified his body. 'Do you know where she is? Please tell me what I must do?' His voice was thick with urgency.

'Your mother is beyond the 'Mist of Time'.'

'The 'Mist of Time'?' repeated Jack. 'I've never heard of this place. Where is it?'

'It is the gateway to other worlds. Some call it the mist between the worlds. It is a very dangerous place and must be approached with great caution.'

'Please, tell me how I find this place?' he begged.

131

She took him by the hand and gently led him across the lake towards the ball of mist that rested there. Amazingly, he didn't sink into the water but walked precariously across its surface. The choking mist wrapped itself around him as soon as he stepped into it and he became totally disorientated. He held onto Breannacht's hand as if his life depended on it.

Ghostly, shadowy figures appeared all around him. They were calling his name. 'Green-Jack – come with us. Let us take care of you.' The voices unnerved him. They were low and enticing. He grasped Breannacht's hand even tighter as he followed her deeper into the mist.

He heard Grimley's voice in his ear. 'You can't get away from us, Green-Jack. We will capture you soon – it's only a matter of time.' His voice was so clear that Jack was convinced he was standing next to him. He looked over his shoulder but there was no sign of Grimley, only the ghostly shadows dancing in the mist.

As the mist gradually began to thin, they emerged into the middle of a dark forest. Not so dark that you couldn't see your way, but dark enough to suggest there was danger there. Birds shrieked in the distance and wild animals howled. Not shrieks or howls of greeting; they were chilling, bloodcurdling cries that called for death.

They left the forest just as suddenly as they entered it, and stood on the edge of a deep valley. They were high up on a plateau. Breannacht pointed across the valley towards a bleak looking castle on the far side. It was dark and foreboding. Three towers surrounded a tall spire in its centre. It was a place that Jack hoped he would never see the inside of.

She let go of his hand and turned towards him. 'I have shown you all that I can. It is now for you to follow your chosen path.'

Jack looked pleadingly into her dark eyes. 'Breannacht – will I find my mother?'

She stared blankly at him and didn't answer.

'Please – tell me which path I should follow.'

Breannacht placed her hands on his shoulders. 'Follow your heart, Jack … your destiny awaits you …' Then she pulled him gently to her and kissed him tenderly on his lips.

*

'Come on, Jack me lad, it's time to get up!'

Jack opened his eyes to see Rory standing by his side holding a mug of steaming tea.

'Shamrock tea – just what you need to kick start your day.'

Jack pulled himself up into a sitting position and took the tea from Rory. 'What time is it?'

'Past eight, and Brendan is just about to serve breakfast.'

Sean and Lilac were busy with Brendan preparing breakfast. Tyler was still tucked up in his sleeping bag, snoring rhythmically. Jack thought about what had happened during the night. It felt real but he'd woken up in his sleeping bag. *It must have been a dream*, he thought.

'Come on me lovely lads,' said Brendan. 'Eat your breakfast while it's hot.'

Jack pulled himself from his sleeping bag and sat on a bench next to Lilac. She handed him a plate full of scrambled egg, fried tomatoes, fried mushrooms and potato cakes. Jack surprised himself at how hungry he was and made short work of it.

Once he'd finished, he sat quietly drinking his Shamrock tea. Lilac had finally managed to wake Tyler, who was now wading his way through a mountain of food, but he wasn't so distracted that he noticed Jack was quiet.

'What ails you Jack?' he asked in between forkfuls.

'To be honest, I'm not sure. I had a strange dream last night, or at least I think I did, and it's bothering me.'

Brendan sat down next to him. 'What sort of dream?' he asked.

'Have you ever heard of a Banshee?'

133

'I have indeed,' said Brendan. 'One resides here in the mountains. In fact, I heard her last night.'

The mention of a Banshee attracted both Sean and Rory's attention. 'Why are you asking about such things?' asked Rory.

'I thought it was a dream,' said Jack, 'but maybe it did happen.'

Rory was beside himself. 'In the name of the great Leprechaun would you ever tell us what happened?'

'I woke in the night and I felt thirsty and restless. I had a drink of water and decided to walk around the lake. At first it was very calm and relaxing, but then the wind suddenly blew up and I heard a spine chilling cry from across the far side of the lake. A white mist drifted across the lake towards me and the Banshee appeared from deep within it.'

Everybody was gripped by his story – in fact Tyler even stopped eating.

'Were you frightened?' asked an increasingly excited Rory.

'At first,' said Jack, 'but then an amazing feeling of calm swept over me. But what surprised me most was that she knew my name.'

'Knew your name!' repeated Rory. 'But how?'

'I don't know – but then she scared the life out of me.'

'Why, what did she do?' asked Sean.

'She told me that she foretells death. I thought that … I thought that she was warning me of my own impending death. I was really frightened.'

'That would scare the life out of anybody,' agreed Rory.

'And then I thought that she may be warning me of my mother's death.' An uneasy silence filled the barn - nobody hardly dare breathe. 'But she wasn't – in fact she told me that my mother is alive …'

The tension in the barn instantly evaporated. 'Oh Jack,' gasped Lilac. 'That's such a relief.'

'Did she mention Seamus or O'Reilly?' asked Sean

excitedly.

'No she didn't, but she said something else about my mother. She said that she was in grave danger.'

'Did she tell you what sort of danger?' asked Rory, his expression rapidly changing from one of excitement to concern.

Jack shook his head solemnly. 'She didn't ...'

'Did she say where Ciara was?' pressed Lilac.

'No she didn't, but she took me on a strange journey into the mist, then through a forest to a valley with a dark castle at the far end. She pointed to the castle and told me to follow my chosen path and that my destiny awaits me. Then she kissed me on my lips and I woke in my sleeping bag this morning. It was all very confusing.'

'Well,' said Rory, 'there's no time to waste. Let's pack our rucksacks and get back on the trail.'

*

Jack stood alone staring across the lake. It looked so different in the sunlight. The silver water glistened like its surface was covered in precious jewels. The mountains stood tall and magnificent like timeless sentries guarding the lake.

There was an emotional conflict raging inside of Jack. He now knew for sure that his mother was alive, but that she was in grave danger. What he didn't know was the nature of the danger she faced. The road ahead was daunting; he was in no doubt about that. But he'd risen to every challenge that had confronted him so far and was ready for whatever lay ahead.

His thoughts were interrupted by Brendan. 'I hope you don't mind me joining you, young Jack. The lake is so beautiful in the sunshine. I find that it feeds my soul just looking at it.'

Jack had lived his whole life in the forest. It was his home and where he felt most at ease. But this wasn't just beautiful, it was spiritual. It soothed his frayed emotions like a healing balm. And he was glad that Brendan had joined him. The old Leprechaun was just the company he needed at that moment.

There were questions Jack needed to ask him. 'I noticed that you were quiet when I was telling my story.'

'I listened to what you said very carefully.'

'There was something the Banshee told me that I didn't tell the others. Have you heard of a place called the 'Mist of Time'?'

Brendan shook his head. 'I have not, but there are many mysterious places in the mountains that I do not know of.'

'She said that it was a gateway to other worlds.'

Brendan pondered Jack's words for several moments. 'And my guess would be that is the way to your Elven homeland.'

Jack hadn't considered that. Had his mother found their homeland? But if she had, why would she be in danger? 'Do you think it's dangerous?'

'There is danger everywhere, young Jack, and I have to admit to spending most of my life avoiding it. But there are times where we have to confront danger, and this may be one of them. Follow your heart, Jack; follow it to wherever it leads you.'

They were similar words to those that Breannacht had used. His mind was made up – he was going to follow his heart, because that was where his mother lay. 'Thanks, Brendan. I really appreciate your advice.'

'You're welcome, young Jack, and just make sure that you return here safely … with your mother and those two rascals Seamus and O'Reilly.'

Chapter Seventeen - The Silent Forest

Jack and his friends had been walking and sleeping in constant rain for two weeks. It started late in the day they left Brendan's and hadn't stopped since. It didn't just dampen their clothes, it dampened their spirits. Even the normally happy-go-lucky Rory found that his sense of fun was seriously waning.

'Would it ever stop, just for a morning or an afternoon? I'm so wet that I don't think it's my boots squelching anymore, I think it's my feet!'

'We're used to this, Rory. Think how hard it must be for the others,' said Sean.

'It's not just the rain,' groaned Tyler, 'it's the rugged terrain. If we're not climbing up the sides of mountains, we're coming back down them again. Do you have any flat ground on this island?'

'Pay no attention to him,' said Lilac. 'He's only happy when he's moaning!'

Jack was lost in his own thoughts. The gloomy weather didn't so much cause his mood as reflect it. The message from the Banshee played on his mind - *Your mother is in grave danger*. If only she could have told him where she was. He needed to find this mysterious place, the 'Mist of Time', not that he'd shared that with his friends. He didn't want to scare them unnecessarily, and decided that he would only tell them when the time came.

And to top it all Sean was struggling to find the forest where his mother's trail ended all those years ago. 'I'm sorry, Jack. But it's so hard to get your bearings in this rain, especially when the cloud is so low. We haven't seen the sun for two weeks.'

Jack understood. It was like they were walking in a permanent mist at times. But he had to stay positive. He had to believe that he was getting nearer to finding his mother. Although the weather dampened his spirits, it was never going to break his resolve.

Then just as suddenly as it started, the rain finally stopped late in the afternoon on the fifteenth day after leaving Brendan's. The low dark clouds moved aside to reveal a clear blue sky. It was like a tonic for them all. The gloom and grumpiness that had affected them evaporated along with the clouds.

'Well,' said Rory cheerily, 'I'm going to make you all one of my famous stews. I think we all need it after the last two weeks.'

And nobody argued with that. But the rain stopping was only part of the good news that day. As the sun headed towards its western resting place at the end of the day, and they were preparing to camp for the night, they came upon a pine forest. But not just any forest – Sean was convinced it was the same one that he'd stumbled across during his last search.

'Are you sure?' asked Rory.

'As I can be,' said Sean. 'It has the same eerie calm about it.'

'Well, we'll set up camp here and discuss what we do next after we've eaten,' said Rory.

Lilac helped Rory unpack the food and prepare the ingredients for the stew, while Jack, Tyler and Sean walked into the forest in search of dry wood for the fire. They were relieved to find plenty of wood lying around on the soft cushion of dead, brown pine needles on the forest floor. The dense forest canopy had proved to be an effective cover as the rain had barely penetrated it.

While Jack and Sean gathered wood, Tyler wandered deeper into the forest.

'Is he OK?' enquired Sean.

'Lilac constantly teases him about his aversion to work so I think he may be avoiding collecting wood,' smiled Jack.

'Well I think we have enough here,' said Sean.

'Tyler,' called Jack. 'We've got enough wood.'

But Tyler wasn't hearing him. He stood by a shallow stream staring into the forest.

'Tyler!' shouted Jack. 'We're going back to the camp.'

Tyler didn't move and continued to stare vacantly into the forest. Jack dropped his wood onto the floor and ran over to him, but Tyler didn't acknowledge him. Jack grabbed him by the shoulders and looked him directly in the eyes.

'Tyler – what's wrong?' But Tyler didn't see him. Jack shook him but he still didn't respond.

'Try slapping him around the face,' suggested Sean.

As much as Jack didn't want to hurt him, what choice did he have? He slapped him around the face, probably a little harder that he intended. Tyler screamed out in pain and grabbed his cheek, and then turned on Jack. 'What did you do that for?'

'I was worried,' said Jack. 'You seemed to be in some sort of trance.'

Tyler was about to argue then thought better of it. He rubbed his cheek which by now had a hand shaped red mark on it. 'I heard voices … someone was calling me. It was the strangest feeling …'

'Sean and I were standing near you and we didn't hear a thing,' said Jack.

Tyler suddenly looked agitated. 'I want to get out of here – it doesn't feel right.'

Jack picked up his wood and the three of them hastily headed out of the forest and joined the others. Jack related the tale to Rory and Lilac, but she showed little sympathy.

'Tyler has an allergy to work, end of. There's nothing he wouldn't do to get out of it.'

Tyler scowled at her. 'Sometimes, Lilac Wildflower, your tongue is as poisonous as a viper's,' and stormed off.

'He was acting very strange, Lilac,' said Jack.

'He's always strange,' said Lilac unsympathetically. 'Let's get the fire lit and the stew cooking.'

*

Tyler sat on his own as he ate his supper and didn't say a

word. It was most unusual behaviour for Tyler, thought Jack. The relationship Tyler had with Lilac was warm even though they teased each other continuously. But there was no warmth between them that evening.

'Can I get anyone an Ishka Baa?' asked Rory trying to lighten the mood.

Tyler didn't respond and kept his back to them all. Sean and Rory both had a glass as Lilac cleared up the dinner things. Jack decided to join Tyler. He sat down next to him and placed a friendly hand on his shoulder. 'I may not have known you that long but it's obvious there is something bothering you.'

Tyler didn't answer straightaway - he continued to stare at the ground. 'Friendships don't always need time to cement them, Jack. I thought I knew Lilac and that she knew me, but I was wrong.'

'I don't think she meant anything by what she said, she was …'

'I'm frightened, Jack,' interrupted Tyler. 'There's something in that forest that really unnerves me. I thought that Lilac being one of my best friends would have seen my fear.'

'What is it that frightened you?' asked Jack.

Tyler didn't answer immediately. 'I could feel something … something very strange. And then the voices calling me.'

Jack could see the fear in Tyler's eyes. He'd never seen him like that before. 'Our path leads us into that forest, I'm sure of it. Are you saying you don't want to go in there?'

'I'm not sure what I'm saying,' said Tyler. 'I just know that I have a very uneasy feeling, the like of which I've never felt before.'

'Let's sleep on it,' suggested Jack. 'We'll decide tomorrow on what path to take.'

*

They were fed and ready to go early the next morning.

They ate a very quiet breakfast as Tyler's unease continued. Lilac still thought he was sulking because she'd teased him the previous evening and made no effort to talk to him. But Jack had a decision to make. They stood in a circle around the remains of their campfire.

'I'm sure that our path leads through the forest. I have no reason other than instinct for thinking this. But Tyler feels uneasy about it, so I'm happy to be guided by you all.'

'I say we go through the forest,' said Sean.

'I agree,' said Rory.

Lilac and Tyler were uncharacteristically quiet.

'Lilac?'

'I'll go with whatever you say.'

Which just left Tyler. Jack addressed him directly. 'If you say no, then it's no. I'm not going to leave you behind. We'll find a way around it.'

Tyler stared at the floor and then looked up at Jack. 'I'll come with you through the forest.'

'Right then,' said Rory. 'Let's be on our way.'

'It's over to you now, Jack,' said Sean. 'I'm afraid my knowledge stops at the edge of the forest.'

And Jack's was no greater. As they walked into the forest he saw a path wind its way through the pine trees. 'We'll follow the path and see where it takes us.'

Jack led the group, followed by Tyler, then Lilac, with Rory and Sean at the rear. This really was a step into the unknown. Jack urged them all to keep vigilant and let him know if they saw or heard anything unusual.

Tyler walked silently by Jack's side, but Jack sensed his unease. He whispered in his ear, 'we can still turn back if you're uncomfortable.'

Tyler shook his head. 'I'll be fine. Just concentrate on getting us through this.'

And that was the limit of Tyler's conversation throughout the whole morning. They stopped to eat early in the afternoon. Rory and Lilac prepared a meal of bread, cheese and dried fruit, all washed down with rhubarb juice.

They ate their meal in silence as none of them were in the mood for small talk.

The afternoon carried on in pretty much the same vein as the morning. They followed the path with very little conversation. Tyler walked by Jack's side locked in his own awareness, and there was little interaction between Lilac, Sean and Rory. Jack sensed all of their unease. He focused on getting them through the forest as quickly as possible.

There had been a close camaraderie within the group since they left Cill-Arney. Yes, there was bickering between Lilac and Tyler, and Sean and Rory, but all good natured. Something had changed since they'd found the forest.

Jack hadn't felt any change in himself although he thought the forest was unusual. He'd grown up in Heywood Forest but there were no similarities in either its look or feel. The forest floor was bare – there was no undergrowth to speak of. It consisted of a dense cluster of tall skinny pines, with florets of green pine needles at the very top of their trunks. They were so tightly packed that it would have been near impossible to find a way through without the pathway.

And then there was the silence. There were no irritating flies buzzing around. There was no birdsong. In fact, he hadn't seen a bird the whole day. And there was no sign of any wildlife in the forest. There were no animal tracks in the dead pine needles. He hadn't seen a rabbit scuttling across the forest floor or a squirrel scampering up the trunk of a tree. It was eerily quiet and empty. Jack didn't discuss it with the others as they were all unsettled enough without him adding to their unease. But it struck him as strange and he would be relieved when they eventually emerged out of the other side.

He kept an eye on the position of the sun through the narrow gaps in the forest canopy as they followed the path westwards. It was ironic that the whole time they were out in the open, it rained, and now they were under the shelter of the forest canopy, the sun shone brightly. But he just concentrated on getting the group away from the strange forest so that they could rediscover the camaraderie that had once held them so closely together.

They all breathed a collective sigh of relief as they emerged from the forest and out into the open. Sean and Rory immediately set about collecting dry wood for a fire so that they could all enjoy their first mug of Shamrock tea since the morning.

But something else happened that lit a spark of joy in Jack's heart. Lilac walked up to Tyler and said, 'I'm really sorry for doubting you last night. It was very insensitive of me.' She swallowed nervously. 'There is definitely something very strange about that forest. I've never felt anything like it in my life. And I thought I heard voices calling my name. I just couldn't wait to get out of there.'

Tyler's stony countenance immediately softened. 'You heard the voices too?'

She nodded. 'Yes I did and it really unnerved me.' Tears welled up in her eyes. 'Please forgive me.'

Tyler stepped forward and embraced her. 'When you've been friends for as long as we have, Lilac Wildflower, you don't have to ask for forgiveness – it's a given.'

Jack walked over and wrapped them both in his arms. 'Please don't fall out again. I need you both so much that I don't think I can do this without you.'

Rory shouted across to them. 'Well I'm just glad to be out of that place. Now the fire's going, I'll soon have a mug of tea for you all.'

The relief was tempered by Sean. 'I think there's something that you should know.'

'Aw, Sean,' said Rory. 'Don't be putting a dampener on the craic.'

'I'm sorry,' said Sean, 'but it's important.'

'What is it?' asked Jack as he walked over to him.

Sean pointed to the remains of a fire. 'We left those this morning.'

'What are you talking about, Sean McSpawn?' said Rory. 'We've been walking all day. We're a long way from where we were this morning.'

Sean pointed to some freshly dug earth just to the side of the ashes. 'That's where I buried the rubbish before we left.' He pointed to the mountains and a dark grey valley. 'That's the way we came yesterday. We've gone in a full circle.'

Jack shook his head. 'That's not possible. I made sure we followed the sun west. We travelled in a straight line.'

'I know,' said Sean. 'Which makes this even more confusing, but I'm sure we're back where we started this morning.'

Jack looked at the surroundings, and as much as he didn't want to believe it, he knew that Sean was right. 'I'm sorry – it looks like I've wasted the whole day.'

Tyler walked over to him and placed a reassuring hand on his shoulder. 'It's not your fault, young Jack. There is something very strange about that forest. Let's have our tea and eat. Better decisions are made on full bellies.'

*

Chapter Eighteen - Morning Dew

'We'll be laughing about it in the morning,' said Rory. 'Come on, Jack me lad, and join us in a drop of Ishka Baa. It will lift the ole spirits.'

Jack shook his head. 'Sorry, Rory, just the smell of alcohol makes me sick. And I'm going to need a clear head to think this through.'

'Tonight is not a time for fretting, it's a time for relaxing, young Jack,' said Tyler. 'We can work out what we're going to do tomorrow.'

'He's right,' said Lilac. 'We're all tired after a long journey. Let's relax and enjoy our evening.'

'I've got just the thing,' said Rory reaching inside his jacket. He pulled out a tin whistle and held it up to his lips. He played a jig and Sean immediately jumped to his feet and started to dance around the camp fire. On his third lap around the fire he pulled Lilac up and they danced together while the others joined in and clapped along.

Rory played one tune after another. Some were light-hearted; some were sad and some were poignant. But it did the trick. It lifted their spirits and any negative thoughts of the strange forest were soon forgotten. Jack's favourite was when Sean sang along to a tune called, 'I wish I was back home in Cill-Arney'. It made you smile; it made you laugh; it made you sad, and he even had a tear in his eye at one point. And they all joined in the chorus:

'Where the lakes are as blue as a summer's sky
The mouth-watering aroma of an Auntie Bridie's pie
The grey misty mountains towering five miles' high
Makes me wish I was back home in Cill-Arney ...'

It was just the tonic that they all needed. The tension that had threatened to swallow them all day had evaporated. Tyler pitched in with a poem and Lilac sang them a song about the hairiest Elf in the world. They all laughed so much that they had tears streaming down their faces.

They took a break from singing and Rory made a pot of Shamrock tea. As he handed the mugs around, they heard a voice from behind them. 'Now I can't believe you're having a party and not invited me.' They all looked towards the forest to see a tall woman with long, dark, wavy hair slowly walking towards them. She hesitated at the edge of the campfire light giving them all a chance to see her more clearly.

She wore a long, flowing, three-quarter length maroon gown, complimented with a lilac chiffon headdress that draped over her shoulders and down her back. Dainty ringlets of dark brown hair hung either side of her face. Her eyes were as dark as the night but as warm as the midday sun.

She walked into the midst of the group and giggled mischievously. 'My, my, it's gone very quiet all of a sudden. Rory McNory, now you're never usually lost for words. And Sean McSpawn isn't exactly known for being backwards in coming forwards.'

Rory was mesmerised. He sat open-mouthed, nervously playing with the tin-whistle in his hands, staring at her. 'You know my name?'

'I do indeed, Rory. Now are you going to sit there gawping or are you going to pour me a mug of that Shamrock tea that's brewing in the pot?' she said, mimicking his accent.

'I will indeed,' said Rory recovering some of his composure. He put his tin whistle back inside his jacket and jumped to his feet and filled a mug with steaming hot tea. He handed it to her and bowed his head. 'A mug of Cill-Arney's best, even though I say so myself.'

She took a sip and smiled. 'It's a grand sup of tea,' she said holding Rory's accent. 'And you, Sean McSpawn, with the dark, brooding looks and the charms to match. Do you have any words for me?'

Sean looked unusually uncomfortable. 'I, er, I'm …'

She giggled again. 'And who else do we have here? Ah yes, Lilac Wildflower, as pretty as a picture and a smile that would melt the hardest heart. And how are you this fine evening?'

'I'm fine, I think … How do you know my name?'

She sipped her tea. 'I know everybody here, including your friend Tyler.' She turned her attention to him. 'I trust you are well?'

'I'm fine, madam,' said Tyler as he nodded his head.

She giggled again. 'You Elves are just so polite.' She set her eyes on Jack who sat quietly by Lilac's side. 'And if it isn't young Green-Jack, my very special guest.'

Jack was hypnotised by her. Not only was she radiantly beautiful but she had an air of mystique that captivated him. He had so many questions spinning around his head but Rory beat him to it.

'Are you going to share your name with us?'

'I was beginning to think that you would never ask.' She placed her tea on the grass next to her, gathered her frock in her hands and curtseyed low. 'My name is Morning-Dew. I'm pleased to make your acquaintance.'

'I don't wish to appear rude,' continued Rory, 'but what are you?'

Morning-Dew giggled. 'What do you think I am?'

Rory shrugged his shoulders and looked to his friends. 'You look like a woman but I suspect that you're not.'

'And you would suspect right,' said Morning-Dew mimicking his accent again.

'And you've no shoes on your feet,' said Rory. 'You'll catch your death of a cold on the damp grass.'

'Your concern is appreciated, Rory, but I can assure you I will neither die nor catch a cold. Does anyone else wish to hazard a guess?'

Tyler tentatively raised his right hand. Morning-Dew looked at him like a school teacher addressing her pupil. 'And your guess is?'

'I think you're a Forest Faery.'

Morning-Dew bounced up and down on the spot and clapped her hands excitedly. 'Well done, Tyler. All that time you've spent reading Faery folklore hasn't been

147

wasted.'

Jack shook his head in disbelief. He'd met Elves, flying horses, Leprechauns, a Banshee and now a Forest Faery. If anyone had told him that any of these existed a few weeks previously he would've thought they were mad. But then something suddenly occurred to him. Why had she shown herself to them?

'Is this your forest?' asked Jack.

'It is indeed,' said Morning-Dew.

'Why have we ended up back where we started this morning after heading west all day?' he ventured.

She sat down in their circle and picked up her mug of tea and sipped it. 'You already know why.'

'I don't understand,' said Jack.

She looked at Tyler. 'Now you should be able to explain it to your friends.'

Tyler contemplated what she'd said as he sipped his tea. 'Is it to do with how I felt, and the voices I heard?'

'It is indeed,' said Morning-Dew.

Tyler looked to Lilac. 'Do you have any idea?' She shrugged her shoulders and shook her head.

'It's something you've lost,' said Morning-Dew. 'Hopefully, only temporarily.'

'Something we've lost,' repeated a mystified Tyler.

'Does that apply to Sean and I?' asked Rory.

'I'm afraid it does,' said Morning-Dew.

Jack remembered what Lomund had told him about the lost art of magic in Waterswood, about how he thought it was wrong. Was that what Tyler was feeling?

'Is it magic?' enquired Jack.

Morning-Dew put her mug down on the grass and once again burst into spontaneous applause. 'Well done, Green-Jack. That's exactly what it is.'

'Of course,' said Tyler. 'How could I have been so stupid?'

'What sort of magic is it?' asked Lilac.

'Now you know the answer to that too,' said Morning-Dew retreating back into her cloak of mystery.

'It didn't harm us so it must be friendly,' said Tyler. He smacked himself on the side of the head. 'Of course! It's Elven magic!'

'Yes!' cried Morning-Dew as she furiously clapped her hands.

'And you allow it in your forest?' asked Lilac.

'It wouldn't be there if I didn't,' she confirmed.

'Grimley has a lot to answer for,' said Tyler. 'We've lost these skills in Waterswood.'

'Perhaps lost is the wrong word,' said Morning-Dew picking up her mug of tea again. 'Mislaid might be more accurate.'

'I can't believe that it frightened me so much,' said an embarrassed Tyler.

'There's nothing about magic to be frightened of,' said Morning-Dew, 'except for that dark stuff … but we won't go there.'

'So how do we get through the forest?' asked Jack.

'You don't need me to answer that.'

Tyler was more animated than Jack had ever seen him. 'Think about it, Jack. If it's Elven magic, we must be near our homeland!'

'Bravo!' cried Morning Dew.

Rory and Sean exchanged confused looks. 'All of this is going right over my head. We've just spent the whole day going around in a circle. How does knowing what it is help us?' asked Rory.

'It's Elven magic,' said an excited Tyler. 'You have three Elves with you. If we can't work this out between us, then … then we should be ashamed of ourselves.'

Morning-Dew drained her mug and put it down by the fire. She stood up and brushed the dead grass from her dress. 'That was a grand sup of tea, Rory. It was nearly as good as Seamus's. Now it's …'

Before she could finish her sentence, Rory was up and beside her. 'Did you say, Seamus?'

'I did,' said Morning-Dew.

'Seamus O'Shoehorn?' pressed Rory.

'The very same,' she confirmed.

Now Jack was on his feet. 'Was my mother with him? She's called Ciara.'

'And O'Reilly?' asked Sean who was now standing next to Rory. Morning-Dew was suddenly surrounded by the whole group.

'They passed this way some time ago. I took the opportunity to share some tea with them.'

'So they were here, on this very spot,' said Jack.

'They were indeed,' said Morning-Dew.

'Where are they now?' asked Jack.

'Now that, I can't answer,' she said.

'Are they OK?' pressed Lilac.

'I'm afraid I can't answer that either.'

'How do we find them?' asked Jack.

'Now you know better than I how to do that,' she replied.

Jack stood in front of her and looked deep into her dark eyes. 'Please help us. I've been told that my mother is in grave danger but that's all I know. Is there anything you can tell us?'

She gently placed her hand on Jack's cheek. 'You are so much like her. You have the same spirit and determination. Let me assure you that you have all that you need to find her. Trust your instincts Jack and follow your heart. Both will always remain true to you.' She kissed him on his forehead. 'And now I must go.'

As she approached the edge of the forest she looked back at them and waved. 'To the next time we meet. But for now, farewell my friends. Always be well and always be happy.' Then she disappeared into the dark gloom of the forest.

*

Jack sat staring into the dying embers of the fire; Tyler was one side of him and Lilac the other. Sean and Rory sat opposite them drinking Ishka Baa. 'What do you think she

150

meant when she said, 'you have all that you need to find her?''

'I wish I knew,' said Tyler.

'I got the feeling that she knew more than she was telling us,' said Rory.

'Me too,' said Sean.

'Well at least we now know we're on the right track,' said Lilac. 'Morning-Dew said that Ciara, Seamus and O'Reilly were here.'

'And we know that we're dealing with Elven magic in the forest and we know that we're near our homeland,' said Tyler. 'So she has helped us a lot.'

They all nodded their agreement and sat in silence for several minutes.

'I guess the first thing we have to work out,' said Jack, 'is how we find our way through that forest. Does anyone have any ideas?' His question was met with four blank faces.

'I always think in situations like this, that the best thing you can do is to sleep on it,' said Tyler. 'Tomorrow is another day, with new opportunities and new ideas.'

'I'll drink to that,' said Rory as he raised his glass.

Chapter Nineteen - The Guiding Light

Jack sat staring at the sun as it rose over the mountains to the east, searching for the flash of inspiration that might tell him how to find the way through Morning-Dew's forest. Lilac and Tyler were washing at the stream while Sean and Rory prepared their breakfast. Rory said that they were all going to need a good Cill-Arney fry inside of them to give them the strength that would sustain them for the challenging day ahead.

Jack desperately wanted to show some leadership and guide his friends safely through the forest. He wanted to prove himself after the disaster of the day before. Despite repeated assurances from his friends that they attached no blame to him, he wanted the opportunity to put it right.

Their homeland was near; of that he was sure. But what he didn't know was how near? There was this place the Mist of Time that they had to negotiate first. How was he going to find it?

Both Breannacht and Morning-Dew had given him the same advice about following his heart. And it resonated within him, because when his grandfather first told him that he was an Elf, he immediately knew that he had to find out who he was. At the time he had no idea of where the journey would take him, but despite all of the dangers he'd faced, he had no regrets.

But it was times like this where he wished his grandfather was with him. He would always have some wise words when Jack needed them – not that he always heeded them, as his grandfather would be quick to remind him.

He thought about the journey that Breannacht had taken him on. He wondered if the forest that she'd shown him was the one he sat near now, but he dismissed the idea. There were clear signs of animal and bird life in that forest which were strangely absent in Morning-Dew's.

And then there was the dark castle that Breannacht

pointed towards. Was his mother being held there? So many questions that he didn't have answers to and it was making his head spin.

A call from Rory brought him back down to Earth. 'Come on, Jack me lad, and get this breakfast down you. You'll be surprised how different the world looks with a full belly.'

Rory and Sean did them proud with a hearty breakfast of Auntie Bridie proportions. Together with several large chunks of soda bread and mugs of Shamrock tea, it did indeed give Jack's spirits a much needed lift.

He sat nursing his mug of tea, alongside Lilac and Tyler as Sean and Rory tidied away the breakfast things. He had the feeling that Tyler had something to tell him, and he wasn't wrong.

'Lilac and I have been talking. Neither of us is an expert regarding Elven magic, but I have studied some of the old texts with Lomund. And Lilac has worked with Crystal in her clinic as her assistant for many years. Healing has its roots in the use of ancient magic and she has a basic understanding of its origins.

I remember some years ago reading about a phenomenon called a Guiding Light. Our ancestors were great explorers. They would travel far and wide across our world. Sometimes they would go so far that they would have trouble finding their way back home. This is when they would summon the Guiding Light.'

'Why is this relevant to our problem with the forest?' asked Jack.

'Because,' said Tyler, 'if we can summon this Guiding Light, it will lead us to our homeland.'

'Do you really think we have the knowledge to summon one?' asked Jack.

'Over to you, Lilac,' said Tyler.

'I have some experience using Earth Magic in my healing work. I wouldn't say that I'm particularly accomplished in the art, but I have worked with it alongside Crystal.'

'So what is the relationship between this Earth Magic and the Guiding Light?' asked Jack.

'Earth Magic is the source from which the elemental world flows,' said Tyler. 'It is derived from the core of our planet. If Lilac can find a way to call on this, we may have a chance of summoning the Guiding Light.'

'What does Earth Magic feel like?' asked Jack.

'It's difficult to explain,' said Lilac. 'I have used it to treat minor ailments, like stomach upsets and headaches. Energy flows up from the Earth's core into your body, and it travels all the way through to your fingertips. You lay your hands on your patient and massage the affected area.'

Jack thought back to when he saved Reggie the fox and Becky. Lilac was describing exactly what happened to him. 'I think I know what you're talking about, Lilac. Unknowingly, I've used Earth Magic. The first time was when I saved a fox that had been hit by a car and the other time was to save the human girl, Becky, when I found her face down in a pond. Her heart had stopped beating and I used this energy that flowed through me to resuscitate her.'

Lilac looked stunned. 'You brought her back from the dead?'

Jack hadn't thought of it in those terms. He'd found a girl who had stopped breathing and revived her. He hadn't thought of her as dead.

'That was some very powerful magic you used there, young Jack,' said Tyler.

'Why didn't you mention this before?' asked Lilac.

'It didn't seem relevant and to be honest I didn't really understand what I was doing, I just did it. All I could think of was saving her life.'

Lilac looked at Tyler with a conflicting mixture of excitement and concern. 'Don't you think it's risky trying to summon this Guiding Light without really understanding Earth Magic? Neither Jack nor I are experts.'

'Do you have any other suggestions as to how we can

get through this forest?' asked Tyler.

Lilac didn't respond. Her silence gave him his answer. 'We can only try,' said Tyler. 'I really don't think trying to summon a Guiding Light could be that dangerous.'

'So how do we do it?' asked Jack.

'I've written some words,' said Tyler. 'It's called an incantation. Rather like what Narky did when he summoned the flying horse.'

'Have you three wizards decided on what we're going to do?' asked a cheerful Rory. 'We're packed and ready to go.'

Tyler looked at Jack and Lilac. 'Well, are we going to do it?' Jack nodded and Lilac shrugged her shoulders. He had his answer. 'Very well,' he said. 'Let's stand in a circle.'

'Does that include Sean and me?' asked Rory.

'I think this is just Elven,' said Tyler, 'although if it doesn't work, we may be glad of your help.'

Jack and Lilac stood in front of Tyler, as Sean and Rory stepped back.

'So what exactly is it you're going to do?' asked Sean.

'You'll soon see ... that is if it works,' said Tyler.

Jack and Lilac stood in front of Tyler, and he formed them in a circle. He held his hands up in the air and closed his eyes, as Narky had done, and recited the following words:

'Oh hear our call great Elven magic
For all we see ahead is tragic
Lead us forth and ease our plight
Please reveal our guiding light'

They stood rock still for several seconds, waiting for something to happen. But nothing did.

'So how long do we have to wait?' asked Rory.

Tyler lowered his arms and opened his eyes. 'Did you feel anything Jack?'

Jack shook his head. 'Not a thing.'

155

'Lilac?'

She shook her head. 'I didn't feel anything either.'

Tyler looked a little downcast. 'This isn't going to be easy, is it?'

'Maybe you should hold hands?' suggested Sean.

'It's got to be worth a try,' said Rory.

'Very well,' said Tyler. He linked hands with Jack and Lilac, and this time they all raised their hands. Tyler closed his eyes and recited the words once again.

Still nothing. Tyler slumped disconsolately onto the ground. 'I was sure that this would work,' he said as he held his head in his hands.

'No offence, Tyler' chirped Rory, 'but I think you're about as good at magic as I am.'

Lilac would normally have joined in and teased Tyler, but she saw how upset he was. 'It was a big ask to expect it to work straightaway. Maybe we should let Jack try; after all, he's the only one here who has actually used powerful magic.'

'I-I'm not sure,' said Jack. 'Perhaps you should try, Lilac.'

'She's right, Jack,' said Tyler glumly. 'You surely can't do any worse.'

'Maybe we should do it together,' said Jack. 'Make it more of a joint thing.'

'What have we got to lose?' said Tyler climbing back to his feet.

They formed a circle again and held hands. Lilac addressed Jack. 'How did you summon the Earth Magic before? Perhaps you should repeat it.'

Jack felt anxious. He was the youngest one there, and had the least experience in all matters to do with Elven culture. But they both seemed keen for him to try. 'Close your eyes and breathe slowly. Just let your breath flow through you and concentrate on your own awareness.' Lilac and Tyler exchanged hopeful looks before closing their eyes and breathing.

'Now, place your feet firmly on the ground like you are

156

taking root. Really feel the connection with the turf that you're standing on. Imagine the Earth's energy flowing into you. At first, all you can feel is a slight tingle in the soles of your feet, but you soon feel it moving up through your legs and to your belly. Feel that warmth slowly building up deep within you.'

Jack concentrated on his own awareness for a second. He could feel all of the things he described. It was just like when he saved Becky. He raised their arms above their heads and leant back. He was sure he could feel a slight tremor in the ground. *Was that the Earth Magic?*

'Feel it building through you. The warmth is spreading itself to your upper body and arms. When you can feel your fingers tingling, it is then you know the Earth Magic is ready.' No-one else spoke. Jack could feel the energy building. He was sure he felt another tremor in the ground, as his own body started to tremble. The moment was on him. He spoke the incantation, very slowly, making sure each word was expressed fully:

> *'Oh hear our call great Elven magic*
> *For all we see ahead is tragic*
> *Lead us forth and ease our plight*
> *Please reveal our guiding light'*

No sooner was the last word out of his mouth, when he felt his whole world start to shudder. It was like an earthquake as the ground below him rumbled like thunder. A burst of energy blasted through the entire length of his body. He felt as if he was on fire, as the energy burned through him and lifted him off his feet.

Then silence. Exhaustion suddenly overwhelmed him and he fell back to the ground. He lay there in a daze and lost all awareness of his surroundings. The next thing he felt was somebody shaking him and he heard a familiar voice.

'Are you all right, Jack me lad?'

He opened his eyes to see the freckly face of Rory

staring down at him. Rory helped him into a sitting position. 'Here drink this.' Jack took the glass from him and sipped the water. His head slowly started to clear.

'Did it work?'

'Did it work?' repeated Rory, and pointed towards the forest. Jack looked over his shoulder and saw a narrow beam of white light piercing the trees. 'You did it Jack me lad; you only went and summoned that Earth Magic stuff you were talking about.'

Jack looked over and saw both Tyler and Lilac sitting on the grass looking in a similar dazed state. 'So what happened?'

'I have to own up to being frightened out of my skin,' said Rory. 'No sooner had you finished your words, when the whole world felt like it was going to implode. The ground shook and I thought we were all doomed. But then this shaft of bright white light burst out of your combined hands and shot up to the sky. It stayed like that for several seconds before turning at right angles and heading straight into the forest. And that's when you all collapsed onto the ground. That was about an hour ago.'

'I've been passed out for an hour?' said a surprised Jack.

'You must have needed the rest,' said Rory. 'I reckon you would have expended a tremendous amount of energy generating that thing.'

Chapter Twenty - Home from Home

They stood at the edge of the forest studying the trajectory of the Guiding Light. It seemed to track the path that they'd followed the previous day.

'Now I'm no genius,' said Rory, 'but I always thought that light travelled in straight lines. Your Guiding Light follows that path with all its twists and turns.'

'Well it just goes to show how potent Elven magic is,' said Tyler proudly.

'Maybe it's because it's an artificial light,' said Jack. 'It's been created by magic. It looks like light but it isn't.'

Both Tyler and Lilac smiled proudly at him. 'How can someone so young be so wise? Tyler and I have lived our whole lives in Waterswood in an Elven community yet we know so little about our magic compared to you.'

'That's just it,' said Jack. 'I don't actually know anything, it's … it's instinct.'

'Whatever it is,' said Tyler, 'it serves you well, young Jack.'

'Well we haven't got time to stand here all day discussing whether it's light or not. Can we get started, as the sooner we start the sooner we get through that forest?' said Rory impatiently.

Jack strapped his rucksack to his back and led them into the forest and along the pathway highlighted by the Guiding Light. Lilac was at his side, followed by Tyler and then Sean and Rory. And they were all pleasantly surprised to find that the strange feelings of the day before had gone.

'I think once you know what's frightening you, it loses its power over you,' said Sean.

'Very true,' said Rory. 'That is unless we come across a lion in the forest. Even though I know what it is, it would still scare the life out of me.'

'Well that's true also,' said Sean. 'But I don't think I've ever heard of a lion in these parts.'

'Better be safe than sorry,' said a smiling Rory. 'Keep an open mind – that's my motto.'

And that's how they passed their day in the forest - light-hearted chat and a lot of laughing. The despair and fear from the previous day had gone, to be replaced by a hopeful optimism that they were near to the Elven homeland and that they were going to find their friends there.

And that optimism was rewarded when, late in the day, they emerged into a beautiful meadow covered in bright yellow flowers. Tyler enthusiastically patted Jack on the back. 'Well done, young Jack, you've got us safely through the forest.'

'And look,' said Rory. 'You can still see the light stretching across the meadow and over the hill. I would bet my gold coin that your homeland is just beyond it.'

'Let's hope so,' said Tyler, 'as my feet are killing me.'

'Now there's a surprise,' said Rory. 'Tyler has sore feet!' Which caused everyone except Tyler to burst into laughter.

They decided against setting up camp and instead carried on across the field and up the hill. Jack knew that there would be no Elven settlement over the brow of the hill as they still had to cross this place Breannacht called the Mist of Time, and his friends were going to have to find out sooner rather than later.

As they strolled through the meadow, Lilac walked alongside Tyler. 'Doesn't this look familiar to you?' she asked.

'Why should it be familiar?' asked a slightly puzzled Tyler.

'Because it's just like Golden Meadow.'

'I'm sure there are many Golden Meadows in the world,' said Tyler dismissively. 'I suggest we relax, enjoy the scenery and breathe in its beauty.'

And that's what they did, but when they reached the brow of the hill, another familiar scene was awaiting them. 'Are you telling me there are many Waterswoods in the world too?' said Lilac.

The pair of them stood looking down into a valley. A picturesque village was tucked neatly in between mountains on one side, and rolling hills on the other. Jack had only experienced the view once in his life before, but it looked identical to the village that he now called home. The Guiding Light followed the path across the meadow and stopped on the outskirts of the village.

'Would somebody mind telling me what's going on?' asked a bemused Rory.

'Look,' said Tyler. 'We're on Emerald Island, hundreds of miles from our home; there is absolutely no way that can be Waterswood. If I know anything about Elves, it's that they like familiarity, and my guess would be that our ancestors, who built Waterswood, built it in similar surroundings to our homeland.'

'But it's absolutely identical,' said Lilac, 'even down to the way that the path winds its way across the meadow.'

Jack didn't know what to think. Lilac was right – it was identical. But Tyler knew more about Elven culture than any of them. Perhaps Elves were creatures of habit.

'Well can I suggest we make our way down there and see what it's like for ourselves,' said Sean.

'Grand idea,' said Rory as he set off down the path.

The walk to the village was a silent one as everyone stayed with their own thoughts. Jack's instincts were telling him that something was seriously amiss, but he decided to keep his own counsel. As they neared the village it was becoming increasingly obvious that it was structurally the same as Waterswood, but with one major difference. It was eerily quiet.

They stood by the lamppost on the village boundary looking suspiciously at the thatched cottages and cobbled lanes.

'This is our home,' said Lilac turning to the others. 'It's exactly the same.'

'But that's impossible,' said Tyler, 'our home is hundreds of …'

'Miles away,' finished Lilac. 'But you have to admit it's identical.'

Tyler didn't respond and shrugged his shoulders in benign resignation.

'If it is Waterswood,' said Lilac, 'my cottage will be just around the corner.'

She set off with purpose across the cobblestones and turned right into a narrow lane, lined with quaint black and white, thatched roof cottages. As they neared the end of the lane, one cottage stood out from the rest. Lilac stopped outside the front gate and looked longingly at it.

Its walls were painted bright pink instead of white, but still had black wooden supports and beams in common with the neighbouring cottages. She opened the gate and walked up to the door and momentarily hesitated, before lifting the latch on the front door and walking in. She stood in the middle of the room and turned in a full circle. Tyler walked gingerly in behind her.

'Well it seems that whoever lives here likes my taste in decorations, even down to my pink and lime green curtains, and light blue carpets. The same furniture, the same layout, the same ...'

Tyler held up his hand. 'OK, I take your point. There's something very strange going on here. But for the life of me, I don't know what.'

'Let's go over to Lomund's cottage,' said Lilac.

'That's just it,' said Tyler. 'It isn't Lomund's cottage.'

'Well, let's head in that direction and see if we can find anyone who lives here.'

As Jack followed Lilac, he studied the surroundings. It certainly looked like Waterswood, but it didn't feel like it. He watched Lilac as she strode on ahead of an unusually quiet Tyler. Sean and Rory looked bemused as they walked beside Jack.

'So what do you think is going on?' whispered Sean.

'I'm not sure,' said Jack. 'I think that Lilac is convinced that this is Waterswood, our home village.'

'What do you think?' asked Rory.

'I barely know Waterswood, but I have to admit that it looks the same.'

'It sounds like there's something bothering you,' said Sean.

'It doesn't feel the same. There's an eeriness about the place that I didn't notice before.'

'Trust your feelings, Jack-me-lad,' said Rory. 'In my experience, they're usually right.'

As they arrived outside Lomund's cottage, Jack noticed the welcoming candle burning brightly in the bay window. Lilac walked up to his front door and hesitated. 'I feel like I should knock.'

'Lomund would never complain if we just walked in. I've done it many times when the LEOs have been after me,' said Tyler as he lifted the latch on the door. They filed in one at a time and stood in the middle of Lomund's living room. Jack was surprised to see the table was laid for five people. A delicious aroma filled the cottage.

'Mushroom soup, if I'm not mistaken,' said Tyler as he walked over to the range and took the lid off the large cooking pot that sat on its surface. He took a ladle full of the soup and tasted it. 'Mmmm, Lomund's best – I can tell it anywhere.'

Lilac sat down at the table and held her head in her hands. 'This doesn't make any sense. This is Lomund's cottage – it's his soup. But where's Lomund?'

'Maybe he's gone out for a stroll in the hills,' said Tyler. 'Perhaps he …' He stopped mid-sentence and shook his head. 'No you're right, Lilac, there's something very strange going on here. We didn't see a soul in the village as we walked along the lanes. When was the last time that either of us strolled through Waterswood without stopping to chat at least half a dozen times?'

'I'm going down to the village centre,' said Lilac. 'I need to clear my head.'

'I'll come with you,' said Jack.

'I'll look after our Leprechaun guests,' said Tyler. 'Lomund always has a bottle of Peardrop to hand. It would be rude not to offer them a drink or two after such a long and demanding journey.'

Lilac's eyes narrowed; suspicion was written all over her face. 'As long as it's only one or two. I need you sober, Tyler Goldsmith!'

*

Lilac and Jack sat on the wall of the wishing-well in the middle of the village square. Jack looked across to the courthouse where he had made his one, solitary appearance all those weeks ago. He thought he would feel dread or some other negative feeling, but surprisingly he didn't. It was triumph and a deep feeling of pride that dominated.

But he could sense that all was not well with Lilac. She'd been uncomfortable ever since they first set eyes on Waterswood, or whatever this place was called. He wanted to help soothe her pain but he wasn't sure how. There wasn't a soul anywhere to be found. Crystal's cottage was empty, as were all of her other friends' homes. And the village centre was strangely deserted; something that Lilac said she'd never seen in her life before.

'I used to throw copper pennies down this well when I was little. I would wish for lots of things … but they never came true.'

'What sort of things?' asked Jack.

Sadness tinged her face. She looked at Jack with misty eyes. 'Mostly I wished that my parents would come to find me.'

Jack wasn't sure how to respond. He'd spent his whole life thinking that Noah was his only family, but now he was on a quest to find his mother. He wanted to say that he knew how she felt, but did he? 'Wouldn't your surname be a clue as to who you are and where you come from?'

Lilac smiled through her tears. 'Wildflower was a name that Crystal gave me. Apparently I always loved to play in them when I was little.'

'I guess the need to find out where we come from is a strong one. I was perfectly happy living with Noah, that was until he told me that I wasn't his grandson. And then when he told me I was an Elf, well … Once I knew that, the desire to find out who I was took over and I set off on this journey.'

'I miss Waterswood so much, Jack. It's all I've ever known. When we saw this place there was a part of me that desperately wanted to believe that it was home. But I knew it couldn't be. And I can see that Tyler is also desperate for it to be Waterswood. He would never say but he is really suffering badly from homesickness.' She reached into her pocket and took out a handkerchief and dabbed her eyes. 'This place is doing something to me, Jack. Something I don't like.'

'What is it?' asked a concerned Jack.

'It's … it's draining me of my desire to carry on the search for Ciara. All I want to do at this moment is go home. I want to sit in Lomund's cottage eating his soup and drinking his Roseleaf. I want to sit around his fire until the early hours, drinking Peardrop and listening to his wondrous tales about the old days.' She looked at Jack as the tears rained down her cheeks. 'I'm sorry Jack but I'm not sure I can do this anymore.'

Her words momentarily stunned him into silence. He wouldn't have got this far without her and Tyler. And for that matter, Rory and Sean. They were a team, and every member was vital to the success of their quest. He knew that it was the Waterswood replica that was draining her resolve.

Replica. The word resonated in his mind. There was something obvious that he was missing. He needed to think – he needed to step back from the situation and take a cool, detached look at things. He placed a comforting arm around Lilac's shoulder. 'Let's go back and join the others.'

Lilac blew her nose and wiped her eyes and put her handkerchief back in her pocket. She did her best to smile and stood up.

'Could I ask you a small favour?' said Jack.

'Of course,' said Lilac.

'Would you refrain from telling Tyler off when we get back and find him drunk?'

A real smile replaced the forced one. 'I'll do my best, but I can't promise.'

Chapter Twenty-One – Illusion

Jack and Lilac walked through Lomund's front door to find Tyler, Rory and Sean sat around the dining table. An unopened bottle of Peardrop stood on its own in the middle of the table.

'Are you OK, Tyler?' asked a concerned looking Lilac.

'I'm absolutely fine,' said Tyler. 'Why do you ask?'

Lilac picked up the bottle of Peardrop. 'This is unopened – I thought you were going to share a few drinks with Sean and Rory.'

'I was,' said Tyler, 'but that was before the three of us decided to put our heads together and work out what's going on here?'

'I'm impressed,' said Lilac as she sat down beside him. 'And what conclusions did you come to?'

'I think before we discuss anything, we need to do justice to this delicious soup that's beckoning me with its inviting aroma. Jack, take your seat at the table and I'll serve it up.'

He filled five bowls full of the thick mushroom soup and sliced several chunks of oatmeal bread for them to dunk. He produced an apple pie from the oven for dessert and smothered each slice with clotted cream. This was all washed down with several glasses of rhubarb juice.

Tyler piled the dirty dishes in the sink and poured them all a mug of Roseleaf before joining them at the table. 'I don't see the point in doing the washing up as I don't think we'll be coming back here again.' He raised his mug. 'To the Elves and the Leprechauns – long may they be friends and long may they enjoy the delights of good food and good company.'

'Now I'm really starting to worry,' said Lilac. 'Not only haven't you opened the Peardrop, but you've served us all a meal, cleared the dishes away, and made us all tea. I don't think I've ever seen any one of those things happen on their own in the past let alone all together.'

'Your cynicism is appreciated and noted,' smiled Tyler.

'Are you going to share your thoughts about this place with us?' asked Jack.

'Of course,' said Tyler, 'although we have our friends Rory and Sean to thank for working out what's going on.'

'Now to be fair,' said Rory, 'I think it was more of a group effort. Sean started the thought process and you and I carried it through.'

'That's very kind of you to say so,' said Tyler.

'You're very welcome,' said Rory.

'Are you going to tell us or spend the evening thanking each other?' said Lilac trying her best to hide her frustration and failing badly.

'Patience isn't just a virtue, it's a blessing,' said Tyler

'So is getting to the point,' said Lilac.

'Sean, would you like to take it from the beginning?' asked Tyler.

'My pleasure,' said Sean bowing his head. 'It struck me that the two people most affected by this place were you and Tyler,' he said addressing Lilac. 'And then I got to thinking why. And the answer was obvious. It's because Waterswood is your home and you're missing it badly.'

'Homesickness,' said Rory. 'I know if this place looked like Cill-Arney I'd be pining for it.'

'So,' carried on Tyler. 'We know this can't really be Waterswood, so it must be an ...'

'Illusion,' interrupted Jack. 'That's what struck me when we sat talking on the wishing-well, Lilac.'

'As all of us sat around this table know, an illusion isn't real. So it must be created by magic,' said Tyler.

'Elven magic?' asked Lilac.

'The very same,' said Tyler. 'It seems our friends in our homeland don't want uninvited visitors, because they're doing everything in their power to put us off.'

'But they've created a perfect replica,' said Lilac. 'How could they do that?'

'They take the details from you and me,' said Tyler. 'The magic just copies what we have deep in our memories – in effect we're creating it, Lilac. It's very clever, of course, and very Elven.'

'The next question must be how we get out of it?' asked Rory.

'I think I might have the answer to that,' said Jack. 'It looked as if the 'Guiding-Light' stopped on the edge of the village. I think the magic has hidden it within the illusion. We need to ask it to show itself again.'

'Problem solved,' said Tyler, reaching for the bottle of Peardrop and pulling out the stopper.

'There is something I've been meaning to tell you all,' said Jack. 'I think you may want to hold off on the Peardrop.'

Tyler replaced the stopper and put the bottle back on the table. The atmosphere changed from light-heartedness to apprehension in an instant.

'There was something the Banshee told me that I didn't share with you. I didn't want to burden you all unnecessarily.'

Lilac looked puzzled. 'We said from the outset that we're all in this together. You should have shared whatever it is with us, Jack.'

'I wasn't sure how to. I thought that you might not come with me if I told you.'

'Jack, would you ever tell us what it is. The tension is killing me,' pleaded Rory.

'She spoke about a place called the Mist of Time. She said that it presented great danger.'

'The Mist of Time,' repeated Rory. 'What sort of place is that?'

'It's the gateway to other worlds. She said that my mother was beyond it. As I believe our homeland is.'

'Ciara is in another world?' questioned Lilac.

'Did she elaborate on the precise nature of the danger?' asked Tyler.

'The Banshee took me on a journey – a dreamlike journey, or to be more accurate, a nightmarish journey. She led me into a mist that was so thick you could hardly see your hand in front of your face. I saw strange shapes dancing around me. Voices called out to me. It was unnerving especially when I heard Grimley's voice in my ear. Then we were in a dark forest. Wild animals howled and birds shrieked. It made the hairs on the back of my neck stand on end.

Finally, she showed me a dark castle. It reminded me of a witch's castle from a fairy-tale. It looked very scary.' He sat back in his chair and breathed deeply. 'I think she was showing me the journey I will take.'

Everybody sat around the table was shocked into silence. Jack wasn't sure what else he could say. He sensed they were disappointed with him – even angry. Tyler spoke first.

'Why didn't you tell us, Jack? That was a huge burden for you to carry on your own. We're your friends – you can tell us anything.'

'Are you angry with me?' asked Jack.

'Of course not,' said Lilac. 'But you need to share these things with us. As Tyler said, it's too much for you to carry on your own.'

'We'll deal with this place, the Mist of Time, don't you worry about that,' said Rory. 'But now isn't the time to think about it,' he said as he reached across to the Peardrop. 'Now is the time to let our hair down and relax. We'll have plenty of time to decide on what to do tomorrow.' He filled five glasses with the golden liquid and handed them around. He raised his own glass. 'A toast to us all – all friends together, and to our quest. But most of all to our dear friends who are waiting for us on the other side of that mist.'

*

Jack was surprised at just how well Tyler, Rory and Sean looked considering they'd got through the best part of 3 bottles of Peardrop the previous evening. Jack took one sip and Lilac one glass, so the rest was consumed by the three of them. Nobody was in the mood for a large breakfast and they settled for porridge and honey, with toasted oatmeal bread and Roseleaf.

The lack of appetite amongst them was down to the day that lay ahead of them. The uncertainty concerning the Mist of Time was at the root of it. Firstly, how were they going to find it? And then, what dangers lay in wait for them?

'So how do we find this Mist of Time?' asked Rory as he sipped his tea.

'We have to relocate the Guiding Light,' said Jack. 'And hope it leads us to, and then through it.'

'To where exactly?' asked Sean.

Jack looked to Tyler and Lilac for reassurance. 'To our homeland?' They both nodded their agreement.

'Do you think Ciara, Seamus and O'Reilly will be there?' asked Rory.

'All that we know is that they are the other side of the Mist of Time. If the legends are true, then that's where our homeland lies also. Let's hope that they're there, but if not, we'll carry on our search.'

'What else can we do?' said Lilac.

Tyler nodded his agreement. 'It seems our only option.'

'So how do we find the Guiding Light again?' asked Rory.

Jack looked to Tyler. 'The poet amongst us has to come up with the words, and I will recite them, just as we did before.'

'In that case it's just as well that I've already written them,' said Tyler looking pleased with himself.

'You've written them,' said Lilac. 'When did you do that?'

'As I was eating my breakfast. I usually find that my creative juices flow when I'm eating.'

'And there's me thinking that you could only ever do one thing at a time,' she smiled.

'You see, Lilac Wildflower, there are depths to me that even you don't know about.'

'And it's probably best that I don't,' whispered Lilac under her breath.

'Well, let's get this over with. There's no point in waiting around. Where do you want to do this?' asked Rory.

'I thought by the wishing-well in the village centre,' suggested Jack.

'It sounds ideal,' said Tyler. 'Shall we go?'

*

The five of them stood on the cobblestones in the village square, just to the side of the wishing-well. Jack, Tyler and Lilac were in a circle holding hands, with Sean and Rory behind them.

'You're sure you've got the words in your head?' asked Tyler.

'I am,' said Jack. 'Are we all ready?'

'As we'll ever be,' said Rory and Sean together.

Jack, Tyler and Lilac raised their hands skywards and closed their eyes. They followed exactly the same procedure as before. 'Breathe calmly and slowly. Feel your feet placed firmly on the ground. Feel the energy from the Earth flowing through your body ... Feel it tingling on the end of your fingertips ...'

Jack leant back and started the incantation:

'Oh 'Guiding-Light' please reveal yourself
Hear the call of this desperate Elf
Show the path that we must roam
And lead us to our ancient home'

The reaction was instant, although a little less violent than the previous occasion. A streak of bright white light burst from their hands and headed straight up to the sky. They waited for it to change to the horizontal plain, and were taken completely by surprise when they were knocked off their feet by an explosion of light all around

172

them.

Jack couldn't see a thing; partly because of the shock of the white light on his eyes and partly because of the thick smoke from the eruption. It took several minutes for his sight to adjust. He was enveloped by a shroud of thick white smoke and had totally lost his bearings. He pulled himself up off his back into a sitting position and called out, 'Lilac, Tyler, are you there?'

There was no reply. He turned onto his hands and knees and crawled to his right. 'Tyler, Lilac,' he hissed. 'Where are you?' He reached ahead into the thick white smoke and made contact with what felt like a leg. He crawled over and peered through the smoky gloom and saw the blotchy round face of Tyler, but his eyes were closed. Jack shook him and whispered into his ear, 'Tyler, wake up.'

Tyler's eyes flickered open but there seemed little recognition in them. He groaned and rubbed the back of his head. 'Where am I? What happened?'

'Tyler, it's me, Jack. There was an explosion of light and it knocked us from our feet.'

'Where's Lilac?' asked Tyler.

'I'm not sure. I think we should wait for the smoke to clear. The others can't be far.'

Tyler struggled up into a sitting position. 'Do you have any water?'

Jack removed his rucksack and pulled out a water bottle. 'Here, take this.'

Tyler took the bottle from Jack and slowly sipped the water. 'I must have banged my head on the ground. All I remember is a blinding white flash of light and then you waking me.'

'Well, as long as we've found the Guiding Light it will be worth it.'

They waited and waited but the smoke showed no sign of clearing.

'How long was I unconscious for?' asked Tyler.

'I'm not sure,' said Jack. 'Maybe a few minutes at the most. The smoke from the explosion will clear soon.'

'It may be my imagination,' said Tyler. 'But I don't see any sign of it thinning.'

Jack looked all around him and had to agree with Tyler. 'What are you suggesting?'

'Smoke from a fire or an explosion isn't damp. My clothes are damp.'

Jack felt his own jacket and slacks. Tyler was right, they were damp.

'This isn't the after effects of an explosion at all,' said Tyler. 'It's a mist, and to be frank, the thickest mist I've ever seen in my life.'

As much as Jack didn't want to believe him, he knew he was right. He wasn't sure how but they had found themselves in the midst of the Mist of Time.

Chapter Twenty-Two - The Mist of Time

'How did we get here?' asked Jack.

'I have no idea,' said Tyler. 'But I think the first thing we need to do is find the Guiding-Light.'

'Surely we need to find the others first,' said Jack.

'Jack, this isn't a mist it's a fog, and to be quite frank, it's the thickest fog I have ever experienced in my entire life. If you take a half a step away from me I'll lose you. Before we think about finding the others we need to get our bearings and the only way we can do that is by locating the 'Guiding-Light'.'

Although Jack was desperately worried about his friends, he knew that Tyler was right. Without the light to guide them, they were going nowhere.

'And I think we should hold hands,' said Tyler. 'The last thing we need is to lose each other.'

They linked hands and started their search for the light. The fog was so thick that it almost choked Jack. It felt like it was sticking in his throat as he breathed. He called on his inner control just like his grandfather had taught him. He breathed slowly and stopped fighting the anxiety that was lurking deep inside him. 'Let it flow through you, Jack, and help focus your mind,' he whispered to himself.

'I didn't get the feeling that the explosion threw us that far,' said Tyler. 'I'm sure the light is nearby; we just have to find it.'

The fog crowded in on Jack – it felt like he was wrapped in a damp blanket. But he kept his focus and studied the swirling mass intently. He cleared his mind and peered deep into the fog, but it was impossible to see anything. It felt like a hopeless task but they were never going to escape the fog without the light.

He closed his eyes and called on his instincts to guide him. *If you can't see the light, then you're going to have to feel it.* He knew it was there – the explosion of light was proof of that. All he had to do was find it. He thought about all of the tight scrapes he'd been in since he'd set out on this journey. He remembered how hopeless he felt when he led his friends in a circle in Morning-Dew's forest. But she had total faith in him. She told him that he knew all that he needed to find his mother.

Believe, Jack, believe ...

He opened his eyes and saw a faint beam of light in front of him. It emanated directly from his body. It cut through the swirling fog like a warm knife through butter – it was the 'Guiding-Light' that was going to lead them to their homeland.

'I've got it, Tyler,' said Jack. 'Now let's find the others.'

'They can't be that far away,' said Tyler. 'Let's search to our left, but make sure you don't lose sight of the light.'

They took a tentative step to their left, and Tyler called out: 'Lilac, Sean, Rory!' There was no response. Tyler's voice was drowned in the thick fog. They took another step to their left and Tyler called out again, but got the same result.

'Don't take your eye off the light, Jack. The last thing we need is for us to get lost as well.'

'That's just it,' said Jack. 'The light is following me.'

Tyler looked at Jack. 'What do you mean it's following you?'

'It seems to be coming from my body.'

Tyler looked down at Jack's stomach and sure enough that's where the light came from. 'I never noticed that in the forest.'

Jack shrugged his shoulders. 'I didn't really think about it. I just followed it.'

'Wait!' said Tyler. 'We might have moved the light away from the others. They'll never find their way out of here without it. We'll have to go back to where we started from.' They took the two steps back in the hope that they would find their friends waiting for them, but they were still on their own surrounded by the thick, foggy blanket.

'I just can't believe they were thrown that far by the

explosion,' said Jack.

'They probably weren't,' agreed Tyler, 'but they could be only a matter of a few metres away from us and we'd never know. We'll have to wait here and hope they find us.'

And wait they did. Every now and again they thought they saw someone coming towards them but it was no more than the fog playing tricks on their eyes. Neither visual nor hearing senses fully functioned in the dense fog. The damp, claustrophobic atmosphere started to drain their spirits. If they were honest, they both just wanted to get out of there as quickly as possible.

'I don't think we're achieving anything by waiting here,' said Jack. 'I think we should follow the light and hope we find the others along the way. If we don't, then we should be able to call on the Elves to help us.'

Tyler reluctantly agreed because he didn't have any alternative suggestions. 'OK, let's hope it doesn't take long to get through this nightmare.'

Jack felt Tyler squeeze his hand even tighter as they followed the light beam into the murky mass. The ground soon changed from firm and damp to wet and boggy. If it wasn't unnerving enough not to be able to see where they were going, they were also unsure of their footing. The muddy water squelched up and over their boots and soaked their feet.

'I can put up with most things,' said Tyler, 'but sore and soaking feet are not a combination I wish to experience again.'

'I have to agree with you,' said Jack. 'But don't tell Lilac, she'll never forgive me.'

'Teasing Lilac is one of my few pleasures in life, young Jack, so I'm afraid I can't promise.'

They carried on chatting as they made their way through the fog. The combination of the marshy ground and the thick foggy blanket made progress painfully slow. They both tried to keep their spirits up but the constant trudging through the muddy morass and the damp fog was starting to wear them down.

'How much longer will this go on for?' groaned Tyler. 'It's not as if we can sit down and take a rest in this bog.'

'I know,' said Jack. 'It's hard enough keeping upright. Surely the end of the mist isn't that much further?'

The question was more in hope than fact. The chat between them dried up and that's when Jack's attention started to drift. He struggled to keep his eye on the light and to stop his mind from wandering. He kept seeing movement out of the corner of his eye, but every time he turned to look all he saw was the fog swirling around him. Ghostly shadows suddenly appeared in the fog and set his nerves on edge.

'Tyler! Can you see them?' he asked.

'See what?'

'I'm sure there are people in the fog.'

'It's your imagination,' dismissed Tyler. 'Just concentrate on the light.'

He was probably right, thought Jack, but it still spooked him. And his unease increased when he heard Grimley's voice in his ear, as clearly as if he was standing right next to him. *'There's no escape for you, Green-Jack. We will find you wherever you go. There are no hiding places. Darkenwold awaits ...'*

Just hearing Grimley's voice again unnerved him. He knew that Grimley couldn't be there in the fog, but it still made him anxious. It was like the fog was trying to goad him; trying to break his resolve. It had become a battle of wills between them.

He remembered his journey with Breannacht. It was exactly the same. He realised that she was trying to prepare him for the ordeal. He turned to Tyler; 'You're right, I'm seeing things, I ...' He suddenly realised that he was no longer holding Tyler's hand. 'Tyler! Where are you?' Jack waived his hands through the swirling fog in a vain attempt to clear it from around him, but it was impossible. The fog instantly filled any gaps he created.

'Tyler!' he shouted again but his voice dissolved into

the thick fog. 'If you're messing around Tyler, I will seriously do something that we'll both regret. TYLER!' But nothing, his friend had disappeared. The shadowy figures that Tyler had said were figments of his imagination returned. The anxiety that had been lurking deep inside Jack threatened to burst through and overwhelm him.

He heard Noah's voice in his head. *'Fear is your friend not your enemy, Jack. Let it work for you. It will protect you if you allow it the space.'*

Jack breathed slowly and composed himself. If there were threats out in the fog it was going to be difficult to protect himself. He removed his backpack and crouched down low. He held the Bloodstone that hung around his neck in his fingers, for no other reason than it gave him comfort. It made him feel close to his mother.

The shadows in the fog surrounded him. He needed to act and act quickly. But then something unexpected happened. He felt the warmth of Earth Magic moving up his lower body – first his legs, then his stomach and finally his neck and shoulders. His anxiety eased as the power channelled through him. The Bloodstone tingled in his hands and the Earth Magic sat poised ready to burst from him.

Then just as quickly as they appeared, the shadowy figures blended back into the fog. Jack didn't hesitate to take his opportunity to escape and headed after the Guiding Light as fast as the marshy conditions would allow. His mind kept focused on the shaft of light and he didn't waiver from its path.

Just as exhaustion was about to take over him, he noticed a change in the fog. He was sure that it was thinning. 'Please let this be the edge of the 'Mist of Time',' he whispered to himself. Even though he felt on the edge of collapse, he kept his legs trudging through the marshy ground. *Keep going, Jack. You're nearly there.*

And his prayers were answered, as the fog slowly dispersed, and he found himself walking on dry ground.

Several steps later he was free of the foggy blanket and threw himself onto the lush, dry grass. He lay there for several minutes, drinking in the fresh air and just enjoying being free of the suffocating fog.

He turned over onto his back and looked up into a clear blue sky. There were times when he was imprisoned within the fog that he thought he would never see such a beautiful sight again. But he'd made it; he'd made it through the 'Mist of Time'. Now the only question that remained was 'where was he?' He was about to find out.

'You look tired and damp after your trek through the mist.'

Jack pulled himself up into a sitting position and saw a tall Elf standing on top of a grassy mound in front of a line of thick green bushes, staring intently at him. His long blond hair rested on broad shoulders, and his bright eyes sparkled like icy blue diamonds. His face was lean and tanned. He wore a black leather sleeveless jerkin over an open necked white shirt and black leggings with knee-length black boots.

Jack surveyed his surroundings. Behind him was the blanket of fog, which he'd just emerged from. A lone, withered old oak tree marked the boundary to the fog. The Elf stood on the edge of a dense green forest. Jack shouted across to him: 'Am I in our homeland?'

The Elf smiled. 'Now that depends on who you are?' He walked over to Jack and helped him to his feet. 'My name is Jack, and I'm an Elf from the human world.'

'In that case, welcome to your homeland, Jack. My name is Tathar Elensar and I am Captain of the Border Guard.'

'Have you seen my friends? A short, chubby Elf with a red face called Tyler: a tall pretty Elf with blond hair called Lilac, and two Leprechauns called Sean and Rory.'

'There will be time enough for questions when we reach Arminas. My orders are to get you there as soon as possible.'

'I'm not going anywhere until I've found my friends,'

said Jack. 'I'll go back into the mist alone if I have to.'

'Only never to find your way out again. I don't think so. I will accompany you to our home city of Arminas. You can ask your questions when we reach there.'

This wasn't going how Jack had hoped. He felt sure the Elves would help him. 'I'm staying put – I need to be here when my friends find their way through the mist.'

The Captain placed a friendly hand on Jack's shoulder. 'I'm sorry but I can't leave you here. I have strict orders that anyone who arrives in our land via the mist must be taken straight to Arminas.'

'They're your orders not mine,' said Jack defiantly. 'I'm waiting for my friends.'

The Captain forced a smile. 'As much as I admire your spirit, you really don't have much choice.' He pointed towards the edge of the forest. A dozen or more Elven warriors suddenly emerged from the bushes, all holding longbows with arrows at the ready. Jack momentarily thought about summoning his Earth Magic but did he really want to unleash it on his own people?

'I promise you,' said Captain Elensar, 'that we will answer all your questions once we arrive in Arminas. It is an hour's journey from here at the most.'

Jack looked at the stony faced archers and instinctively knew that any one of them could pierce him with an arrow in the blink of an eye. It pained him to leave the mist without his friends but it was looking like he had little choice. 'Will there be guards waiting here in case my friends turn up?'

'There are always guards posted here.' The captain turned to his warriors. He addressed a morose looking Elf with short, cropped, dark hair. 'Elladan, you will take command while I escort Jack to the city. I need six guards as an escort.'

He chose six of the Elven warriors and turned to Jack. 'We will leave now. I hope you are as fit as you look as we will be setting a healthy pace.' The guards lined up in three pairs behind him. 'I will be back before nightfall,

Elladan. Send a messenger if you need me.'

Elladan nodded and blended back into the forest with the rest of the guards. 'Right, Jack,' said Elensar, 'let's see what you're made of.' And set off along a compacted dirt pathway through the forest.

Chapter Twenty-Three – Arminas

Elensar wasn't joking when he said they would set a healthy pace. Jack was fit and it was just as well as they were running at what for him was half pace, but for the guards, looked like a jog. The sweat soon started to stream down his face in the hot midday sun. His head was bursting with questions but he didn't have the breath or the energy spare to ask them. Instead he chose to take in his surroundings.

The forest looked green and lush – it was an environment that Jack was used to and loved. Tall pines lined one side of the track and a combination of beech and elm the other. Jack had exactly the same feeling as when he first saw Waterswood. All of the colours were richer and the forest seemed even more alive than his beloved Heywood Forest back home.

The birdsong was loud and resonant and unlike anything he'd ever heard before. And when he saw a brightly coloured bird fly across the track in front of him, he realised why. Its body was bright blue and yellow, with red and green wings. Its wingspan was at least a metre and Jack wondered if it was some sort of parrot as it squawked in delight as it weaved its way in and out of the trees around them.

'It's looking for food,' said Elensar as he ran by Jack's side. 'Make sure you don't slow too much as you could be its dinner.'

'Are you being serious?' gasped Jack.

A huge grin spread across Elensar's face. 'They're not carnivores. They live off fruit and nuts.'

It seemed that the Elven Captain had a sense of humour. He hoped that he had an equal sense of care and would help Jack find his friends. His initial feeling was that Elensar had been evasive but Jack tried to suspend his judgement. They were all Elves and surely they would want to help find their fellow kindred.

They eventually emerged from the forest and descended into a long deep valley that was flanked either side by tall, jagged, snow-capped mountain ranges. Elensar pointed towards a blue lake at the far end of the valley.

'Arminas is on a raised island in the middle of that lake. We will be there in less than thirty minutes. 'You will see a golden dome perched on top of a tall building at the city's centre. That is the King's palace and that is where I will be taking you.'

'I'll be seeing the King,' said a surprised Jack. 'Why would he want to see me?'

'He likes to welcome all of our guests personally. Do not worry, Jack, he is a fine Elf and you will find him friendly, although a little forthright.'

Jack was uneasy about his friends still wandering lost in the 'Mist of Time'. He guessed that if he was going to get the assistance he needed he would have to convince the King. He hoped his powers of persuasion were up to the task.

As they neared the end of the valley, Jack got his first clear view of the city that Elensar called Arminas, and it was spectacular. A tall stone wall surrounded the city and the palace stood high and proud at its centre. The gold dome glistened brightly in the sun and provided a magnificent focal point.

They stopped on the edge of the blue lake and boarded a long flat boat that was crewed by several burly Elves. Jack sat on a bench next to Elensar and took in the scenery as they slowly glided across the lake.

'You've hardly said a word since we left the mist,' said Elensar.

'That's because I couldn't catch my breath,' said Jack with a wry smile.

'That was just a pleasant trot,' said Elensar. 'You must join us when we're hunting Wood Trolls in the lowlands. We run at twice that pace for days. And it pays not to get left behind as Wood Trolls aren't known for their fondness of Elves.'

'I'll give the Wood Troll hunting a miss if you don't mind,' said Jack with a smile.

'Living in the human world has made you soft,' joked Elensar as he playfully slapped Jack on his back.

The boat pulled into a small jetty and Jack disembarked along with his escort. He looked along the path that wound its way upwards towards the city and was overwhelmed at the sheer size of the vast stone structure. It was like a medieval castle, thought Jack. Something that he'd only ever seen in the history books his grandfather used when he was teaching him.

They marched up to tall wooden gates that were flanked either side by two Elven guards. As the Captain approached they stood to attention and saluted him. Elensar waved his acknowledgement and strode through the gates into the city. Jack found himself in a large square that was filled with market traders. They barely took any notice of the group as they forced their way through the crowds.

Elensar led them up some stone steps at the far end of the square towards a stone arch. As they walked underneath it Jack noticed some words and symbols carved into the stone. He stopped to read them and they made him shudder. The words: 'In Freedom We Trust' stared back down at him - exactly the same words that were carved into the 'Arch of Peace'.

'Has something disturbed you?' asked Elensar. 'You look like you've just seen a ghost.'

'It's the words on the arch,' said Jack. 'They're exactly the same words that are carved into the 'Arch of Peace' in my home village of Waterswood.'

Elensar smiled. 'All Elves treasure their freedom, Jack, so it comes as no surprise to me.'

'And those symbols,' continued Jack. 'What do they mean?'

'They are Elven runes. Our ancestors would use them on ancient manuscripts and monuments like this stone arch. They are symbols of peace and freedom. We can discuss in more detail another time. Now come, we must not keep the King waiting. He will know that we're here by now.'

Jack followed Elensar through the arch and across another courtyard and through a series of narrow cobblestone streets that climbed steadily towards the palace at the summit of the city. The Elven escort remained behind them and stared impassively ahead at all times. Not one of them had spoken to Jack, or even acknowledged him since they left the mist.

As Jack's legs started to ache through the constant uphill trek, Elensar stopped at the foot of a long stone staircase that stretched up towards a pair of large wooden doors. Guards stood either side of the stairs, staring impassively ahead of them.

'The Royal Palace,' said Elensar, 'The home of our ruler, King Erenin. He will meet us in the throne room and you must remember to bow when he enters. You will address him as 'Your Majesty' and only speak when he speaks directly to you.' He turned to the escort. 'Return to the mist and re-join Elladan. Tell him I expect to be back before nightfall. I will send a messenger if I'm delayed.'

They all stood to attention and saluted their Captain, before running back down the cobblestone streets. Elensar placed his arm around Jack's shoulder and said, 'now we meet the King.'

They walked up the steps and the Elven guards pulled open the tall wooden doors. Elensar led Jack into a grey, marble-floored hall, with a magnificent wide mahogany staircase facing them. They climbed the stairs and walked through another pair of double doors and along a wide door-lined corridor towards another set of closed doors.

The only sound in the corridor was the clatter of Jack and Elensar's boots on the hard wooden floor. Jack felt the tension increase in his stomach as the doors approached. He guessed that the throne room was directly ahead. Never in his wildest dreams did he imagine that he would meet a

King, let alone an Elven one.

They stopped outside the doors and Elensar straightened his jacket and dusted himself down. He adjusted the knife in his belt and turned towards Jack. 'Remember what I told you – respect at all times.'

Jack nodded that he understood and Elensar knocked on the door. It opened immediately and two Elven guards stood stony faced to attention and saluted Elensar. He led Jack into a large chamber with a domed ceiling. A regal throne sat upon a dais against the wall facing them. Long maroon velvet drapes that covered the walls and surrounded the dais matched the upholstery on the throne chair.

He looked up into the gold dome that he'd first seen from the other side of the lake as he approached the city. It was like looking up into the ceiling of a cathedral, it stretched so high. A shield hung from the wall over the throne. Two red griffins stood upright on their hind legs on either side of the shield; a white dove in between wrapped them both in its wings.

'That is the coat of arms for the House of Erenin,' said Elensar. 'It symbolises strength and compassion.'

'It's very striking,' said Jack, 'as is the whole room.'

Just at that moment a door opened to one side of the throne and an Elven guard strode in. 'Please be upstanding for King Erenin.'

Jack stood up straight; his heart thumped in his chest as he fought to stay calm. An elderly Elf dressed in a green tunic, black leggings and a long dark cloak draped over his shoulders, walked into the room. His long, grey hair hung loose on his shoulders. It was still thick and strong; it was only its colour that suggested old age. He held himself erect and had an aura of strength and wisdom. He climbed the steps on the dais and took his seat on the throne.

'Bow,' whispered Elensar. Jack followed Elensar's lead and bowed from the waist.

'Captain Elensar, it is good to see you again.' The King turned his attention to Jack. 'And who is it we have here?'

His voice was deep and commanding and resonated around the chamber. It was the voice of a King.

Jack's throat had dried and he wasn't sure any words would come from his mouth. *Stay calm, Jack ... breathe ...* He swallowed deeply and spoke as calmly as he could.

'Your Majesty, my name is Jack and I'm an Elf from the human world.'

The King nodded his acknowledgment. 'Welcome, Jack. Welcome to my kingdom. Please tell me what brings you here.'

'Thank you, Your Majesty,' said Jack bowing again.

'Before we continue, Jack, let us dispense with formalities. I find the constant use of 'Your Majesty' very cumbersome. So, continue ...'

'Thank you, Your Maj ...' Jack felt his face flush. He took another deep breath and continued. 'I am looking for my mother. She came in search of our homeland with two Leprechaun friends many years ago.'

'And you think they are in Arminas?'

'It's more a case of hope. I was told that she was on the other side of the 'Mist of Time'. It would come as a great relief to me if she and her friends were here.'

'And what are their names?'

'Her name is Ciara and the two Leprechauns are Seamus and O'Reilly.'

The King looked towards the Captain who shook his head. 'I'm afraid that they are not here and if they had entered our land via the mist, I can assure you that they would have been apprehended by our Border Guard. I think it safe to assume that they did not find their way to this land.'

Jack was disappointed but not surprised. As much as he hoped his mother was in Arminas, the warning from the Banshee about her being in grave danger suggested she was not. He changed his tack and foolishly pressed the King about Tyler and the others. 'My friends who came with me are lost in the mist. I need your help to find them. We have already lost too much time – we need to leave now.'

Elensar reacted instantly – his face looked like thunder. 'Do not speak until spoken to …'

The King raised his right hand. 'Jack has spirit and is not used to our ways. He is worried about his friends and understandably so.' He focused his attention on Jack. 'But what you need to understand is that we only have your word for who you say you are. We live in dangerous times and are vulnerable to attack from enemies who enter our land through the mist. We must be sure of who and what we're dealing with before we decide upon any course of action.'

Jack understood his concern, but his friends were lost in an impenetrable mist, and the longer they were left in there, the harder it was going to be to find them. 'I apologise, Your Majesty,' said Jack bowing low.

'I ask you to bear with me, Jack, while I ask you some questions,' said the King.

As frustrated as he was, Jack nodded his agreement.

'I'm told that you possess great magic.'

Jack was confused. How would the King know that? 'I'm not sure how to answer, I …'

The King smiled enigmatically. 'You found your way through the various traps that our Artisans set for uninvited visitors, and you found your way through the 'Mist of Time'. I'm intrigued as to how you managed that.'

Elensar and the King studied him intently while the guard stood impassively staring into space. 'I used a 'Guiding-Light', Your Majesty.'

The King looked astonished. 'But you are still just a young Elf. I have known Artisans who have practiced the art of magic all of their life who have never achieved such a feat.'

'It was Tyler's idea. He gave me the words for the incantation and I called on the Earth Magic. I didn't realise what it was until I met Lilac and Tyler, but I've been able to do it since I was very young.'

'You called on it in the mist,' said Elensar.

189

'Not consciously,' said Jack. 'I saw shadows circling me and I was frightened. I held onto my Bloodstone to give me comfort. It made me feel close to my mother. Then I felt stirrings of Earth Magic but it melted away when the shadows disappeared.'

'They were my Border Guard,' said Elensar. 'They were attempting to apprehend you.'

'I'm sorry,' said Jack, 'I didn't realise; I thought they were a threat to me.'

'That's understandable in the circumstances,' said the King. 'You mentioned a Bloodstone. Would you mind showing it to me?'

Jack reached inside his shirt and pulled out his Bloodstone and held it out to the King. He leant forward and carefully studied it. A look of disbelief suddenly crossed his face. His friendly countenance became serious.

'Where did you get this?' he asked firmly.

'It was my mother's. I was only a baby when she left so I don't remember her. Noah, the man who brought me up, gave it to me when he told me I was an Elf.'

'You were raised by a human?' asked a surprised Elensar.

'I thought he was my grandfather. He was very kind to me but when I found out I was an Elf, I decided I wanted to find my mother.'

The King fired a series of questions at Jack.

'Why would your mother leave you with a human?'

'I don't know,' said Jack. 'My grandfather said that she seemed frightened. She said that she would come back for me one day, but …'

'What made your grandfather tell you this? He could have waited until your mother returned.'

The question brought back bad memories to Jack, but he had to tell them the truth. 'Elves tried to kill me in the night – they burnt our cottage down. He knew that my life was in danger so he had no choice other than to tell me who I was.'

'And who were these Elves who tried to kill you?'

'It was ordered by the Head of the Council of Elders in Waterswood. His name is Grimley. The search for my mother led me to my home village. I knew that it was dangerous but I had to find out where I came from. I was arrested within a day of arriving there and Grimley planned to send me to a place called Darkenwold. I'm told that it was unlikely that I would have survived it.

My friends helped me to escape. I ran back to the human world and Lilac and Tyler eventually followed me. It was decided that the only way we could find out why Grimley wanted me dead was to find my mother and that search eventually brought us here.'

The King sat back in his throne. Jack thought that he looked troubled. He rubbed his chin as he digested what he'd just heard. He eventually turned to Jack. 'If your Bloodstone is genuine, and I believe that it is, then you are descended from one of the five High Elven families.'

Jack looked to Elensar for guidance. 'I don't understand, I …'

'The Elves of the House of Sarmondian left these lands many centuries ago following a disagreement between the high families,' said the King. 'There has been no trace of any of them since, that is, until you arrived here today.'

Jack stood in stunned silence. So that's what the 'S' in the stone stood for – Sarmondian. Was he really descended from a High Elven family? Did his mother know? Did Grimley know? Maybe he'd just found out the reason why Grimley wanted him dead.

Chapter Twenty-Four - The Council of the Elves and Leprechauns

King Erenin pulled a long rope sash that hung by the side of his throne. 'You need refreshment, Jack, and you need to rest. Elensar, pull up a chair for our young friend.'

Elensar fetched a chair from across the other side of the chamber and placed it behind Jack. He slumped into it and held his head in his hands. 'I'm not sure I can take this all in. I wish Lilac and Tyler were here to talk to.'

A maid appeared in the chamber. 'Angara, please bring refreshments. Our guest is tired and hungry.' The maid disappeared out of the door that she entered through as the King whispered to the guard standing by his throne, who also promptly left the chamber through another door.

'This has been a very trying time for you, Jack,' said the King. 'You have been on a long and arduous journey of discovery. But let me assure you that you are now amongst friends and we will do our best to help you.'

'You will help me find my friends and my mother?'

Before the King could answer, a door opened across the other side of the chamber and a guard stepped through. Jack heard a familiar voice from outside. 'Get your hands off me. I'll have you know that I am a distinguished citizen of the Elven community of Waterswood. I object to being manhandled in this manner and demand that you treat me with the respect that I deserve.'

Jack leapt to his feet and ran across towards the door just as a short stout Elf with a rosy red face stepped through. 'Tyler!'

Before Tyler realised what was happening, he was enveloped in a hug that nearly broke his back. 'Jack! I thought I'd lost you forever.' Tyler returned the hug with interest and held Jack's face in his hands. 'These ruffians kidnapped me in the mist and brought me here. No matter how much I protested they ignored me. Did you find Lilac?'

Jack's answer was drowned out by a loud voice from behind him. 'I may be half your size but I can look after myself. Get your hands off me you ugly brute. Nobody pushes a Leprechaun around.'

Jack saw Rory dragged through an open doorway by a tall Elf, quickly followed by Sean and a pensive looking Lilac. But her demeanour changed instantly when she saw Jack and Tyler. She screamed out loud and ran towards them wrapping them both in her embrace. 'I thought I'd never see you both again!'

'How did you find your way through the mist?' asked Tyler.

'We followed the 'Guiding-Light',' said Lilac.

Jack and Tyler looked puzzled. 'But that's what we followed,' said Tyler, 'that was until I was kidnapped.'

'It was very strange,' said Lilac. 'The three of us were knocked from our feet by the blinding white flash. When we came to, we were in the middle of a thick fog. It was Sean who guessed it was the 'Mist of Time', so we called out your names but the sound barely got out of our mouths before it was absorbed by the fog. It was then the light seemed to find us. It came out of nowhere from the mist and then moved away again but we followed it all the way to the oak tree. That's when the Elven guards arrested us and brought us here and locked us in a room. They interrogated us but refused to answer any of our questions.'

Jack and Tyler looked at each other in amazement. 'It must have been when we went looking for them that they found the light,' said Jack.

The King rose to his feet and raised his right hand. 'I will arrange for a meal to be served in the banqueting chamber. I think that it's the least I can do in the circumstances.'

*

Tyler sat back in his chair holding a goblet of wine. 'Well, that was one of the best meals I've ever had in my entire life. If I eat one more thing I think I will burst.'

'And that's something you don't often hear Tyler say,' said Lilac.

'It was a grand meal,' said Rory. 'Up to Auntie Bridie's standard but twice as much!'

'I still can't believe that we all found our way through the mist,' said Jack.

'Ah, there's a bond between us all,' said Rory, 'a bond that will never be broken.' He raised his goblet: 'To good food and good friends.'

'To good food and good friends,' they all repeated.

The door at the end of the chamber opened and Elensar strode in. 'I trust that you've all had sufficient to eat and drink?'

'A banquet fit for Kings and Queens,' said Tyler. 'The least you could do in the circumstances.'

Elensar nodded. 'I apologise for the lack of hospitality when you first arrived, but as I explained to your friend Jack, these are dangerous times we live in. We had to be sure of who you were before we could welcome you properly. And as a way of making amends, the King would like to invite you all to his private chambers.'

'Tell the King we would be delighted to accept his gracious offer,' said Rory bowing low.

'Then follow me,' smiled Elensar.

He led them along a dimly lit corridor and up some stone stairs. When they reached the top, there were two Elven guards standing either side of double wooden doors. They saluted Elensar and pulled the doors open. Elensar led the group into a large square chamber with a long mahogany table in its centre and several comfy armchairs strategically placed around the walls. A blazing log fire burned in an open grate and candles flickered in a candelabra hanging from the ceiling.

The wooden floors were covered by thick, maroon velvet carpets and the King's coat of arms was fixed to the wall above the open fireplace. The King sat at the head of the table, with a beautiful dark-haired female Elf sat to one side of him, and a strange looking Elf with manic eyes and a full, grey beard wearing a long, white robe, sat the other.

The King rose slowly from his chair and welcomed them. 'I hope you are all sufficiently fed and rested. Please take a seat at the table and we will serve you further refreshments if you desire them.'

Jack sat to one side of the King with Lilac and Tyler. Rory and Sean sat opposite them. A maid appeared with a tray and offered them drinks. Jack went for a cup of Roseleaf, as did Lilac, but Tyler and the Leprechauns plumped for the wine.

'Please let me introduce you to my daughter, the Princess Larien. The Princess stood up and bowed to them all. 'I'm pleased to make your acquaintance. I hope we can make your stay a little more pleasant than your welcome.'

'Aw, that's all forgotten now,' said Rory. 'I don't see the point in dwelling on the past. Let the past stay where it is and enjoy the present, is my motto.'

The King bowed his head. 'I thank you for your understanding.' He turned to the Elf in the robes. 'Could I also introduce you to Meredin – he is our Master Artisan. He and his colleagues are responsible for the magic that sustains and protects our Kingdom.'

As the King spoke, Meredin didn't take his eyes away from Jack. He studied him like a scientist might study an experiment. It made Jack feel quite uncomfortable. The King resumed his seat and picked up a silver goblet from the table in front of him. 'I would like to propose a toast. To our Elven cousins from Waterswood, and to our Leprechaun friends – may they always be welcome in Arminas.'

'I'll drink to that,' said Rory as he took a large mouthful of wine. 'And to our Elven friends in Arminas - they will always find a warm welcome waiting for them in Cill-Arney.'

Meredin barely acknowledged what was happening around the table. He continued to stare at Jack. He uttered some words that were out of context with the conversation. 'He is who he seems …'

The King turned his attention to him. 'Could you explain yourself, Meredin?'

'The young Elf is heir to the House of Sarmondian. I can see it in his eyes and I can feel it. He has the gift to summon great magic.'

This stopped Tyler mid-flow as he was emptying his wine goblet. 'The House of Sarmondian?'

'It is one of the five high Elven families,' said the King. 'Four of them reside here in our homeland. The fifth, the House of Sarmondian left these lands many centuries ago. Your friend Jack wears the Sarmondian Bloodstone.'

Tyler looked genuinely shocked. He turned to Lilac. 'Did you know about this? Did Ciara ever discuss it?'

Lilac shook her head. 'She never told me. I'm not sure if she was even aware of it.'

'Do you think that would explain why Grimley wants me dead?' asked Jack.

A look of realisation spread across Tyler's face. 'Yes it would and why Ciara ran from Waterswood and wanted you to be born away from there. Grimley would see you as a threat to his authority in Waterswood.'

Princess Larien addressed Jack directly. 'How can we help you? Tell me what you need from us.'

'My mother and her two Leprechaun friends left Cill-Arney many years ago in search of this land. There have been several attempts to find them, but without success.'

'I can assure you that they have not found their way to our land. We constantly patrol the 'Mist of Time' and know of all who enter here,' said the Princess.

'I'm sure that they found the 'Mist of Time' but lost their way while in there,' said Jack. 'I think they may have accidently found another land. I believe that my mother is in great danger.' He swallowed nervously before continuing. 'We need your help to find her.'

'We have great tracking skills in my Guard, but we would never be able to track your mother to a land on the other side of the mist,' said Elensar.

'And you will have no need of your tracking skills,' said Meredin mysteriously.

'Why so, Meredin?' asked the King.

'Jack has the Sarmondian Bloodstone – this will enhance his magical powers. It will lead him to his mother just like it led him here.'

'Of course,' said Tyler. 'I should have thought of that. I'm afraid that we are not encouraged to work with Earth Magic in our community. In fact, the use of magic is banned.'

Meredin had a face that didn't show either what he was feeling or thinking. His expression never changed. 'All Elven communities are sustained by Earth Magic. We are creatures of Faery and magic is a part of us all. The roots of all magic lie in the Earth Magic, or to use the Elven word, Koehtia. Your leaders are taking great risks with the safety of your people and need to change their ways before it is too late.'

'Well you'll find no disagreement on that from me,' said Tyler. 'I've always known that Grimley's ideas were dangerous.'

Elensar addressed the King. 'Your Majesty, will you authorise an expedition to find Jack's mother? If so, I would like to lead it.'

The King didn't hesitate. 'Of course, and I agree that you must lead it.'

'I will need a dozen warriors. I will choose these from my Border Guard. We need to travel light and we need to travel fast. Including Jack, there will be fourteen of us.'

Rory was onto his feet in an instant. 'When we set out on this quest, it was agreed that we were all in it together no matter where it led us to. And I see no reason why that should change now. We came here as a group and we leave here as a group.'

'This is too dangerous a mission to take non-combat individuals on,' said Elensar. 'I must insist that I have full authority on the make-up of the group.'

Tyler sprang to his feet. 'Lilac and I both gave our words to Jack that we would stay with him no matter the risks involved and the dangers we faced. I must insist that we also come with you.'

Elensar was about to refuse but Jack interrupted him. 'I appreciate what you're about to do for me, Captain Elensar, and I appreciate the dangers we face. But my friends have stuck loyally by my side ever since I started this quest and I will never leave them. They are the bravest and most loyal friends an Elf could ever hope to have. Please reconsider and allow them to join us.'

'I don't think you're going to persuade them otherwise, Captain Elensar,' said the Princess. 'And you also need to know that I will be joining you.'

'Absolutely not!' said Elensar. 'I will draw the line at that.'

'You have a short memory, Captain. Do you not remember who it was who saved you from that Wood-Troll when we were travelling in the Southern lands?' A confident smile spread across her face. 'And I have healing skills that will be vital when we go to this place, wherever it is.'

Elensar looked to the King for support. 'Is there anything I can say that will dissuade you from this?'

She shook her head. 'My mind is made up, Father. I will be going on this quest.'

Chapter Twenty-Five - Journey into the Unknown

Elensar reluctantly gave in to the demands of Rory and the others, but he insisted that they were all trained in self-defence. This comprised of learning judo-like skills as well as being able to handle a short sword. Jack took to it like a duck to water, as did Lilac and Sean, but Tyler and Rory struggled with the unarmed side of things.

'I'm afraid my skills are more in tune with the artistic side of life,' said Tyler. 'I can just about use the sword, but I think throwing someone over my shoulder is beyond me.'

In the end, even Elensar was impressed with how they reacted to the hard discipline from his guards, Tyler and Rory excepted. 'I think Jack and Lilac have what it takes to be fully trained Border Guards, as does Sean, though on a smaller scale. Tyler and Rory are best suited to cooking duties,' he joked.

'I can live with that,' smiled Rory. 'I make a grand stew, even though I say so myself.'

Meredin spent time with Jack to help him with his Earth Magic, or Koehtia. Jack's ability to use this in conjunction with his Bloodstone was the key to them finding his mother. 'The Bloodstone is of the blood of your ancestors. It is more than just an artefact – it will enhance your ability to work with Koehtia. There is but one for every Elven family. It is very precious, Green-Jack. Always keep it close to you.

No one ever gets to be the master of Koehtia and the magic that it gives us, but we can learn to work with it, and more importantly to work within ourselves. Although your experiences so far have been positive, you need to refine your technique so that you gain the maximum benefit from it. I will show you how to do this. Our time is limited but you start from a very advanced place.'

Meredin went on to explain that Jack had no need of an

incantation to summon the Koehtia. It was this which caused the flash of power and the resulting explosions of light. He told him that if he built it up slowly and allowed it to find its own way through him, it would be much more controlled. Although Meredin was an understated type of character, he was full of praise for Jack's abilities.

'Trust your senses and feel it, Jack. It will build to the level that you need and you can use it as you see fit. I have a strong sense that you will you grow into this the more you use it. You will be as I one day, a Master Artisan, but don't be fooled by the word 'Master' – it merely means that you are at the peak of your skills and not the master of the magic.

Go forth, Jack, and find your mother. Go back to your community and take your rightful place as their leader. But most importantly of all, reintroduce the practice of Koehtia and magic and make sure that these skills are inherent in your new found society.'

*

Two days after arriving in Arminas, the small group of Elves and Leprechauns were gathered at the city gates. Captain Elensar stood at their head and the King faced them. An air of anticipation and optimism surrounded the group.

'It is with mixed feelings that I stand here today,' said the King. 'I truly hope that you find your mother, Jack, and that she is safe along with her two Leprechaun friends, Seamus and O'Reilly. But I urge you all to take extreme care, and listen carefully to what Captain Elensar tells you. He is a fine Elf and a fine warrior. I could not entrust your safety to anyone more worthy.

So, all that remains to be said is that I wish you all well and please return safely to Arminas.' He shook them all warmly by the hand and hugged his daughter. Jack was sure he saw the trace of a tear in his eye.

They marched down to the jetty and climbed into two

large flatboats that were tied there. The Elven guards took up the oars and pushed them away from the jetty and out and across the lake. Nobody knew where they were headed to, or what dangers awaited them, but there was an air of steely determination about them that showed they were ready for whatever challenges lay ahead.

They disembarked at the far end of the lake and headed towards the valley. Jack looked back as they reached the mouth of the valley and admired the splendid Elven city of Arminas. He wished more than anything that the next time he stood in that same place, his mother and Seamus and O'Reilly would be standing beside him.

The walk back to the 'Mist of Time' was much more relaxed than his trek of two days earlier. They had time to take in their surroundings and admire the picturesque scenery. But the nearer they got to the mist, the more the anticipation and anxiety built. Jack tried to focus his mind on the task in hand and concentrate on how he was going to summon the Koehtia.

They were met by the Border Guard at the mist, and Elensar named a tall blond Elf, called Firlas, as their temporary commander. In normal circumstances Elladan would have fulfilled that role but he'd insisted that he join the quest, and after a long and protracted negotiation, Elensar finally relented.

Jack stood by the old oak tree and studied the swirling fog. It was so dense that it looked like a moving wall. But he knew what he had to do and mentally prepared himself for the task.

'Are you ready, Jack?' asked Elensar.

Jack nodded. 'I'm ready.'

He closed his eyes and breathed steadily. *Compose yourself, Jack. Feel your feet planted firmly on the ground. Make your connection ...*

He blanked out his surroundings and reached deep down within himself. He felt the first stirrings of Koehtia in the soles of his feet. He remembered Meredin's words: *'Let it build slowly – it will find its own way through your body'.*

And it did. Jack felt it move up his legs, through his stomach and into his upper body. He didn't force it; he just allowed it to move freely within him. He thought of his mother. He built a picture of what she looked like in his mind. *Help me find my mother.*

He felt a warm sensation deep inside. It felt natural, almost familiar. *Be at one with it.* Meredin's words continued to echo through his mind. An image started to take shape. He saw a petite, female Elf with shoulder length, wavy, brown hair. He knew instinctively that it was his mother. He saw a beam of light reach out to her and cover her in its warm glow. It was the Guiding Light. He opened his eyes and saw a shaft of bright, white light disappearing into the foggy gloom. He'd done it.

Tyler and Lilac both hugged him. 'We knew you could do it, young Jack,' said Tyler.

'Jack and I will lead, followed by Rory and Sean, then Tyler and Lilac,' said Elensar. 'The warriors will cover our rear. It's important to hold onto the person directly in front of you at all times. If one stops, we all stop. I have no idea how long we will be in there, so please be vigilant at all times.'

They moved into the fog as one, Jack and Elensar leading them into the murky gloom. In a matter of seconds, they were engulfed in the thick, swirling, foggy blanket. The firm ground soon gave way to a marshy, thick sludge. It was like wading through a swamp. But at least this time they knew what they were dealing with and Jack felt reassured having the Elven Captain by his side.

He thought about the image of his mother generated by the Koehtia. Did that mean she was still alive? He certainly hoped so. She seemed so far away at times but he now had a strong feeling that she was getting nearer. The light would lead him to her, of that he was sure. And even if there was danger, he knew that between them they would be able to deal with whatever lay ahead.

He wasn't the same person that had left his grandfather

all those weeks ago. He could hardly believe some of the experiences he'd faced. But he'd found some true friends – friends that he knew would stay with him throughout his journey no matter what. And he didn't just mean the journey to find his mother; he was referring to his journey through life.

Meredin told him that when he returned to Waterswood he should take up his rightful place as their leader. Crystal had told him the same when he left Waterswood, and she didn't know then that he was descended from one of the high Elven families. But he had to dismiss that from his mind for the time being. He had to focus on finding his mother and that was what he was going to do.

There was no sense of time in the fog; there was no sense of anything. No visibility; no sound; no awareness of your surroundings. It was like walking blind into a foggy wall, but Jack kept focused on the light. He felt Lilac's hand holding tightly onto the back of his jacket but there were no spoken words between them. You were in your own foggy world even though you were surrounded by your friends.

He was disturbed to find that Grimley joined him once again. The image of the leader of the Council of Elders appeared clearly in the fog beside him and his words were equally scathing. 'So you think you're a King, Green-Jack. You think that you will one day rule Waterswood. I will make sure that never happens. You are an outsider to our community and your destiny is Darkenwold.'

As much as he tried not to let them, the words disturbed him. He knew that it was the fog playing tricks with his mind. It was as if it could reach inside him and see his deepest fears. As much as he didn't want to admit it to himself, Grimley frightened him. He caught a grip of himself and reined in his imagination. *Just keep focused on the light.*

The trek through the swamp seemed to go on forever. His feet were soaking and the fog dampened his clothes. As much as he tried to fight it, the trying conditions drained his resolve. He was physically and mentally tired. He was surprised that Tyler hadn't already stopped them.

Then just as he thought he was going to have to ask Elensar to rest, the fog started to thin giving him a much needed boost of energy. He felt a huge weight lift from his shoulders – they were nearly through.

They emerged into a narrow ravine between two sheer walls of grey rock. Once they were all out of the fog, Elensar waved for them to stop. The relief in the group was palpable. Poor Rory and Sean were soaked nearly up to their waists. And Jack saw the reason why Tyler hadn't asked to stop. Elladan was carrying him.

The stocky warrior placed him gently on his feet and a grateful Tyler breathed a huge sigh of relief. 'Thank you, my friend. I must apologise for my bad manners the last time you carried me through the mist.'

The Elf nodded his acknowledgment but his stony countenance never wavered.

'We'll find somewhere to set up camp,' said Elensar. 'I think we're all tired after our long trek through the fog.'

'I'll second that,' said Rory. 'I have some Shamrock tea in my rucksack. I'll make a pot for us all and a thick, creamy mushroom soup.'

They followed the ravine into a stony valley surrounded by tall, granite, grey mountains. There was little shelter for them; Elensar pointed to a forest at the far end of the valley.

'We'll make camp by the forest. There should be plenty of dry wood to build a fire.'

It was a humid, overcast day and although the sun never quite managed to break through the heavy grey clouds, by the time they arrived at the forest edge, they were all drenched in an uncomfortable, clammy sweat. Elensar found a clear pool hidden within the rocks on the valley edge and they all took turns to bathe in the cool, clear water.

As they dried themselves down, the guards gathered wood for a fire, and in no time at all, they were sitting on the ground nursing the mugs of Shamrock tea that Rory had promised them earlier. They were all tired but relieved that the journey through the 'Mist of Time' had been uneventful. They didn't know the exact nature of the land that they'd just entered, and at that precise moment, were too tired to care.

Following a delicious meal of mushroom soup and bread prepared by Rory and Lilac, Elensar and the Princess took Jack to one side. They sat on granite boulders on the edge of the stone valley.

'I didn't want to say this in front of the others,' said Elensar, 'as I don't want to concern them unnecessarily. Have you noticed that the 'Guiding-Light' has disappeared?'

Jack looked down at his stomach. The Captain was right, it had gone. He'd been so pleased to be through the mist that he'd lost his concentration. 'I don't understand ...'

'It went the moment we stepped into the ravine,' said Elensar. He turned to the Princess. 'Have you any idea why?'

'I don't, but I'm no expert on the ways of magic. It could be as simple as the fact that we're in another land. Maybe Jack has to reconnect with it?'

It made sense, thought Jack. 'Do you want me to try now?'

'There's no point,' said Elensar. 'You need to gather yourself after a long, hard journey, Jack. Tomorrow is a new day and you will be rested and ready.'

Chapter Twenty- Six – Lestrada

Jack woke to an unfamiliar sun – it was deep red and shed a soft, early morning crimson glow across the landscape. He sat up, yawned and rubbed the sleep from his eyes. The dull, grey valley that they crossed the previous day came alive in the shallow red light. The forest looked green and serious. The place had a look and feel unlike anything that Jack had ever experienced before.

Rory suddenly appeared by his side with a welcoming mug of Shamrock tea. 'Did you sleep well, Jack me lad?'

'Very well,' said Jack. 'I always do after I've used Koehtia. It seems to drain me.'

'Well, I don't begin to understand that stuff, but as long as you're OK with it, that's fine by me. We have bread and dried fruit for breakfast – it will be ready as soon as you've finished your tea.'

Jack sat next to Lilac and Tyler as he ate his breakfast. He was pleased that they were their normal selves teasing each other as it helped take his mind off the day ahead. He felt on edge, even anxious. He was sure that they were getting nearer to his mother, but the words of the Banshee kept coming back to him: *'She is alive but in grave danger.'* How much time did they have to find her?

They quickly cleared up after their breakfast and Jack prepared himself to re-summon the 'Guiding-Light'. He followed exactly the same procedure as the previous day and he was relieved when the light appeared on cue and shone directly into the forest.

But then something strange happened. Within a few seconds, the light gradually faded away. Jack was bewildered and looked to the Princess for guidance.

'Should I try again?' he asked.

'It takes a long time to master the magic, Jack. I think you should try again but maybe you should take a little longer building up the Koehtia.'

And that's exactly what he did, and a clear, bright, shaft

of light penetrated the forest once again, but within a few seconds it faded just like its predecessor. Jack felt deflated; it felt as if he'd failed. He was so sure that he was coming to terms with the Koehtia.

Princess Larien put a consoling arm around his shoulder. 'Don't be too hard on yourself, Jack. It can take years to master magic. Meredin is an Artisan and he would be the first to say that he is not its master.'

'She's right, Jack,' said Elensar. 'The light has given us the general direction through the forest. That is the path we will take.'

The Princess walked alongside Jack as they entered the forest. As much as he liked her company he stayed lost within his own thoughts. All of the feelings he had with the Koehtia were the same as the day before when he'd summoned it to guide them through the 'Mist of Time'. It built up inside him in exactly the same way. The light came as strong and sharp but inexplicably faded back into the daylight.

'There are many things that we don't understand about our magic,' said the Princess. 'And we know little about this land we have entered. Let it rest with you Jack and don't dwell on it. The best answers come when we don't search for them.'

Jack had felt out of sorts the moment he'd arrived in this land. There was something that he couldn't put his finger on. Jack had always loved walking through a forest; it is where he felt most at ease, but for some reason he felt nothing like relaxed as he followed the path that wound its way in between the trees and shrubbery. The failure of the Guiding-Light had unsettled him. Perhaps that was the reason for his unease, he wondered?

Rory and Tyler chatted innocently as they strolled along behind him, both seemingly oblivious to Jack's concerns. Elensar strode purposefully ahead, his warrior's instincts on full alert, constantly encouraging his Border Guard to keep vigilant.

Lilac appeared by Jack's side and grabbed his hand.

'Stop beating yourself up about the light. You did your best and that's all anyone can ever ask of you. We are getting nearer to Ciara – don't ask me how I know but I can feel it. I feel excited but I'm anxious too. We have the right people with us, I know it.' She gave his hand a reassuring squeeze. 'I promise you that we will get through this together.'

They continued along the path through the forest and by mid-morning they emerged into a rolling green meadow that was covered with brightly coloured flowers. The anxiety that clouded their journey through the forest eased slightly as they drank in the beautiful scenery.

'Now that's more like it,' said Tyler. 'That view inspires words in me … I amble through the meadow green, To behold the beauty of a dream, The colours gleaming both bold and bright, Have you ever seen such a gladdening sight …?'

The Princess clapped her hands enthusiastically. 'Bravo – you are a great poet, Tyler.'

Tyler bowed low. 'Why thank you, Princess.'

'Don't tell him that,' pleaded Lilac, 'or he'll carry on …'

'I'm afraid my friend has never appreciated my artistic side, Princess Larien. It is an honour to share a journey with someone who has an eye and an ear for such beauty.'

They followed a path across the meadow and onto sprawling green hills that stretched for as far as the eye could see. Jack tried to summon the light once again and the same thing happened, but at least it showed them they were headed in the right direction.

The intensity of the red sun increased steadily during the day, and by early afternoon, the heat was sweltering. There was little cover from the burning sunrays so when they came across a solitary oak tree by the side of the trail, they decided to make camp, sheltering in the welcome shade beneath its branches.

'We will rest here a while,' said Elensar. 'It's too tiring to travel in this heat. We will wait until late afternoon when it's cooler and then resume our journey.'

They found a running stream at the foot of the hills and filled their canteens with fresh water. Tyler removed his boots and bathed his feet.

'My poor feet feel like they're swollen to twice their normal size,' he complained. 'A poet's feet aren't made for walking.'

'No, but his tongue is made for complaining,' whispered Lilac to Jack.

Jack smiled but it didn't reflect his inner feelings. He'd felt uncomfortable all day and it wasn't just down to the failure of the Guiding-Light. He unenthusiastically ate a lunch of bread and cheese, followed by dried fruit. He sipped on a mug of Shamrock tea as he pondered the situation. His thoughts were interrupted by a cheery voice from behind him.

'Good day to you all. I trust that this heat isn't too overbearing?'

They all turned around to see a tall man with a neatly trimmed silver-white beard and short white hair, wearing dark robes, standing on the trail. He was holding a long wooden staff.

The guards were on their feet in an instant, their longbows primed and at the ready. The stranger raised his right arm. 'Please, there is no need for mistrust or violence. I come in peace and only wish to offer you a warm welcome and a friendly face.'

Elensar cautiously approached the stranger; his right hand poised on the short sword hanging from his belt. 'And who is it that welcomes us?'

A broad smile crossed the man's lips. 'My name is Korrian and I am as you, a traveller in this land.'

'And what land is this?' asked Elensar.

'Lestrada,' replied Korrian. 'A land full of rolling hills, forests and deep blue lakes. It is a place of great peace and beauty. All are welcome in Lestrada.'

'And where do you come from?' asked Elensar.

'From a place a long, long way from here; a place that

could only dream of the beauty that is Lestrada.' Korrian noticed Rory drinking his tea. 'That tea smells inviting, my friend. Could you spare a cup for a thirsty traveller?'

'Of course,' chirped Rory, and filled a mug and handed it to him. Korrian sipped it and said, 'that tastes as good as it smells. I thank you for your kindness.'

'Don't mention it,' said Rory. 'Anyone who appreciates the cultured taste of the Shamrock tea is fine by me.'

'Would you mind if I take a seat amongst you?' asked Korrian. Elensar nodded and Korrian sat down on an upturned log next to Jack. 'Would you indulge me and introduce your friends?'

'I am Captain Tathar Elensar of the Elven city of Arminas.' He pointed to the guards. 'They are Elven warriors from our Border Guard, and this is Princess Larien. Rory and Sean are Leprechauns from Cill-Arney, and Jack, Tyler and Lilac are Elves from the human world.'

Korrian turned his nose up in distaste. 'I have never been interested in the human world. Humans have always struck me as uncultured beings. But I'm told that Arminas is a beautiful city and represents the best of Elven architecture. I must take the time to visit your land one day, Captain.'

'All are welcome,' said the Captain, 'as long as they come in peace.'

Korrian nodded his agreement. 'So what brings you all to Lestrada?'

Before anyone else could answer, Rory blurted out, 'we're looking for our friends.'

Elensar shot Rory a withering look. Rory blushed with embarrassment and dropped his gaze to the floor.

'So who are these friends you're looking for?' asked Korrian.

Elensar momentarily hesitated before answering. 'An Elf and two Leprechauns. We believe that they may have accidently entered Lestrada some time ago.'

Korrian thoughtfully sipped his tea and didn't respond

immediately. 'I am a regular visitor to this land and I have never come across these people. Why do you think they are in Lestrada?'

'We tracked them here,' said Elensar.

'That would have taken some tracking through the 'Mist of Time', Captain. No doubt you called upon some of that magic that you Elves are so renowned for.'

'We have our ways and means,' said Elensar.

'It's OK, Captain, I'm not prying into your affairs.' Korrian turned his attention to Jack. 'You have an air of knowledge and wisdom about you. A potent combination for someone so young I would say.'

Jack wasn't sure how to respond, so he mumbled 'thank-you,' and carried on drinking his tea.

Korrian finished his tea and placed his mug on the log beside him. He used his staff to help him back to his feet and looked down at Jack, and reached inside his shirt and pulled out his Bloodstone. He caressed it in his fingers before holding it in the palm of his hand. 'A very precious jewel if I may say, a very precious jewel indeed. If I'm not mistaken, it's an Elven Bloodstone that's handed down through the generations.'

Jack wasn't sure what to say and looked across to Elensar for guidance. Korrian picked up on his reticence. 'There is no need for concern. It's just that I appreciate beauty, and this jewel is indeed beautiful.' He replaced the Bloodstone back inside Jack's shirt. 'Thank you all for your tea and hospitality. I truly hope that you find your friends. But now, I must be on my way.' He bowed his head and walked slowly from the shade of the oak tree and onto the path through the hills.

Elensar watched him until he disappeared from view and turned to his friends. 'It's time for us to resume our journey,' said Elensar. 'There's only a few hours of daylight left so we need to make the most of it.'

*

'I thought yer one, Korrian, seemed a nice enough sort,' said Rory as he strolled alongside Jack and Lilac.

'When you've travelled in strange lands as often as I have,' said Elensar, 'you learn to be suspicious of everyone.'

'He asked a lot of questions,' said Tyler, 'and he locked straight onto your Bloodstone, Jack.'

'I think he noticed it in my shirt as he stood up,' said Jack.

'I didn't like him,' said Lilac. 'He seemed almost too friendly.'

'Well we probably won't see him again,' said Elensar, 'but if we do, I think we need to be careful what we say around him.'

As the dark red sun set to the west they descended down the twisting path from the hills towards a dense green forest that stretched for as far as the eye could see. They stopped at the foot of the hills alongside a shallow stream. None of them particularly wanted to camp in the forest so Elensar chose a spot near to the stream. Rory and Lilac soon had a fire blazing and cooked a delicious vegetable stew for their supper, followed by dried fruit.

As Rory, Sean and Lilac cleaned up after their meal, Elensar and the Princess sat down by Jack as he drank his tea.

'Have you had any further thoughts about your magic?' asked the Princess.

'Not really,' said Jack. 'I just can't understand why it's not working. I'm doing all the same things as before.'

'I think it is working,' said the Princess. 'It's just that we can't see it. It's the atmosphere here masking it.'

'But how?' asked Jack.

'There is magic at play, of that I'm sure,' said the Princess. 'I don't think that this land is as friendly as Korrian would have us all believe.'

Chapter Twenty-Seven –
Attack in the Night

Jack lay on his blanket by the side of the campfire. Lilac and Tyler sat one side of him with Sean and Rory on the other. No one was in the mood for small talk. The guards circled the camp continuously, their eyes permanently scouring their surroundings for signs of any threats.

The Princess came and joined them by the fire. 'All Elven warriors are highly trained but the Border Guard are the best. No one will get near this camp without them knowing.'

'That is very reassuring, Princess,' said Tyler. 'I'm exhausted after that journey today, so I can rest easy knowing the Border Guard is looking after us.'

'You will need a good night's rest as we will have another long day on the trail tomorrow.'

'As tired as I am,' said Rory, 'I don't feel the slightest bit sleepy. I'm going to have a nip of Poteen to help me relax. Is anybody going to join me?' He reached into his rucksack and took out a small bottle. He pulled out the stopper and was just about to take a drink when Elensar knelt down by his side. 'I think we all need to keep our wits about us, Rory. As tempting as it may be, I'd prefer it if you didn't drink any alcohol while we're in Lestrada.'

Rory was just about to protest when the silence was broken by a blood curdling howl from deep within the forest. He replaced the stopper and put the bottle back in his rucksack. 'In the name of the great Leprechaun, what was that?'

Elensar was on his feet in an instant. He pulled a burning branch from the fire and strode over to the edge of the camp and peered into the dark gloom of the forest. 'Elladan! Place all the guards on full alert. I want ten facing the forest and two at our rear.'

The words were no sooner out of his mouth when the guards sprang into action like a well-oiled machine. They took up their positions and crouched low as they focused all of their attention on the forest.

Another blood chilling howl came from deep within the forest but from a different direction. Jack jumped to his feet and joined Elensar. 'Do you have any idea what that was?'

Elensar continued to study the forest. 'They sound like wolves, but who knows in this land?' He turned to Rory. 'Can you and Sean keep the fire burning? We will have need of it before this night is out. Princess, keep a close eye on our friends.'

More howls echoed around the forest. They were calling out to each other, and what was more worrying, they were getting nearer. 'Guards – prime your longbows,' hissed Elensar. 'Make sure that every arrow counts.'

The guards did as he asked and loaded their longbows. Their faces were masked with a steely determination and showed no trace of any fear.

'Stay close to the Princess, Jack,' said Elensar. 'And be ready to use that sword just the way I showed you in Arminas. If anything breaks through our front-line defences you know what to do.' Elensar prowled the camp perimeter like a wild animal searching for its prey, continually whispering words of encouragement to his guards.

Lilac, Tyler, Sean and Rory were huddled together by the fire. Jack stood one side of them and the Princess the other. Sean and Rory held on to their short swords. 'You know, when the Captain showed us how to use these things, I never really thought we'd have to. I just hope I can remember it all,' said Rory.

'Instinct takes over in the heat of battle,' reassured the Princess. 'Your training will see you through.'

Jack kept his eyes and ears on full alert as Elensar circled the camp. Each new cry from within the forest sounded more chilling and was getting nearer and nearer. He was sure they were going to be attacked. But what he didn't know was by what?

'Should we move further back from the forest?' asked the Princess. 'It will give us more time to defend ourselves.'

'There's no moonlight,' said Elensar. 'We need the light of the fire.'

Jack knew that the Captain would weigh up all of the options. He'd set the camp nearer to the stream than the forest. A thick bramble hedge on the other side of the stream would have been almost impossible for anyone or anything to break through, so any attack would come from the forest.

The howls gradually grew in volume and intensity, before reaching an ear piercing summit.

And then silence.

'Ready yourselves,' urged Elensar.

Jack felt the cold clammy sweat on the back of his neck. He'd never faced anything like this before in his entire life. As frightening as Finn Tarr was, at least he was human. Whatever it was out there was definitely not human. The silence screamed at him. It tried to paralyze him. *Remember your training, Jack. Let your instincts take over.*

Elensar forensically surveyed the forest for any sign of movement. He removed his sword from its sheath and held it tightly in his right hand. 'Hold your line,' he whispered to his guards. They didn't acknowledge him – they didn't have to. Each one knew exactly what was expected of them. They carefully studied the forest, looking for any sign that warned them of attack.

They waited minutes, but it seemed like hours. Sean and Rory stood like animals trapped in bright lights. Lilac and Tyler held onto each other as if their lives depended on it. Jack took out his sword and held it in both hands. He would deal with anything that broke through the line of guards.

And when the attack came it was terrifying. A pack of snarling, grey wolves came charging out of the forest like a tidal wave. The Elven guards had only seconds to take aim and unleash their arrows. But they didn't hesitate – ten arrows hissed towards the wolves and each one felled its intended target.

The guards reloaded instantly, unleashing another wave of arrows and ten more wolves fell, but the remainder of the pack were upon them before they could reload again. The guards swapped their longbows for their swords and hacked at the raging pack. Elensar joined them and fought like a demon. A wolf jumped on his back, ripping at his leather jerkin with its razor sharp teeth. The Princess leapt forward and hacked at it with her sword. The wolf fell backwards and Elensar was onto it in an instant, finishing it off.

Then, just as suddenly as they attacked, the wolves withdrew back into the forest. The chaos and madness became deathly silence. Jack stared out onto a sea of dead wolves. He could taste the atmosphere and it unnerved him. He never knew that death smelt so bad.

'Regroup,' hissed Elensar. 'Are there any injuries?'

'Only minor, Captain,' shouted Elladan.

'Reclaim the arrows!' ordered Elensar, and the warriors withdrew the spent arrows from the dead wolves. They retook their positions and primed their longbows. 'Vigilance!' hissed Elensar. 'They will attack again at any moment.'

And they did. They came streaming out of the forest, a slavering mass of razor sharp white teeth and blood red gums. The hiss of arrows filled the air again and another ten wolves perished. But they seemed even more bent on death than the previous charge and were on top of the guards before they could reload their longbows.

The guards stood as one and repelled the attack with a deadly combination of skill and bravery. Wave after wave of rabid wolves threw themselves at them but they couldn't break through the solid Elven wall. Jack had no previous experience of battle but was amazed at the ruthless efficiency of the guards. The suicidal assault fell away as the pile of dead wolves grew. Once again they withdrew into the forest and the screaming hell was replaced by an uneasy silence.

'I don't understand it,' said Elensar. 'A pack of wolves will fight until the last. It doesn't make any sense for them to keep withdrawing.'

'But the numbers don't seem to be reducing,' said the Princess.

'You're right,' said Elensar. 'And it's almost as if they are being controlled.'

The words were no sooner out of his mouth when another onslaught began. This was the most ferocious and for the first time, the defensive line fractured and two wolves broke through and closed in on Lilac and Tyler. But Jack and the Princess were onto them in a flash and both wolves fell under the joint impact of their swords.

Jack staggered backwards, hardly daring to believe that he'd just killed an animal. But he knew that if he didn't, his two friends would have been torn to pieces. He had no choice but it didn't help soothe his conscience. The two Elves at the back of the camp ran forward and joined the fray. The wolves were stretching the guards to breaking point.

Just as the battle reached its peak, the wolves once again withdrew. Jack could see that the guards were tiring; they were tiring fast. They were being slowly broken down by the continuing attacks. Jack knew it was only a matter of time before they started to take casualties, and there was no obvious way out.

The wolves came streaming out of the forest again, a snarling mass of hatred. The arrows from the guards cut them down like tenpins but they still kept coming. All twelve guards joined Elensar in the desperate fight to keep the wolves at bay. Wave after wave descended upon the line of guards but they just managed to hold their position.

Jack and the Princess stood just behind them ready to pick off any wolf that broke through. Their whole focus was concentrated on the bloody fray in front of them. The manic sound of the wolves baying for blood filled the air along with the cries of the guards shouting to each other. Jack had loved the rare occasions when his grandfather had taken him to the cinema. It was always to see war films and Jack would daydream that he was in the midst of the action.

But the films were nothing like the reality. The pitiful sound of the dying wolves would stay with him forever. He knew that the guards had no choice but it didn't make it any easier. He just wanted the carnage to end but the wolves showed little sign of giving up their assault.

Once again the wolves withdrew to regroup in the forest. Each fresh assault seemed to swell their numbers. Jack looked at the guards' faces and could see that their resolve was breaking down. But Elensar didn't let up and rallied them.

'Use the breaks to rest and take on water. Conserve every bit of energy – you will need it my friends. Keep strong and keep brave - we are breaking down their will, I can feel it. Remember, you are the Border Guard – you are the best!'

And that was obvious to Jack. How they'd suffered no casualties was purely down to their fighting skills and resolute determination. Jack fought to stop his mind projecting forward but he feared the worse. How were they going to continue to fight off the wolves?

A blood chilling chorus of howls told him that the wolves were charging again. Each time they attacked with a renewed vigour and battered the iron line of guards. But there was no strategy to the attacks – they just threw themselves mindlessly at the warriors. The area between the camp and the forest was littered with the bloodied bodies of the dead wolves. It made Jack sick to the stomach.

His attention was suddenly diverted by an ear shattering shriek from behind him. He turned around just as a giant black bird swooped down onto him. He tried to move but his feet were rooted to the spot. Razor sharp talons grabbed at his clothes. But the Princess hacked at its

218

foot with her sword and the bird screamed out in agony before flying back off into the night sky.

Another giant bird came at him from the other side and knocked him from his feet with a swipe of its long black wing, sending his sword flying from his hands. The Princess swung her sword at the bird but it rose up into the air avoiding the blow. 'Elensar!' screamed the Princess. But her voice was lost in the chaos of the battle.

Jack turned to her just as a giant wing swatted her across the camp like a fly. He felt razor sharp talons grab at his jacket and he was yanked to his feet and off the ground. But the bird shrieked in agony and he felt the talons lose their grip and he fell to the ground. Tyler pulled him to his feet and was holding a sword with the bird's dark red blood dripping from its blade.

'It's surprising how brave you are when someone you love is in danger.' He handed his sword to Jack. 'Here, this can be put to much better use in your hands.'

Jack took the sword and hugged him. But he had no time to dwell on Tyler's bravery and avoided the clutches of another giant bird as it swooped low over the camp. A dazed Princess struggled to her feet, sword in hand. Jack ran over to her and steadied her. 'Are you OK?'

She nodded her head and he handed her his canteen. 'Here, drink some water.' As the Princess raised the canteen to her lips, Lilac screamed, 'Jack!' He turned towards her and suddenly felt the iron grip of bony talons clamp onto his shoulders and whisk him up into the air. He tried to hack at the bird with his sword, but its claws held his arms tight. In desperation, he shouted out as loud as he could:

'E-L-E-N-S-A-RRRRR!'

The Elven Captain reacted instantly and grabbed a longbow from one of his guards. He loaded an arrow and took careful aim. Lilac ran forward and cried, 'NO! You'll hit Jack,' and knocked him off balance. The taught bowstring slipped from Elensar's fingers and the arrow hissed past the bird and sped harmlessly into the night-time sky.

Jack rose into the darkness and looked down at the camp rapidly disappearing below him. The massive wings of the bird beat steadily against the night air, lifting him further and further away from his friends. Where was the bird taking him? Why didn't it kill him while it had the chance? Questions that he had no answers to.

The bird flew over the forest and towards a mountain range in the distance. It flew with speed and purpose. It obviously knew where it was heading for, and Jack guessed that wherever that was, the welcome was unlikely to be either a warm or a friendly one.

Chapter Twenty-Eight - The Dark Castle

The vice-like grip of the bird's claws held Jack firmly, and he was glad of that as it climbed higher and higher into the dark sky. The low cloud gradually thinned and the moon and stars made a welcome appearance casting their white, luminous light across the landscape below. They flew over the forest and across a vast lake as they steadily approached the mountains.

Jack's shoulders ached but he was relieved that the razor sharp talons hadn't punctured his skin. He tightened his grip on his sword as he was sure he would have need of it when he arrived at wherever it was the bird was taking him. He just hoped that his arms weren't completely wrenched from their sockets by the time he arrived there!

As the bird flew high over the mountain range, Jack looked ahead towards a castle perched on top of a lonely plateau on the far side of a deep, misty valley. The grey mist crawled across the valley floor and surrounded the base of the plateau. The castle looked dark and foreboding. Three towers surrounded a tall spire at its centre. It was the same grim scene that Breannacht the Banshee had shown him. Is this where his mother was imprisoned?

A spine-tingling anticipation filled him – could she really be within those bleak walls? The anticipation was quickly replaced by fear. He thought that he would meet this challenge with his friends by his side, but the giant bird had changed that. This was a challenge that he was going to have to meet on his own.

The castle loomed large and daunting in front of him, and the nearer it got, the bleaker and more threatening it looked. *Steel yourself, Jack. Be ready to face whatever threats lay within that dark, depressing place.*

The bird flew over the outer walls and swooped down low into a wide courtyard in the heart of the castle. Jack suddenly felt its claws let go of his shoulders and he dropped like a stone onto the courtyard below. His sword flew from his hand as he ended up in a heap on the hard cobblestones. He looked up just as the bird perched itself on top of the castle wall.

Jack quickly scrambled to his feet and picked up his sword. He held it out in front of him as he checked out his surroundings. A dark stone statue of an angel mounted on a stone plinth in the centre of the courtyard was looking down at him. She had a fixed, anguished look that told of terror. He turned around and saw a closed portcullis that led onto a walkway. The opposite wall had a solitary door at the top of a stone staircase. Dark shadows covered over half of the courtyard, masking whatever lay within them.

As he considered his options, he heard a low, threatening voice come from within the shadows. 'I smell Elf …'

Jack tightened his grip on his sword and peered into the darkness.

'The Elf thinks he can defend himself. I have to tell him that if he even tries, I will cleave him into small pieces.'

Jack pointed his sword towards the shadows. 'If you're so sure of that, why don't you come out of your hiding place and show yourself.'

A short, stocky figure moved from the shadows towards him. It emerged into the moonlight and hesitated as it studied him. It was just over a metre tall and a thick black beard covered its face. It was holding an axe.

'An Elf will never be a match for a Dwarf. Drop your sword or I will carry out my threat.'

Jack's heart pounded like a drum in his chest but he was determined not to show any fear. 'If you want my sword you're going to have to take it from me,' he said as calmly as he could.

'Very well,' said the Dwarf as it strode menacingly towards Jack. He raised his axe in the air and lunged at him. But Jack was too quick and easily side-stepped the assault. The Dwarf's axe hit the cobblestones with an almighty clang and flew from his hand. Jack quickly stepped forward and held his sword to the back of the Dwarf's neck.

'I believe that I now have the upper hand.'

The Dwarf didn't dare to move as Jack pressed the tip of the sword against his neck. Jack heard a voice from behind him.

'Please forgive my friend – he has an aversion to Elves.' Jack turned around to see Korrian standing at the top of the stone staircase, holding his wooden staff in his right hand. 'Glimring – pick up your axe and return to your duties. Jack is a friend of mine and will be accorded a welcome befitting that status.'

Jack stepped back from the Dwarf but kept his sword at the ready. Glimring glared at him before picking up his axe. He reluctantly put it back in his belt and skulked back into the shadows. Korrian walked down the steps and held out his hand to Jack. 'Welcome to my humble home. I'm glad that you were able to make it.'

'I wasn't given much choice in the matter,' said Jack still holding onto his sword.

'Please,' said Korrian, 'put your sword away. You have no need of it here.'

Jack carefully studied Korrian looking for any clue that may tell him something. He still had the same friendly smile that he wore when they first met, but Jack suspected that it was no more than a mask that he wore for convenience. 'Why did you bring me here against my will?'

'I wanted the opportunity to meet with you without your friends. It will allow us the opportunity to get to know each other better. Please put your sword away, Jack. I promise you that you will come to no harm.'

Jack's choices were limited to say the least so he reluctantly put his sword back into his belt.

'If you would like to come with me, I have refreshments waiting.'

Korrian walked up the stone steps and Jack made sure that the Dwarf wasn't around before following him.

Korrian pushed open the heavy wooden door at the top and stood to one side. Jack walked past him and found himself in a narrow, dimly lit corridor, the only light coming from the flickering, flame torches in metal holders on the wall. Korrian led him along the corridor and up a narrow stone spiral staircase. They eventually came out into an open chamber with several lounge chairs and a long chaise longue in front of a low, carved, wooden table.

Korrian walked up to the table and picked up a cut glass decanter. 'Wine?'

Jack shook his head. 'I don't touch the stuff.'

'Very wise,' said Korrian. He replaced the decanter on the table and filled the glass with water from a stone jug and handed it to Jack. 'Please, take a seat and make yourself comfortable.'

Jack sat on the chaise longue and placed the glass on the low table in front of him. There were colourful tapestries hanging all around the walls. They showed a bearded character in a long dark robe holding a long wooden staff. Each tapestry depicted a different scene but had Korrian as its focus.

'They tell the story of Lestrada,' said Korrian as he sat down in the chair opposite him. 'From its inception to the present day.'

'You make it sound like it was made rather than evolved,' said Jack.

'And that's exactly what happened,' said Korrian mysteriously. 'I am the creator of all that you see.'

'You created this land?' said Jack.

'I did indeed,' said Korrian. 'It is a land that I made in the image of myself and of all the things I value.'

'Like kidnapping innocent young Elves.'

'Nothing is ever innocent, Jack. You are here for a purpose as we both well know.'

What is it he thinks he knows? wondered Jack.

'You were accompanied by a group of Elven warriors. The Elves don't send their best warriors into other lands for no reason. No Jack, there is purpose to your visit to

Lestrada.'

Jack picked up his glass and sipped his water, not because he was particularly thirsty but it gave him time to think. 'The Captain already told you that we're looking for our friends.'

Korrian studied Jack intently for several moments. 'Why don't you tell me something about yourself?'

Jack wasn't sure he wanted to tell him anything about himself, but he needed time to decide what he was going to do. Perhaps it wasn't such a bad idea to try to win Korrian's trust. 'I was brought up in the human world. I only found my Elven home, Waterswood, a matter of months ago. I am on a journey of discovery.'

Korrian turned his nose up in disgust. 'Humans are such primitive creatures. They understand little of the world they inhabit. I am glad to be able to say that no humans have ever found their way into Lestrada. I would give them short shrift if they did.'

'So you must have visited the human world,' said Jack.

'I entered it once by mistake. I did not particularly enjoy the experience and have no intention of repeating it.'

Jack needed to find out as much as he could about Korrian. He needed to keep him talking. There was something he needed to ask him first. 'You orchestrated the attack in the forest?'

An enigmatic smile crossed Korrian's lips. 'Yes I did. Elves never cease to amaze me. They revel in aggression and violence and they never know when to give up. So they reacted just as I knew they would by throwing everything into fighting the wolves.' His smile turned to one of satisfaction. 'Which made it easy for my birds to take you.'

'But why did you only want me? Why didn't you capture us all?'

'Your friends are of no interest to me, Jack. They are as insignificant as the insects that crawl under a stone.' He leant forward and stared deep into Jack's eyes. 'You stand out like a precious shining jewel, Jack. As precious as that jewel that hangs around your neck.'

A sudden dark thought disturbed Jack. 'Did you leave my friends at the mercy of the wolves?'

'I did not,' said Korrian. 'Once my birds had captured you, I called off the pack. Your friends will be safe as long as they are not foolish enough to try to find you.'

And that's exactly what they will do, thought Jack. *I must keep him occupied.* 'You still haven't told me why you brought me here?'

'There is no urgency, Jack. I want you to make yourself at home and enjoy the comforts of my castle. You can have anything you want.'

'The only thing I want is my freedom. Am I free to come and go as I please?'

Korrian didn't answer and stared back impassively at Jack.

'I thought not. I come from an oppressive regime in Waterswood. I have no intention of subjecting myself to another equally oppressive regime. I will not cooperate with you and I will do my utmost to escape from this place.'

Korrian sighed wearily. 'You disappoint me, Jack. I'd hoped that you would recognise the benefits I offer. I have great power and can share it with you. Together you and I can rule, not only Lestrada, but other lands that lay beyond the 'Mist of Time'. We could even conquer the Elven city of Arminas and you could be King.'

'I'm not interested in great power. I'm interested in the people I care about and who care about me.'

Korrian reached forward to the table and filled a silver goblet with wine. He sat back in his chair and thoughtfully sipped it. 'Oh the naiveté of youth. If you had lived as long as I have, Jack, and seen the greed and corruption that infests societies, you would change your mind. Yes, even the Elves are as prone to corruption as the rest of us. You've seen that first hand in your own community. Rule or be ruled Jack, those are the choices we face. And take it from me, it is far better to be the ruler.'

'There is good and bad in all – my grandfather taught me that. I prefer to concentrate on the good in me and in others. It makes for a fairer society where everyone can be the people they wish to be. We learn to tolerate and accept each other rather than judge each other.'

'Fairness! What is fairness?' spat Korrian. 'Is it fair to be exiled from your own people because you dare to question their antiquated ways; because you dare to show them opportunities way beyond their wildest dreams. I could have led my people to a brave and exciting new world.' He drained his wine goblet and slammed it back down on the table. 'Fairness and stupidity are bed mates, Jack, and I will have no truck with either.'

Jack wanted to keep Korrian talking. He needed to find out as much as he could about him. He still didn't know why he kidnapped him. 'Perhaps what you were proposing was dangerous? Perhaps you were a threat to them?'

'They were fools and one day I will prove it to them.'

'So where is your home?' asked Jack.

Korrian smiled. 'Very good, Jack, I'm impressed. The more you can find out about me the more likely you will find my weaknesses. Let me save you the trouble … I have none. I have power beyond your imagination and there is no escape for you. You will eventually bend to my will – you have no choice in the matter.'

'I think not,' said Jack as he sprang to his feet and pulled his sword from its belt. 'I would rather die than cooperate with you.'

A flick of Korrian's staff and Jack's sword evaporated into a wisp of purple smoke. Jack didn't hesitate and lunged at Korrian, but another flick of the staff sent him sprawling across the floor and he ended up dazed on his back. Jack felt like he'd been floored by a charging bull.

'I didn't have you down as a fool, Jack, and that was foolish,' said Korrian. He picked up a small brass bell and rang it. A Dwarf appeared in the doorway and bowed his head. 'Runding – take our guest to one of our special rooms in the bowels of the castle.'

'Yes master,' said Runding and dragged Jack to his feet.

Korrian flicked his staff again and Jack's hands were pulled behind his back by an invisible force and bound with course rope. 'You need time to calm down, Jack, and think about our discussion. The offer is still there if you choose to see sense.'

Runding threw Jack through the door and half-dragged him along the corridor and down several flights of stone stairs. It was as dark and oppressive as it looked from the outside – Jack fought hard to stop it from infecting his spirits. Runding pushed him along a narrow, dimly lit corridor. He opened a rusty, iron door and threw Jack into a small, damp, empty cell.

As Runding was about to leave, Jack called after him: 'Are you going to untie my hands?'

The Dwarf roughly threw Jack on his front and pulled off the rope that bound his hands. 'Even think about attacking me and I will break your neck,' growled the Dwarf. He strode out of the cell and slammed the iron door shut and bolted it. Jack heard the sound of his boots disappearing back down the corridor.

He was in virtual darkness – the only light coming from under the door. He sat on the floor and leant against the cold, damp wall and rubbed his wrists where the coarse rope had burned them. His options were limited to say the least. Perhaps he could go along with Korrian? But he instantly dismissed the idea. He could never sell himself to such corruption.

No, he had to hope that his friends would come for him. But how were they going to find the castle and how were they going to combat the great power that Korrian commanded? Surely Elensar would know what to do, after all, he was Captain of the Border Guard, and they were the best …

Chapter Twenty-Nine –
The Corruption of Power

Jack had no idea of whether it was night or day in his cell. The Dwarf had shoved some stale bread and water through a flap in the door and that was his only contact with the outside world. There was no chance of sleep on the cold, damp floor, but he did his best to occupy himself by thinking through what Korrian had told him.

He was an outcast from his people, whoever they were, and it was obvious that bitterness drove him, along with a thirst for power. He could muster some pretty serious magic with his staff. Disarming Jack and throwing him across the floor was one thing, but controlling a blood-thirsty pack of wolves was something else.

And there was the Guiding Light. Princess Larien had been right when she suspected that there was magic at play masking it. Lestrada was created by magic and would resist magic that was brought into the land. Korrian said that he had chosen Jack because he was different to the others. Jack had found out the reason why during his stay in Arminas. He was descended from the high Elven House of Sarmondian – a House that had great magic according to the Artisan, Meredin. Magic that Korrian would use to supplement his own, so that together, they could rule other worlds.

To Jack that was a total abuse of power. He was still coming to terms with the Koehtia that was his heritage. It almost seemed to have a will of its own. If Jack was honest, at times it felt more like it controlled him. The time with Meredin was well spent but Jack was still a novice.

And then there was his mother. Was she also being held at the castle as suggested by Breannacht's vision? If she was, why would Korrian keep her prisoner for so long? She had been gone from Cill-Arney for over fifteen years. There were more questions than answers and at this precise moment, he needed the council of his friends.

The door to the cell suddenly burst open and the two Dwarves, Glimring and Runding strode in. 'Stand up!' barked Glimring. As Jack was about to stand a strong hand grabbed his jacket and dragged him on to his feet. 'Don't try anything, Elf,' he growled as he held up his axe, 'as nothing would give me more pleasure than cracking your head open.'

Glimring stood behind him as Runding roughly pulled him from the cell into the corridor and back up the several flights of stone steps before knocking on the heavy wooden door that Jack had been unceremoniously dragged out of several hours previously.

The door opened and Korrian stood there with a broad smile across his face. 'Did you like your room, Jack? I chose it especially for you.'

Jack didn't answer and stared impassively at him. He felt a heavy blow to the back of his head. 'Answer the master when he asks you a question!'

Korrian raised his hand. 'Please, Glimring, no violence. Bring our guest into my chambers and seat him on the chaise longue.'

Jack was dragged through the door and thrown onto the seat. Korrian sat on the chair opposite him as the Dwarves took up positions either side of the door.

'Now, Jack, have you had a chance to reconsider my earlier offer?'

'There was nothing to consider.'

'You disappoint me, Jack. I thought a spell in my dungeons may change your mind.'

'Power has corrupted you, Korrian, and I will have nothing to do with your insane plans.'

Korrian sat back in his chair and thoughtfully stroked his beard. 'A noble sentiment, Jack, but incredibly naïve. I will get my way whether you cooperate or not so why don't you save yourself a lot of unnecessary pain and discomfort and give me that jewel that hangs around your neck.'

Jack laughed mockingly. 'And you think I'm naïve.'

'Brave words, Jack,' said Korrian calmly, 'but incredibly foolish ones.' He turned to the Glimring. 'I think it is time to fetch one of our other guests.'

Glimring bowed his head. 'Yes master,' and strode purposefully out of the room.

'You see, Jack,' continued Korrian, 'I always get what I want, as you're about to find out.'

Jack eyed him suspiciously. Who was the Dwarf going to bring into the room? It was almost certainly someone who would cause him great pain, but he was ready for it. How he could do with Elensar and the Border Guard by his side at that precise moment. He breathed deeply and steeled himself to his fate.

Glimring came back into the room leading an old woman by her arm. Her long grey hair was a tangled mess that covered her face. She was stooped and frail and was dressed in what only could be described as rags. Her head hung on her right shoulder as if she was on the point of exhaustion.

'Sit her down next to Jack,' said Korrian.

The Dwarf did as he asked and pushed her down on the chaise longue. Who was this poor soul, thought Jack? And why would Korrian bring her into the room? He was about to find out.

'Let me introduce you to your mother,' said Korrian.

Jack was looking at an old, haggard female. His mother was only eighteen years older than him. There was no way that this poor soul could be his mother.

'You look like you don't believe me, Jack,' said Korrian. 'Pull her hair away from her face. You will see what I'm saying is true.'

Jack reached forward and did as he asked. Her hair was dry and felt like straw. Her skin was wrinkled and pallid. Her eyes were shut as if she was asleep. Jack could see that she was an Elf by her facial features and pointy ears.

Korrian addressed her directly. 'Wake up; we have someone to see you. It's your son, Jack.'

Her eyes flickered open but they were tired and vacant.

She stared at Jack but there was no sign of any recognition. Jack leant forward to have a closer look at her. Could it really be his mother? She looked so old – what had happened to her? Or was Korrian playing a game with him. 'How do you know she's my mother?'

'It is obvious to any outside observer – you are facially identical.'

'But why does she look so old? And she doesn't even seem to be aware of me,' said Jack.

'She has been with us for only a short time. I found her wondering in the hills not far from here. She was as she is now – very frail and not aware of her surroundings. I took her in and looked after her.'

'Were there two Leprechauns with her?'

'They are insignificant and unimportant. They have no bearing on what happens between us.'

Jack needed a plan. He needed to play for time. He needed to know if the poor unfortunate sitting next to him really was his mother. 'Show me that they are safe and unharmed.'

'I think you forget your place, Jack. It is I who make the demands, not you.'

'If you bring the Leprechauns to me, and allow the four of us to leave, and promise not to pursue us,' he swallowed deeply, 'I will give you the jewel.'

Korrian studied him intently. His dark, evil eyes bored deep into Jack's soul, but he held firm. 'Don't play games with me, Elf, or you will find that I don't play to the rules.'

'I'm not playing games. It is an honest and sincere offer based on what you've told me.'

Korrian stood up and walked over to a window and looked out in silence for several moments. 'Runding – fetch the Leprechauns.'

'Yes master,' said Runding as he ran from the room.

Jack turned to his mother, if indeed it was her, and took hold of her hand. It was cold and lifeless. What had happened to her? He didn't believe Korrian's story; he was sure that he was responsible for the state she was in. Once he saw the Leprechauns he would know for sure that he was holding the hand of his mother. It hadn't been the reunion he'd dreamt about but all he wanted to do was to get her away from Korrian and back to the people that loved her.

Runding appeared at the door holding two Leprechauns by their collars. Neither of them seemed aware of their surroundings. The Dwarf dragged them into the room and left them standing halfway between Jack and Korrian. Jack had the confirmation that he needed – he could tell from Rory's descriptions that he was looking at Seamus and O'Reilly. And the poor soul sat next to him on the sofa was his mother.

'I have kept my side of the bargain, Jack. Now give me the jewel.'

Jack stood up and walked over to the Leprechauns. 'Seamus, O'Reilly – I am Jack, Ciara's son. I have come to take you back home.'

But the two of them stared blankly ahead of them. There was no acknowledgement of Jack or anyone else in the room for that matter.

'What has happened to them all? It seems strange that not one of them is capable of speech or is even aware of their surroundings.'

'It is obvious that they have been subjected to some great trauma,' said Korrian. 'I and my servants took them in and looked after them.'

Jack didn't believe a word of it. He needed to get them all away from that dark place. He sat back down next to his mother and took her in his arms and wrapped himself around her. He tenderly kissed her hair and whispered in her ear; 'Mother, it's your son, Jack. I have come to take you back home to Waterswood. I will make sure that you and I are never separated again.'

'As touching as this is,' said Korrian, 'it is time for you to keep your side of our bargain and give me the jewel.'

But Jack ignored him. He was going to savour the time with his mother, even though she wasn't aware of him.

He'd been forced to spend nearly the whole of his life away from her and wasn't about to let anyone interrupt this moment. He closed his eyes and cradled her in his arms. Everyone else in the room faded away, it was just him and his mother.

And then he felt it. At first just a slight tingling in the soles of his feet, but then the warmth moved slowly up his legs. It was Koehtia. He hadn't summoned it or even thought about it. The Koehtia had found him and gradually worked its way through the whole of his body. Then it moved across to his mother – joining the two of them together in a magical union. They were both covered in the warm glow of the magic.

He used the Koehtia to search for her – even though he held her in his arms, he looked for any sign that she was with him. *Mother, can you hear me?* He listened intently; he felt for a response, but nothing. *It's me, your son Jack.* He reached deep into her with the Koehtia. He felt it repairing her. He felt it healing her. *Mother come to me.*

He waited and waited but she didn't respond. He was sure that the magic was working its way through her, knitting together all of the fragmented parts. She'd become disconnected but what he didn't know was how. Was it a major trauma? Was it other magic? The Koehtia couldn't tell him but it could heal. He held her more tightly in the hope that it touched her awareness.

Then he heard it. Very faint at first, but it was definitely a voice. *Help me ...*

I'm here, Mother. It's your son, Jack. I will heal you.

Jack? My son, Jack?

You left me with Noah many years ago, but I've come to find you. I've come to take you home.

He felt her arms wrap around him. *Jack, my son.*

Rest, Mother. You are very weak; let the Earth Magic heal you.

Earth Magic? You can summon Earth Magic?

I've been doing it all of my life without knowing. I have the jewel you left with Noah. I have the Bloodstone.

234

It will always protect you, my son. It will keep you safe.

Jack suddenly felt strong hands grab his arm and throw him across the floor. 'You must not ignore my master!'

Glimring stood over Jack holding his axe above him. Jack felt invigorated – he felt the energy charging through his body like electricity. He tripped the Dwarf up with his feet and snatched the axe away from him. He jumped up and stood on the Dwarf's throat. Glimring gasped for breath as Jack threw the axe across the room and watched it embed itself in the wall. Korrian stood glaring at Jack holding his staff out in front of him.

'You're testing my patience, Elf! Just give me the jewel or I will destroy you all.'

'Don't do it, Jack!'

He looked across the room and Ciara was standing in front of the chaise longue, but she wasn't the wreck that Korrian had brought to him. Her hair was dark and shiny and her skin was smooth and wrinkle free. She stood straight and determined. Her dark eyes blazed with passion. She was a young, beautiful Elf again.

'He's a vampire, Jack. He feeds on other's magic. It's what sustains him. Do not give him the Bloodstone under any circumstances. He can only use its power if you give it to him.'

Korrian waved his staff and sent a bolt of purple fire surging at Ciara. It caught her on her shoulder and she was thrown off her feet and onto the chaise longue. She lay still on her back.

'Mother!' screamed Jack and ran at Korrian. But the sorcerer was too quick and threw another bolt of dark fire at Jack; it hit him a glancing blow and he was thrown across the floor. He lay dazed for a moment but amazingly the bolt hadn't done him any permanent damage.

Korrian strode menacingly towards him, his eyes growing darker and more threatening by the second. 'Just give me the jewel!' he demanded.

But Jack was back on his feet in an instant and ran across to the other side of the chamber. The Leprechauns

235

stood impassively, totally unaware of what was happening as the Dwarves cowered in the corner behind a chair. Korrian threw another bolt of fire at Jack but it slammed harmlessly into the wall leaving a black charred hole in the stone. Jack darted across to the other side of the room, and Korrian continued to throw bolt after bolt at him but Jack danced around them all.

But it was only a matter of time before one caught Jack, and when it did, it caught him full in the chest and sent him flying across the room, leaving him in a crumpled heap on the floor. Korrian held his staff out in front of him looking menacingly at Jack. 'I will ask you one more time - give me the jewel.'

As disorientated as he was, Jack raised himself on his elbows, and his answer was defiant: 'Never!'

'And then it's death,' said Korrian as he raised his staff. But Ciara suddenly leapt to her feet and flew at him and made a grab for his staff. Korrian was knocked off balance and sent a bolt of deep purple fire crashing into the ceiling, showering the room in a cloud of stone dust. Jack struggled to get back to his feet but his legs felt like they were made of lead. Ciara continued to wrestle with Korrian, desperately trying to prise the staff from his iron grip.

She was only half the size of Korrian and couldn't match his physical strength, but she fought like a tiger. Jack needed to help her before it was too late. He climbed to his feet and staggered towards them, but the whole room felt like it was spinning.

Korrian managed to push Ciara away but she flew at him again and scratched at his face. It was the fury of a mother who was determined to protect her son at any cost. But Korrian eventually repelled the attack and threw her across the floor. His face turned white with anger and he waved his staff and sent a bolt of black fire flying towards her. It hit her squarely in her chest as she scrambled back up and it lifted her off her feet and sent her slamming into the wall. Her lifeless body slumped to the floor and lay motionless.

'Mother!' screamed Jack. He staggered over to her and took her in his arms and embraced her. He knew instantly that she was dead. He tilted her head back and kissed her tenderly on her cheek, his grief stricken tears raining down onto her. He gently lifted her body and laid it on the chaise longue and turned to Korrian.

The sorcerer looked contemptuously at Jack. 'Your thoughtlessness has killed your mother. If you'd given me the jewel as I asked, she would still be alive.'

Jack felt a rage burning through the entire length of his body. He'd never ever hated anyone in his life, but it was blind hatred fuelling the anger that was building deep inside of him. Jack walked slowly towards Korrian and let the red fire build within him. The sorcerer, for the first time, looked afraid. He raised his staff and threw another bolt of black fire at Jack, but Jack raised his hand and contemptuously deflected it.

Korrian tried to run towards the door but Jack threw a bolt of red fire towards him and his staff evaporated in a wisp of black smoke. Korrian looked frightened, even terrified and once again ran for the door, but Jack threw another bolt of red fire at him. A ball of red fire engulfed Korrian and suspended him in mid-air. He screamed for mercy but Jack didn't hear him. Rage threatened to drown Jack as he held Korrian in the midst of the glowing ball of red fire. He wanted to hurt him; he wanted to destroy him. All reason had left him when he saw his mother's lifeless body lying on the floor. He had to rid the world of this hideous sorcerer.

But something flickered deep down within him. Was it pity? Perhaps it was compassion? He somehow managed to find himself and allowed the fire to slowly die. Korrian slumped to the floor – his robe hanging off his limp body like a burnt rag. Jack walked back to the chaise longue and took his mother in his arms and cradled her. His grief had been momentarily held back by his burning anger but the sight of the beautiful Elf he held in his arms melted it away and he sobbed so hard that he thought he would die.

He heard a voice from behind him. It was a soft voice, laden with concern. 'Are you Jack? I'm Seamus and this is O'Reilly. Is Ciara OK?'

A distraught Jack turned to them. 'She's dead – Korrian killed her.'

Seamus's face crumpled into tears. 'Oh my beautiful Elf; my poor, poor, beautiful Ciara.'

O'Reilly stood impassively by Seamus's side looking down at her. 'I really liked your mother, Jack. She was an inspiration to Seamus and me.' He looked over to Korrian's body. 'Is he dead?'

Jack shook his head. 'I wanted to kill him, but that would have made me like him.'

'But he could come after us, and capture us again,' said a worried Seamus.

'His power is gone. I destroyed it along with his staff. He will never threaten anyone again.' Jack looked across to where the two Dwarves skulked behind the chair. 'Take your master away and tend to him.' They both stood up and walked over to Korrian. 'And don't ever come near me again.' Neither of them spoke or looked at Jack. They lifted Korrian between them and carried him out of the door.

Jack gently lifted Ciara into his arms and stood up and turned solemnly to Seamus and O'Reilly. 'Let's get out of this place.'

*

Jack stood on top of a plateau looking across the valley towards the dark castle. It was the same view that Breannacht had shown him in her vision. They didn't see either the Dwarves or Korrian as they left the castle and had an uneventful journey across the valley. Jack only had a rough idea of the direction they needed to take to find his friends. He hoped that they would be looking for him because at that moment he felt at the point of exhaustion.

A combination of grief and the exertions of the Koehtia had totally drained him.

'I wish we'd never set eyes on this place,' said Seamus.

Jack sat down next to his mother's body and leant back against a rock. 'Why did you come here?'

'We were trying to find your Elven homeland. We got lost in that mist and spent years wandering from land to land. We eventually ended up here and at first we thought Korrian was OK, because he took us into his castle and looked after us. He even told us he would help us find the Elven homeland, but it was all lies. He was only after your mother's magic.

She was like an empty shell once he'd got that and he turned O'Reilly and me into zombies. We were no more than slaves. But once you'd destroyed his power, his hold on us went.'

'Why did my mother want to find our homeland?'

'It was because of you, Jack. She wanted them to help her get rid of those nasty characters that govern Waterswood so she could come back for you. She never stopped talking about you, Jack. It broke her heart leaving you.'

'Did she ever tell you why she was so frightened?'

'Never,' said Seamus. 'I asked her many times, but she always refused to tell me.'

Jack sat back and closed his eyes. The only reason that he'd set out on this journey was to find his mother and bring her back to Waterswood, and now she was dead. He'd failed in his quest. He felt like he'd let her down. All of the fight had gone from him. He had no idea of where he was going anymore. His direction in life had been taken from him the moment Korrian took his mother's life.

'I'm sorry to interrupt you,' said O'Reilly. Jack opened his eyes and looked up at the Leprechaun. 'There's a huge black bird flying this way. I think that we should take cover.'

Jack knew exactly what it wanted. Maybe Korrian's power wasn't finished. Perhaps he'd left some small vestige for him to start all over again. But he no longer cared. He leant back against the rock and closed his eyes and waited for the end. His life was over.

Then he felt somebody shaking him. 'Jack,' said Seamus. 'I don't think it's a bird at all – it's a horse, one that I think you might be glad to see.'

Jack opened his eyes to see Troy gliding gracefully towards the plateau. As depleted as he was, the sight of the beautiful black horse coming towards him lifted his spirits. He climbed unsteadily to his feet with his mother in his arms. Troy landed barely twenty metres from them and trotted over to where they stood. He stopped in front of Jack and nuzzled against Ciara's head. Jack saw tears in his eyes.

Seamus appeared by Jack's side and tenderly touched his arm. 'Come, young Jack, let's take yer mammy home.'

Chapter Thirty - A Day called Hope

Tyler and Lilac sat together and watched the flames as they danced in the campfire. The Leprechauns were making tea as the Border Guard and Elensar prepared once again to go out into the forest in search of Jack. Princess Larien joined Tyler and Lilac and sat down next to them.

'It's only a matter of time before the Guard find Jack. Elensar and Elladan have great instincts when it comes to tracking people.'

'I shouldn't have pushed Elensar when he fired that arrow at the bird,' said Lilac. 'I only did it because I thought he would hit Jack. I feel so guilty.'

'They say that Elensar can split a hair on a Wood Troll's head from one hundred paces with an arrow. But you weren't to know that and only did what you thought was right,' said the Princess sympathetically.

'But Jack's been gone for two days now and we're no nearer to finding him,' said Lilac.

'We must retain faith in Elensar and the Guard,' said Tyler. 'They won't give up on Jack and nor will we.'

Lilac did her best to smile but her heart ached. Just as Rory handed her a cup of tea, one of the guards called out. 'Captain! Another bird approaches.' He pointed towards the hills that lay to the west of them, to what was no more than a black dot on the horizon.

'Guards! Take your positions and ready your longbows,' shouted Elensar. 'Princess, guard our friends while we deal with this threat.'

The Princess took her short sword from her belt and took up a position alongside Lilac, Tyler and the Leprechauns. They all scanned the skies for more birds.

'Keep steady,' urged Elensar. 'Don't fire until I tell you.'

The Princess shouted across to him. 'It looks even bigger than the one that took Jack.'

'Yes it does,' said Elensar, 'but it can still be taken

down by several well placed arrows.'

It was Rory who was first to realise that the creature flying towards them wasn't a threat. 'That's no bird and if I'm not mistaken, that's a flying horse and there are people on its back.'

'He's right,' said Lilac. 'It could be Troy.'

'Keep your longbows trained on the target as it approaches,' said Elensar. 'We cannot afford to take any chances.'

As the horse glided gracefully towards them, it became clear who the horse was and who he was carrying.

'That is Troy!' said Lilac unable to contain her excitement. 'And that's Jack at the front holding somebody.'

'And I'd recognise Seamus and O'Reilly from a mile away. Jack's only gone and rescued them all,' said Rory dancing a jig of joy around the campfire.

Troy landed as elegantly as ever and trotted to a standstill just in front of the waiting group. Lilac screamed for joy as she ran up to Jack. Troy gently lowered himself to his knees enabling his passengers to climb off. Lilac was the first to reach Jack and swallowed him and Ciara in a huge hug and was quickly followed by Tyler.

Seamus and O'Reilly were similarly engulfed by Rory and Sean. The guards watched on impassively as the Princess and Elensar exchanged relieved looks. Lilac stepped back from Jack and suddenly realised that something was wrong.

'What is it, Jack? You don't look happy and why is Ciara sleeping?'

'She's not sleeping,' said Jack solemnly. 'She's dead.'

A look of horror swept across Lilac's face. 'Dead? But how?'

'Korrian killed her.'

Elensar laid out some blankets on the ground. 'Lay her here, Jack.'

Jack didn't respond. He held onto his mother as if he would never let her go. Elensar walked up to him and placed his hand on his shoulder. 'Please, Jack, let the Princess tend to her.'

He gently took her from Jack and laid her on the blanket. The Princess knelt down by Ciara's side and placed her hand on her forehead. Lilac and Tyler sat Jack down by the fire and gave him a mug of tea.

'What happened – where did that bird take you?' asked Tyler.

'To Korrian's castle - Elensar was right to be suspicious of him, he was a sorcerer. He'd imprisoned my mother along with Seamus and Rory. He drained her of her magic and she became a lifeless shell. He planned to do the same to me – he was after my Bloodstone. I was able to use the Koehtia to build my mother up again, but once Korrian realised that I wasn't going to give him my Bloodstone, he tried to kill me. He threw bolt after bolt of dark fire at me but I managed to avoid them. One eventually hit me in the chest and knocked me to the floor. As he moved in for the kill, my mother attacked him.' Jack swallowed deeply. 'She diverted the bolt that would have killed me, but then … but then he threw a bolt of dark fire at her and …'

Tears streamed down Lilac's face as she embraced him. 'Oh Jack, I am so sorry. Ciara must have loved you very much.'

'Life can be so cruel at times,' said Tyler. 'I wish I could find the words to help sooth your pain, but at times like this, words can be a burden. Lilac and I will always be here for you; anything you want from us, you only have to ask.'

'Jack! Can you please come over?' shouted the Princess, her voice filled with urgency. He looked across to her. 'What is it?'

'I'm as certain as I can be that your mother isn't dead.'

Jack didn't comprehend her words. What was it she was saying?

'I can feel a pulse, a very faint pulse, but a pulse nonetheless.'

Jack jumped to his feet and ran over and dropped to his knees beside her. 'Are you sure?'

'Absolutely,' said the Princess, 'but we must get her back to Arminas as quickly as possible.'

Jack took hold of his mother's hand – it was still warm. Why hadn't he noticed before? He held her in his arms and reached deep down inside of himself – he needed the Koehtia to join them again as it did in Korrian's castle. He breathed slowly and composed himself and felt the connection to the earth below him. Meredin's words came back to him: *Trust your senses and feel it, Jack. It will build to the level you need and you can use it as you see fit.*

He focused everything onto his mother. Nothing else existed other than the two of them. He felt the tingle of Koehtia moving from his feet, through his legs and into his body, until it covered him from head to toe. He felt vibrant; he felt alive. He was ready to join with her.

He reached out for her; tried to feel her; called out to her – *Mother?* He found himself confronted by an impenetrable wall of darkness. The Koehtia took control and probed the dark wall that confronted it. Jack realised he was being challenged by the poison from Korrian's dark magic that had infected his mother. It felt pervasive and obscene. He knew he had to break through it to save her.

The blackness tried to swallow him but the Koehtia smothered him in its warmth and protection. The dark magic withdrew but Jack knew it wasn't defeated. His instincts took over and he placed himself in the protective embrace of the Koehtia. The blackness suddenly turned into a dark, menacing serpent and leapt at him, its bloodthirsty fangs trying to suck away at his protection.

But the Koehtia stood strong and repelled the beastly attack. Jack was safe but how was he going to break through the dark magic that gripped his mother? He searched for her again but she was still outside of his reach. *Keep patient, Jack. Let the Koehtia find its way.* But it felt like standstill – he had to break down the dark wall or his mother would be lost forever.

Fire surrounded Jack, great swathes of flames leapt at him. The sweltering heat was suffocating, sucking the oxygen from his lungs. But a sudden downpour of Koehtia rained down on him, instantly extinguishing the flames. It was like a game of chess being played out between the two conflicting powers fighting for his mother. But Jack was tired – the exertions at Korrian's castle had left him on the point of exhaustion. He needed a quick breakthrough.

The blackness seemed to sense his vulnerability and attacked once again. Invisible shafts of dark energy assailed him from all directions, trying to pierce through the layers of Koehtia that protected him. The icy cold bursts of dark magic burnt through his body trying to paralyse him. But the Koehtia closed around them once again, diffusing the corrosive barbs before they penetrated deeper into Jack

Jack recoiled back into himself. He needed to gather himself, to regroup. The dark magic inside his mother was strong and he knew it was slowly draining her life away. Time was running out and he needed to act, and act quickly. The bones of an idea started to form in his head. He was going about this in the wrong way. Yes, the Koehtia would protect him and could save his mother, but he had to direct it. He remembered Meredin's words again: *It will build to the level that you need and dispense as you see fit.*

He knew what he had to do.

He reached into his mother once again but this time he held the Koehtia back. The darkness lurked in the background waiting to pounce. Jack's plan had to work or they were both doomed. He and his mother would be lost. But he'd made up his mind and moved towards the darkness, inviting it to come for him. The Koehtia strained to protect him but he pushed it back. He felt vulnerable and exposed and the dark magic sensed its moment and came for him.

The attack when it hit was devastating, Jack was enveloped in a sea of pain and screamed out from the depths of his soul. It consumed him and began to break down his resolve. *Hang on, Jack, for as long as you dare.* And he did. The Koehtia continuously tried to cover him in its protective shield but he kept it at bay. He had to get the timing just right.

Just at the point where he was about to drown in the sea of darkness he reached out for his mother. His heart leapt in his chest when he felt her presence. The dark magic had given him the glimpse he needed. He let the Koehtia flood through him, and a tidal wave of warmth and light swallowed the darkness. Exhaustion was about to take him, but he summoned his last ounce of energy and reached out: *Mother?*

*

Jack heard voices echo in the distance, like they were at the end of a long tunnel. He drifted in and out of consciousness, completely unaware of where he was. He recognised Lilac – her voice thick with concern. Tyler was there also, and the Leprechauns jabbering away in the background.

But there was another voice – soft and gentle and soothing him. It was a voice full of tenderness and love and it was vaguely familiar. Somebody held him and gently stroked his hair. He opened his eyes and saw the most beautiful, tearful face staring back down at him.

'My beautiful, brave son. No one will ever part us again.'

'Mother?'

Ciara gently placed her index finger on his lips. 'Just rest, my son. You have taken yourself beyond exhaustion. You need to replenish yourself.' She moistened his lips with water and pulled him tightly to her breast.

'You gave us all a rare ole fright just then, Jack me lad,' said Rory. 'I thought we'd lost you.'

246

The Princess appeared in the periphery of his vision. 'We need to get you back to Arminas, and put you in the care of our Healers. You have both been through a horrendous ordeal.'

Lilac knelt down beside him. 'I can't tell you how good it feels to see you both together. It's like you were never apart. This has to be the happiest day of my life.'

'I'll second that,' said Tyler.

'O'Reilly and I owe you our lives, Jack,' said Seamus. 'There isn't anything that either of us wouldn't do for you.'

Jack laid back in the comfort of his mother's arms. How long had he waited for this moment? It was a moment he'd dreamed about from when he first learnt of her existence. And now it was happening. He closed his eyes and drifted off into a deep and restful sleep.'

Chapter Thirty-One – Homecomings

Jack sat back in his bed propped up on pillows as his mother spoon fed him vegetable broth. He'd slept through the whole journey back from Lestrada to Arminas. When he eventually woke he was in the secure comfort of the Healers' clinic, safely within the city walls. He'd been in the clinic for two days and his mother hadn't left his side.

There was an instant bond between the two of them – it was as if they had never been apart. They were similar physically, as were their mannerisms. Now he knew why everyone said that he was the image of his mother. As much as he loved his grandfather and appreciated everything that he'd done for him, the relationship with his mother was on a totally different plane.

Baelsar, the Healer entered the room and sat down on the side of Jack's bed.

'Well I have to say that you are looking better, Jack. I think the rest has been good for you, although I suspect that the real healing is because of your mother.'

Ciara put the soup bowl down on the bedside cabinet and took hold of Jack's hand. 'I left my son once – I will make sure that nothing ever gets in the way of our relationship again.' She squeezed his hand. 'We have much time to make up for, my son, and I think we will both relish every minute.'

'Your friends are keen to see you,' said Baelsar. 'Are you up to a visit?'

Ciara was about to say no, but Jack pleaded with her. 'Please, Mother. They kept me going through some very dark times.'

'Very well,' she said, 'but you must tell me the moment you feel tired and I will send them away.'

'I will,' promised Jack.

Baelsar walked over to the door and opened it. 'You can come in but must promise not to tire them.'

'We won't,' said Lilac as she almost ran into the room.

She wrapped Jack and Ciara in a hug. She playfully pinched Jack's cheek. 'You have your old colour back. You worried us all half to death back in Lestrada.'

'It's not a place I'll be hurrying back to,' said Jack.

Tyler, Seamus, Rory, O'Reilly, Sean, Elensar and the Princess all trooped into the room. 'Young Jack,' beamed Tyler. 'It's good to see you looking so well. And as for you, Ciara, I will personally make sure that you never ever go any further than Badger's Fall again.'

'Don't worry, Tyler, my travelling days are behind me.'

'That's good to hear,' said Tyler, 'because I'm looking forward to seeing the look on Grimley's face when we all walk back into Waterswood.'

*

Jack woke in the night to see his mother standing by the window staring out across Arminas. He climbed out of bed and walked over to her. 'Can't you sleep?'

She smiled. 'I've done nothing but sleep for the last few days.'

Jack put his arm around her and pulled her slender body close. He was well over one and a half metres tall and still growing. Ciara was petite in comparison; a mini version of Jack. She rested her head against his arm as she looked across the city. 'It is beautiful here, don't you think?'

'I haven't seen that much of it,' said Jack. 'They've all treated us so well. I will be sad to leave.'

Ciara looked up at him through tearful eyes. 'But we don't have to – we could stay here.'

'But I thought you'd want to go back to Waterswood. After all, it is our home.'

'Maybe once, Jack, but I never want to see Grimley again.'

Jack walked over to a stone jug and poured himself a glass of water and slowly sipped it. 'I always imagined when I found you that we would go home together.'

'Grimley isn't just devious, he is dangerous. I will never trust him again.'

'Why are you so frightened of him? What made you run away from Waterswood?' asked Jack.

Ciara turned away from Jack and looked out over Arminas again. Jack could see that painful memories troubled her. 'I was close to him once. He seemed to take a special interest in me. He once told me that I was different to the other Elves in Waterswood and that one day I would play an important role in the community.'

'Did he know that you were descended from the House of Sarmondian?'

'I didn't know until I came here so I doubt if Grimley did. But you could never be sure with him.'

'So what made him change towards you?'

A solitary tear trickled down her cheek. 'I'd confided in Rosebud that I was pregnant and she took it upon herself to tell Grimley. He was absolutely furious and said that I had brought disgrace onto our community. He ordered me not to tell anybody and sent me home. But I didn't go home. I had an uneasy feeling about the whole situation so I ran away to a village further down the valley called Greenwood. But Grimley sent his spies after me so I decided to go to the human forest. I found a women's hostel in a small town near to the forest and they looked after me. You were born in a human hospital. The nurses couldn't get over your thick mop of brown hair and your pointy ears. We stayed there for just over a week but they started asking me awkward questions about my background so I had no choice other than to move on.

I took you to the forest as there was nowhere else to go. I spent one cold and very lonely night with you sheltering under a tree. But it wasn't right, you were only a baby; you needed warmth and a roof over your head. I'd seen Noah and his wife, Rosie, many times in the forest. They seemed nice, kind people.

The idea of leaving you with them came to me as I watched them both sitting in the midday sun outside their cottage. I was going to have to keep on the run if I was to avoid Grimley's spies, and that was no life for a young baby. And if they did capture me I would have told them that you died at birth so you could live a free and happy life away from the oppression of Grimley and the Elders.' She grabbed Jack's hand and looked directly into his eyes. 'I know that it sounds cruel and callous, my son, but I would do anything to keep you safe, including sacrificing my own life.'

As painful as it was, Jack nodded that he understood.

'I took you to Noah and Rosie and told them I was in great danger and had to get away. I asked them to look after you and promised that I would be back to get you as soon as I found somewhere safe for us both to stay. I left my Bloodstone with them to give to you just in case anything happened to me. I never even told them my name.'

'How did you get the Bloodstone?' asked Jack.

'It was my mother's; she died shortly after giving birth to me. No-one knew who my father was and my mother had no family so I ended up in an orphanage until Crystal took me in. The Bloodstone was the only link to my past.'

Jack momentarily dwelt on what she had just told him and how they had both grown up without mothers, but there was something bothering him that he needed to ask her. 'Why didn't you come back for me?'

'When I left you I found Syd Gumboot and stayed with him and at first it was safe. I was planning to tell Syd about you but then a nasty character called Finn Tarr came looking for me. Grimley had paid him to bring me back to Waterswood. Syd said it was too dangerous for me to stay with him so he took me to Narky's. I was safe there for a while but Finn was on my trail. Seamus came across Narky's cottage on his travels one day and stayed with us. He told me amazing stories about how beautiful it was in Cill-Arney and invited me to go back there with him. As frightened as I was I couldn't contemplate being so far away from you.

But then he told me about the legend of the Elven homeland. Faery folklore said that it was on Emerald Island. I decided that I should go there and try to persuade our Elven cousins to help me.' She looked at Jack through tearful eyes. 'I think you know the rest of the story.'

Jack wrapped his mother in his arms and kissed her tenderly on her forehead. 'You did what you thought was best for me. Noah treated me like his own and I will always be grateful to him. Sadly, Rosie died when I was a baby and I never got to know her. I always called Noah, Grandfather, and I just accepted the situation – I never asked about my parents. And I would still be none the wiser if Grimley hadn't sent those Elves to kill me.'

Ciara looked horrified. 'Grimley did what?'

'He sent the LEOs to burn down our cottage. If Noah hadn't been so alert, we'd both have been killed.'

'And you know it was Grimley?'

'I didn't until I found my way to Waterswood. He had me arrested and was going to send me to Darkenwold.'

'He knew who you were?'

'I could tell when first I met him that he recognised me. He put me on trial but Lomund planned my escape and I returned to the human forest. Lilac and Tyler came after me and it was decided that we would come to find you. We all felt that you were the key to why Grimley wanted me dead.'

Ciara lowered her gaze to the floor. She sat in silence for several moments then looked up at Jack with a burning intensity. 'I knew that Grimley was capable of many things, but murder?'

'Lomund and Crystal found it hard to believe but when they found out Grimley planned to send me to Darkenwold, they both realised that he didn't intend for me to come out of there alive. For some reason Grimley thinks that I'm a danger to Waterswood. Do you have any idea why?'

Ciara hesitated for a second before answering. 'Who knows what insane thoughts run through his mind?' She took hold of Jack's hand. 'Do you still wish to return there even though you know that your life is in danger?'

'It's our home, Mother. It's where we belong.'

'Very well, we shall both return to Waterswood. It is time we rid our home village of that evil regime. It is one thing hounding me, but when Grimley tries to kill my son, he has crossed a line, and he will live to regret it one day.'

Jack could hear the determination in her voice. He was fast learning that his mother was a formidable Elf. 'When do we leave?'

'We leave for Cill-Arney tomorrow.'

*

They arrived in Cill-Arney two weeks after they left Arminas. King Erenin insisted that Elensar and several members of the Border Guard escorted them, along with Princess Larien. They stayed a night with Brendan and needless to say the old Leprechaun was absolutely thrilled when he saw Seamus, O'Reilly and Ciara.

But his welcome was sedate in comparison to the reception they received when they arrived in Cill-Arney. The whole village came out to greet them and the revelries started the moment they arrived. The Muldoon was moved to tears when he set eyes on Seamus and O'Reilly. But as glad as he was to see them he made them promise that their travelling days were over.

The welcome home party, or ceilidh, as the Leprechauns call it, started in the early evening and didn't finish until the next morning. Below is an extract from Seamus O'Shoehorn's diary, who will describe the events better than I ever could:

'The craic was mighty (translation – they had a great time!). We danced and sang until the sun came up. Auntie Bridie was in top form and danced so much her bloomers ended up around her ankles! The Elves surprised everyone with their dancing and singing skills. Yer one Princess Larien can belt out a grand song when the mood takes her.

And Rory and I were made up when we got Tyler to try the Poteen again – but I think it must have been after the fourth glass that he collapsed and we had to put him to bed! O'Reilly was in grand form – I've known him all of my life and have never seen him dance. Well he did last night – he jigged for Cill-Arney. He's a deep one that O'Reilly but he loves his friends, and he will miss the Elves when they go back home.

Now Cara seems to have taken a bit of a shine to Jack. She danced with him the whole night; I don't think he managed to get more than a metre away from her! But something amazing happened – Jack went to give back her gold coin that she'd given him before he left Cill-Arney. When he took it out of his breast pocket, it was as flat as a pancake. It suddenly dawned on him that it must have absorbed the bolts of fire that Korrian was firing at him in the Dark Castle. The coin had saved his life. Cara insisted that Jack should keep it and he promised that it would always stay close to his heart. Needless to say that Cara was made up. Rory and I tried to tell her that Jack would be going home soon and not to get too attached but would she listen?

Now I've always thought that the Elven guards were a serious bunch and I can't say that I had any sort of conversations with them as we travelled home. They surprised us all, not least by the amount of Poteen they could drink, but by their dancing skills, and one of them, a fairly rough looking character called Elros, surprised us all over again when he pulled out a tin whistle and played a series of jigs.

And last but not least there was the Muldoon. He's not just our leader he's a father figure to us all. I'll never forget the relief on his face when he saw us all back home safely. He drank more Poteen than he has for years and he sang a song and I can never remember him doing that before. Although Auntie Bridie says he was the regular turn when he was a young Leprechaun … So that was the home coming ceilidh in Cill-Arney. I'm going to miss

Ciara terribly when she goes home as I've got used to having her around. But I suppose I could always take a trip over to Brittany Island again if the mood takes me … now there's a thought.'

Reprinted with the kind permission of Seamus O'Shoehorn, resident of Cill-Arney, Emerald Island.

*

Jack sat on a rock on the edge of the village staring down at the Great Blue Lake and the mountains beyond. It was two days since the welcome home party and he was still feeling the effects of his one and only glass of Poteen. But despite his slightly fragile condition, the breath-taking view lifted his spirits. He was at home when he was amongst nature.

His mother suddenly appeared by his side and sat down next to him. 'Are you OK, my son?'

'I'm a little tired but other than that I'm fine.'

'Are you ready to go home?' she asked.

'I think so,' said Jack. 'I just hope I'm up to whatever challenges lay ahead.'

Ciara smiled. 'Of that I have no doubt. Neither of us are the same people that were forced to leave our home behind. I was scared for both of our lives when I ran from Waterswood, but that has all changed. We are both older, wiser and stronger for our experiences. You, my son, have grown into a fine Elf. I feel it in my heart that one day you will take your rightful place at the head of our community in Waterswood. And then together with our people, we can build a strong society that values justice and freedom, just as they do here in Cill-Arney and our ancient home city of Arminas.'

She stood up and held her hand out to him. 'Come, I will tell the others and summon Troy. We're going home, my son. We're going home to Waterswood … together.'

*

To be continued …